A PRICKLY PAIR

"Remember what happens when you pull a knife on someone stronger? They use it against you."

Camile wasn't afraid of him. He was making a point. Teaching her a lesson. "If you plan on spanking me again, you might as well kill me. I won't sit still for it."

He smiled. "You didn't sit still last time, either." In a lightning fast motion, he threw the knife he'd held against her throat. It landed point down in the soft mud. "I'm not going to kill you."

Camile began to feel strange again. His tall frame was stretched out on top of her. She felt his heart pounding. "And you're not going to spank me, right?"

"I'm not going to kill you, and if I'd known you were a woman, I'd have never spanked you to begin with."

"Then why are you looking at me like that?" she demanded.

His gaze lowered to her mouth. "Because I'll be damned if I'm not going to kiss you."

Other *Leisure* books by Ronda Thompson:
COUGAR'S WOMAN

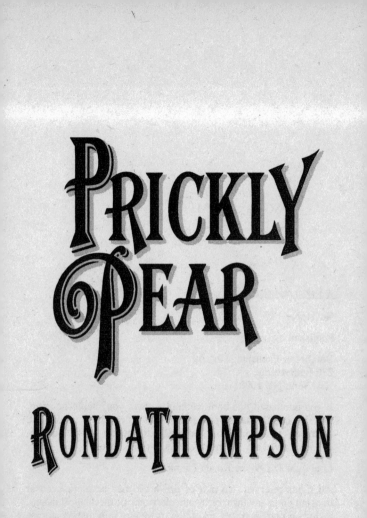

PRICKLY PEAR

RONDA THOMPSON

LEISURE BOOKS NEW YORK CITY

A LEISURE BOOK®

November 1999

Published by

Dorchester Publishing Co., Inc.
276 Fifth Avenue
New York, NY 10001

ISBN 0-8439-4624-5

The name "Leisure Books" and the stylized "L" with design are
trademarks of Dorchester Publishing Co., Inc.

Printed in the United States of America.

To Charlotte Goebel, a talented author and true friend. Over the years, we've plotted, schemed and dreamed together. Thank you for sharing your compassion, encouragement, and wisdom with me, but most importantly, thanks for sharing your chocolate.

ACKNOWLEDGMENT

A special thanks to Jennifer Archer, a wonderful friend, and an invaluable critique partner. To Christine Scheel, who offered me her proofing skills as well as her friendship, and by doing so, aided my journey down the path to publication. To Jean Price, my agent, for standing by me all of these years. And to Christopher Keeslar, my editor, for his belief in me and in my talent. It is often said the journey of a writer is a lonely one, but publication is not a goal that can be achieved without the help of many. In my case, there are too many to thank. You know who you are, and I hope all of you know how truly grateful I am.

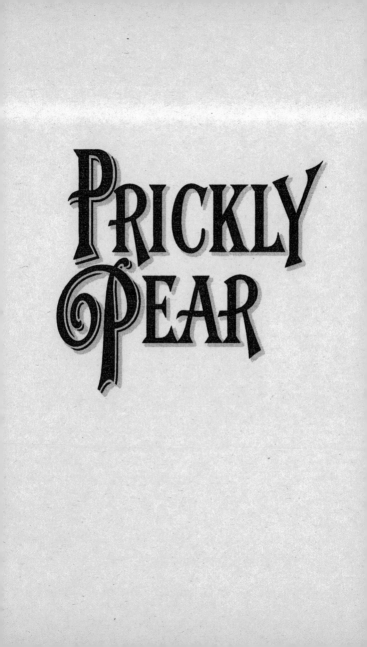

PRICKLY PEAR

Chapter One

1883 Texas

It was a whorehouse. Smoke hung in the air, thick as the smell of too many warm bodies crowded together. Men sat at crudely built tables drinking, laughing, or waiting for a turn with a woman. A card game was in progress. Nothing out of the ordinary, Wade Langtry imagined, for a small town in the Texas Panhandle.

He dusted off his clothes and approached the bar, silently cursing his past, his present, and his future, all of which were tied to this godforsaken territory.

"Get you something, mister?" a woman asked from behind the bar.

"Whiskey."

"Ain't seen you around these parts before." Her gaze

roamed over him boldly. "I'd remember. Show me the color of your money first."

Wade removed a gold piece from his pocket and placed it on the bar. The woman snatched it up. She tested the coin's authenticity with her teeth, then grinned.

"Even an *ugly* cuss who pays with gold is welcome in Tascosa. A face like yours will get you more than decent liquor." She dropped the coin between her full breasts, wiggling suggestively. "I'm Rosie. I own this watering hole, but gold or no gold, dimples or not, I demand a man's name before inviting him to the back."

Back rooms and women of easy virtue were no strangers to Wade. Before Atlanta, before he'd ceased to make a living with a gun and instead vowed to make one with his brains, he'd shared many a back room with women such as Rosie.

"Much as I appreciate your offer, I came inside to drown the dirt in my mouth and ask for information. How far is the Cordell place?"

The brunette's smile faded. "Information ain't gonna keep you warm tonight. You don't look like a cowhand. You don't look much like a rancher, either. What are you?"

"Thirsty." He raised the glass to his lips. "I'd appreciate directions. I'll pay you for your trouble."

Rosie frowned. "It's your own damn trouble you'll be paying for if you have business with the Cordells. The ranch isn't far. If you're set on going, those two will be headed that way tonight. You can ride with them."

He followed her nod to a nearby table where a leather-faced man laid down his cards, grinning with tobacco-filled jaws.

"You can't beat a full house, Cam."

Cam, a boy Wade guessed to be about sixteen, and that would be stretching it, took a long draw on a black cigarillo.

"Not unless four ladies are smiling back at me, Hank," the boy said.

"It's a bluff," another man snorted. "No one is that lucky. I lost my whole stake to that ruffian. Take the brat down a notch or two, Hank."

"Watch your mouth, Jake." Hank cast the cowboy a dark look. "Cam's a fair player. If you lost, it's 'cause you got beat." The old man's gaze swung back to the boy. "I'm calling you, Cam. If you've got the ladies, show 'em."

The kid pulled a black Stetson lower over his eyes. He blew a stream of smoke into the older man's face. "Not just yet. Let's up the pot before I show my cards." He threw in another coin.

"He must have the queens," a pockmarked man drawled. "I think he's a little too lucky. Didn't four queens take our money two rounds ago, partner?" He threw his cards down.

A man to his left nodded and did the same. "Eight queens in one night is more than luck."

"If you're calling Cam a cheat, it ain't a smart thing to do," Hank warned the men. "But since you two are strangers, I'll let it slide."

"We have ourselves an old man sticking up for a wet-behind-the-ears pup, Sam." The pock-faced man laughed. "That ain't much to be afraid of, is it?"

Sam grinned. "Which one you reckon yelps the loudest, Lenny? The old dog, or the puppy?"

Silence fell over the noisy room. Wade knew the scene well. It usually ended with a grave-digger's profit. Hank's face turned an angry shade of red. The kid seemed uncon-

15

cerned; he took a drink and pulled his jacket tighter around him.

"Have you ever noticed that a pup's teeth are sharp as pin ends?" the boy asked softly.

It wasn't the wisest threat to hurl at two rough-looking characters such as Sam and Lenny, Wade thought.

Hank shifted nervously in his chair. "Come on, Cam, let's take our winnings and go home."

Lenny, the pock-faced man, scrambled to his feet. "Hold on a minute. I want to see those cards first."

"I told you—"

The kid shushed his bluster, waving a hand in the air. "If he wants to see my cards, it's fine by me." A cocky grin settled over his lips as he laid down his hand. "I only had three queens. Now, if you'll excuse us, Hank and I'll be on our way." He rose, gathering his pile, as Hank reached for his own.

Wade turned back to his drink. Rosie's gaze stared past him.

"Them drifters won't let it be," she said, "Mark my words, there'll be trouble and someone will end up getting hurt."

"The old man and the kid," Wade predicted.

"Care to wager on the outcome?"

"Trail scum like those two don't fight fair. You'd be betting against bad odds."

"That hellion ain't being fair, either," Rosie grumbled. "The brat cheats. Been cheating all night, although Hank don't know it."

Card cheats rated right up there with hired guns in Wade's altered opinion. Before he gave the situation much consideration, Rosie's prediction came true.

"What do you have under that jacket?" Lenny demanded. "The fourth queen? Take it off and prove you ain't got a card up your sleeve."

"Cam's word is good enough," Hank insisted. "You two are headed for trouble if you keep on."

"How much?" Rosie asked Wade when he turned to watch the inevitable confrontation.

"That gold piece between your breasts, and the right to remove it with my teeth when I have the time."

She chuckled. "When I make a bet with a man, even if it's a wager I won't mind losing, I want his name."

Wade introduced himself seconds before Lenny lunged for the kid and Sam went for Hank. The steel of a blade flashed. Lenny yelped. His hand flew to a cut dripping blood down the side of his cheek. The kid had cut him.

"You're gonna pay for that, smart-mouth!"

Given the unfair odds, Wade admired the kid for his spunk. Still, Cam's eyes were huge, as if he'd cut Lenny by accident. A boy that age had no business playing a man's game. Hank wasn't much help. He kept watching the kid, and his opponent's fist kept connecting with his face. Wade flexed his fingers, annoyed. The older man represented what was known in the gunman's profession as easy pickings.

A bottle over the head sent Hank to the floor. When he didn't get up, those previously content to mind their own business began inching forward.

"All bets are off if anyone steps in," Wade said to Rosie.

"It wasn't part of the agreement. I warned you it wouldn't be a fair fight."

"You did for a fact," he admitted, content to lose a gold coin for the sake of a life. Card cheat or not, every kid had the right to grow up.

17

Lenny lunged for Cam, wresting the knife from his hand. He grabbed the kid by the collar and poised the knife at his throat. The fight had taken an ugly turn. Unconsciously, Wade moved his duster behind the Colt strapped to his thigh.

"Get back, all of you!" Lenny shouted. "I'll cut him if anyone comes closer. Take the money, Sam."

His partner drew his revolver, aiming at the crowd while gathering the currency.

"You cut me, smart-mouth," Lenny said to the kid. "I'm gonna teach you a lesson about taking a knife to a man bigger than you. First, I'll prove you cheated me."

The kid no longer appeared cocky. His eyes were round, his smooth cheeks pale. He struggled when Lenny tried to remove his jacket.

"You're hidin' something all right, boy. I aim to see what!"

"We've got the money. Leave the brat be," Sam snarled. "That cut on your cheek don't make you any uglier than you already were."

Lenny's lips puckered into a pout. "I say an eye for an eye. This boy's a little too pretty. I'm gonna give him a lesson he won't forget."

Tauntingly, Lenny waved the knife before the kid's face. If the pock-faced man would lower the blade, Wade could disarm him. Wade caressed the polished walnut handle of his Colt, waiting.

"Ain't no woman gonna take you willingly between her legs after I get through with you," Lenny said with a laugh. "Maybe I should just slit your throat and save you the heartbreak."

Cam came down hard with his boot heel against Lenny's

foot. The knife barely missed the kid's throat as he twisted away. Lenny made a desperate attempt to recapture his hostage, but a gun shot to the knee crippled his efforts. He fell to the floor, howling with pain while Sam, noting the Colt leveled on him from the bar, slowly lowered his own weapon.

Placing himself above Lenny, Wade trained his revolver on Sam. "I think you two should count your blessings and get out." He glanced down. A card lay at his feet. A queen. "Take the money and go."

"Take the money?" Cam knelt beside Hank, glaring up at him. "That no good egg-sucker put his hands on me. He deserves to die, not be rewarded!"

Bending, Wade retrieved the card. "This look familiar? In most states they hang card cheats the same as horse thieves."

"You shot me, and he was guilty just like I said!" the pock-faced man shouted at Wade.

Wade glanced at Lenny. "A good swat to his backside would whittle him down to size. He didn't cut you on purpose, did you, boy?"

The kid rose, retrieving the knife Lenny had dropped. "Maybe I did, and maybe I didn't." He slid the knife into the top of his boot. "Either way, it's no business of yours. I didn't need you to step in on my behalf. I drew those three queens fair. I stashed the fourth one earlier, but didn't plan to use it until the strangers had moved on. Just wanted to pull one over on old Hank."

"Hank doesn't look amused." With a nod, Wade indicated the unconscious man. "Guess you've learned a lesson."

Color exploded in the kid's cheeks. He stuck a slender finger in Wade's face. "You interfered, greenhorn! Hank's

19

got a skull thick as they come. If he couldn't handle his own man, he deserved a bottle over the head. This was our fight, not yours." He glanced toward the strangers. "Those two didn't have more than five bits between them in the game. The way I see it, you either tell them to give us our money back, or replace what you let them take!"

With every "you" the kid poked him in the chest. He truly was a brat, Wade thought. One who needed the whittling down he'd spoken of earlier. "I'll give you your due," Wade said. He tossed his gun to the nearest man. "See that the drifters stay put. I'll see to the kid."

Calmly, he removed his hat and set it on a nearby table. Wade pulled out a chair, grabbed the kid by the arm, and seated himself. He slung the boy over his knee, jerked up the heavy jacket, then whacked him on the bottom. The kid stiffened. A second later, he sank his teeth through the rough fabric of Wade's pants. The next blow fell harder.

"Someone shoot him!" the kid screeched.

His voice sounded suspiciously high. Wade glanced down at the round bottom beneath his hand. Something wasn't right. Before he could identify exactly what was out of place, the kid began to struggle. His Stetson fell away. Long, honey-colored hair brushed the floor. Hair that looked too pretty on a snot-nosed, smart-mouthed boy. Wade quickly pulled the kid into a sitting position.

His gaze locked with a pair of thickly lashed blue eyes. Without thought to the impropriety of doing so, he yanked open the jacket. One glance cleared his confusion. The kid was no kid. Not by a far stretch of the imagination. And *he* was a *she*.

"I'll be damned," Lenny whispered from his position of

the ground. "Didn't know I was tangling with a she-cat."

Wade hadn't known either. Staring at her at that moment, however, he wondered how he'd ever mistaken that rosebud mouth for a boy's. Her full lips turned up slightly.

"You should have never given your gun away," she said.

Now wary, Wade glanced at the man holding his Colt. The weapon was still trained on Lenny and Sam. But for how long?

"And you should have kept yourself to the back rooms where you belong," Wade countered softly.

She followed his nod, then frowned. Suddenly, her face registered understanding. "Do you think I'm a whore?"

In truth, Wade didn't know what to think. One thing had become perfectly obvious to him. Cam, smart-mouth, card cheat, and whatever else she might be, was a looker. She'd made a pretty boy, but she was a beautiful woman.

"Wishful thinking maybe," he answered, his gaze lowering to a mouth that promised all manner of pleasure.

The man holding his gun stepped forward. "Now listen here, mister!"

A deadly glare from Cam halted him. "You stay out of this, Grady. I can handle the greenhorn."

"First things first," Wade said. "What are you going to do about those two?"

She eyed the strangers thoughtfully. "Grady, give them their five bits and throw in a little extra to see that the one who tangled with me gets care for his injuries."

Sam scowled, then reached to help his partner from the floor. Once on his feet, Lenny ran a heated glance over Cam.

"We ain't through tangling yet, girlie. You owe me for

the scar your knife's gonna leave." His gaze lowered to the front of her jacket. "I got me some good ideas on how I'm gonna collect, too."

"Come near her and we'll fill you full of lead," Grady, the man who held Wade's revolver, warned. "Both of you, take your money and move on."

Wade watched the pair, tensed for trouble, uncomfortable because Cam hadn't moved from his lap. Very uncomfortable.

Once Sam had gathered their money, Lenny leaned on his partner for support, limping toward the door. The pock-faced man turned.

"Watch your back, girlie. You, too," he said to Wade.

"Shut up," Sam instructed harshly. "No female is worth the trouble that one has cost us."

Only after the two left the cantina did Wade breathe a sigh of relief. Next problem. The woman was snuggled into his lap. And she fit there. Perfectly. She also had trouble sitting still. He clamped his teeth together when she ground her round bottom into him.

"So, you like women of easy virtue?" she asked, as if their conversation hadn't been interrupted.

Wade didn't answer. He continued to stare into her frosty blue eyes until they began to widen.

"Guess that answers your question," he said dryly.

She jumped up. Fast as his reflexes were, hers were quicker. With a sweep of her foot, she knocked the rickety chair from beneath him. Wade Langtry, once a hired gun, a bounty hunter, a Pinkerton operative—whatever the money had led him to five years ago—found himself on his back, a woman's foot against his throat.

"I ain't no light skirt," she said, applying slight pressure with her foot. "Now, I suggest you ride out the same as you rode in. We don't take to strangers meddling in our affairs in Tascosa. First, say you're sorry for laying a hand on me."

"Like hell I will," Wade responded. If she were a man, he'd shoot her. He didn't have to lie there with her foot on his throat. One strong tug of her leg would send her backward. His fingers inched toward her boot. The click of a revolver stopped him. Wade glanced at the man holding his Colt. His gray eyes warned him to stay down.

There was a time when the man would have just dug his own grave. A time when Wade went by another name; when hunger ruled his conscience; when only his soul was at stake. But he'd come to Tascosa to do a job. One his future rested upon. This man probably handed for the Circle C Ranch.

According to Gregory Kline, the person who'd blackmailed Wade into taking this assignment, Tom Cordell set store by his men. It wouldn't be wise to ride the wrong side of anyone affiliated with the ranch. Not just yet, anyway.

"You've humiliated him enough, Cam," the man holding the revolver said. "We need to tend to Hank. The stranger knows you can handle yourself. Let him go."

"That right?" she asked, staring down at Wade.

He allowed his gaze to roam the length of her leg, over the ripe mounds of her breasts, then smiled slightly. "For the time being."

Rosie appeared with a bucket. "That's as good as he's giving you, Cactus. Let the man up. It could have ended with worse than a smack to your backside. You keep causing trouble in my place, and I'll tell Hank he can't bring you in here no more."

Cam reluctantly removed her foot. "I guess the green-

23

horn learned a lesson, too. Next time, he'll think twice about manhandling females who give as good as they get."

"Next time"—Wade rose from the floor—"and I hope there isn't one, I'll give you more than a smack to the backside. It's easy to be brave when you've got a man holding a gun for you."

She whirled around. The gray-eyed man blushed, then handed the Colt back to Wade.

"Sorry, Cam," he mumbled. "Hank would skin us alive if something happened to you."

"Once I'm on my feet, I don't need you to watch my back, Grady," she growled. "Hellfire, I'll skin you myself if you pull a stunt like that again. Get Hank and come on."

Without a glance in Wade's direction, the firebrand took off, moving across the floor with unladylike strides. Wade watched the sway of her slim hips longer than he intended. She had legs that went all the way to Heaven.

"Best forget those thoughts." Rosie laughed, then sloshed the bucket's contents into Hank's face.

The man sat up abruptly. "What happened?" Hank brought a hand to the back of his head. He stared blankly at the smear of blood against his palm.

"Cam," Grady explained. "The stranger stepped in after you went down, but she ain't too beholden. We'd better get her home."

Hank lumbered to his feet, regarding Wade curiously. "Name's Hank Riley. Thanks for watching out for Cam. Grady, you'd better go wait with her."

Wade slid his Colt into the holster and took the hand Hank offered. "Wade Langtry."

The older man released his grip and bent to scoop up his hat. "Sorry you had to step in. I wouldn't stick around if I was you. Cam don't care for men defending her."

"He found out," a man said. "She took him down in exchange for the spanking."

"You hit her?" Hank frowned. "Reckon I'll have to kill you then."

"Ain't no killing going on in my place," Rosie snapped. "He gave her less than she deserved. Cam had a card up her sleeve, Hank."

His face paled. "Is that right, boys? Cam cheated?"

A man shuffled uncomfortably. "You shouldn't have taught her how if you didn't want her doing it."

"Damn," Hank swore. "I'm getting too old for this." He ran a hand over his eyes. "I taught her so she'd know when someone else was cheating. Should have known Cam would turn the tables on me. She's spirited," he explained to Wade. "Her mama died when she was two, and she's been running loco ever since."

"It's time someone broke her," Wade suggested.

Hank snorted. "Ain't a man in the territory brave enough to try that—no one usually dumb enough to stay in Tascosa long after they've riled her, either. I'll say my thanks now. Don't figure I'll see you again."

Wade touched his hat in parting, but said nothing. He would be seeing Hank again. Soon.

"Will you be staying then?" Rosie asked when Hank departed, a hopeful gleam in her dark eyes.

"It's tempting." Wade removed another gold coin from his pocket and handed it to her. "But I'd better make sure they get home safely. Those drifters might be waiting for them."

"Not if they have the sense God gave a chicken. You seem smart. I'd think twice about trailing after her. She looks female, but she ain't."

"I'm interested in Hank," Wade reminded her. "To be more exact, in where he's going. The ranch, remember?"

She sighed loudly. "I don't know what business you've got at the Circle C, but I'd stay clear of that ranch. The last man through here looking for the Cordells left lickety-split. Some Easterner sniffing out land—as if the greedy investors haven't all but bought it up.

"Guess he sniffed down the wrong barrel. Besides," Rosie continued as she walked to the bar and poured two drinks, "the Cactus won't be happy to see that handsome face of yours. Old Hank's had about a gullet full of keeping her out of trouble. He'd hang up his saddle tomorrow if Tom could find an able man to take his place. Cam gave him every one of them gray hairs."

"Then, Hank is Cam's father?"

"Might as well be. He dotes on her like one. Hank Riley has been Tom Cordell's legs since an accident left him crippled. Chasing after that feisty miss comes with the job. Hank's the Circle C foreman."

Hackles rose on the back of Wade's neck. "And she is?"

"Camile Cordell, but folks around here call her Prickly Pear. The cowhands call her Cam. Only her pa and that Mexican housekeeper they have got the nerve to call her Camile."

Wade had quit listening. Cordell echoed through his mind. *That was the helpless daughter Gregory Kline had briefly mentioned?* Kline said "convincing" a crippled old man and his mousy daughter to sign over the deed to their ranch would be a simple job for a man of Wade's former talents. Like hell she was mousy!

Maybe Kline had said mouthy, and Wade had misunderstood him. This job might not be as easy as Kline had indicated. Not if the father and daughter were cut from the same cloth. Wade swore softly, retraced his steps to the bar, and downed in one gulp the glass of whiskey Rosie handed him.

Chapter Two

Camile Cordell's mouth felt as if a wad of cotton had been stuffed inside. Her head hurt. Her stomach churned. Rarely had she raised a bottle to her lips. Since Hank had insisted she tuck her hair up and act like a man around strangers, she'd done just that. Now she wished she'd left the liquor alone. Camile threw the covers back. She sat up, then groaned when the action made her head feel worse.

Last night seemed like a dream. A nightmare. Hank was angry with her. He'd told her she couldn't go into Rosie's anymore; couldn't play cards, or smoke, or cuss, or have any fun. But old Hank would settle down and forget his pledge to see her hobbled, Camile assured herself.

He'd ranted all the way home, but now it was morning, and things never seemed as bad during the daylight. Bile rose in her throat. Camile clamped a hand over her mouth and stumbled out of bed. She moved to the washbasin, hurriedly splashing her face with cold water. After a second, she felt somewhat better.

Snatching up a brush, she tried to tame her unruly mane. She vowed she'd be at Rosie's next Saturday night come hell or high water. There were few enough distractions to entertain a woman raised around men all her life. Even if things had gotten out of hand with the drifters, she deserved a night in town, same as the other hands. Hank would see reason.

"I heard you creeping upstairs at some unholy hour last night."

She jumped, then winced, raising a hand to her pounding forehead. "Don't sneak up on me, Maria. And don't talk so loud. It's too damn hot to sleep at night. I felt restless and went out for some fresh air."

Maria Theresa Ortega, the housekeeper and closest thing to a mother Camile had been given, eyed her reproachfully. "Watch your mouth, miss. I know good and well where you went last night. You would put your father into an early grave if he knew half of your doings."

Lifting discarded buckskins with a frown, Maria continued to fuss. "This card playing and running around dressed like a cowhand is no life for a proper lady. When will you find yourself a nice man and settle down—have children the way God intended?"

"I'm not like other women," Camile declared. "Why would I want some scratching, smelly man giving me orders? A house full of squawking brats sounds as pleasant as coffee on a summer afternoon, too. I have plenty to keep me busy."

Maria clucked while straightening out the room's haphazard condition. "Mr. Riley can run things without your help. You have no business prodding cattle and breaking horses. Thomas wants what every father wants, to see his daughter happily settled."

"I'm only twenty," Camile said dryly. "I think I have a few years left."

"Why make him wait? He has little else to look forward to, sitting in that dark study with nothing but ledgers and financial worries during the prime of his life. He needs more, Camile. He needs a son. . . . " Maria quickly closed her mouth.

"A son-in-law to replace the real son I took from him," Camile finished softly. "That's what he needs, isn't it, Maria?"

The housekeeper lowered her gaze. "Forgive me, Camile. You were only eight. The stallion was too much horse for you. You must forget—"

"Forget?" she interrupted. "Forget that I crippled my father and killed my brother? How do you forget something like that?"

Maria approached her, gently placing a hand on her arm. "The horse did those things, not you. If your brother had not pushed you from the stallion's path, you would have been killed."

"Father told me to stay clear of the stallion, but he let Clint ride him, and I wanted to show him I could, too. I wanted him to be proud of me—to notice me."

"And you still want that from him," Maria said, sighing sadly. "But this ranch needs a man to run it, Camile. A fine, strong son-in-law to relieve poor Hank of the burden age places on him. A husband would ease the strain for both Hank and your father."

Camile walked away from her. "I don't need a husband to relieve them, or me, of anything. I realize Hank intends to retire someday. I look for him to hang up his saddle soon and let me take over."

"You?" Maria asked, her surprise evident. "As much as Hank Riley dotes upon you, he knows the men will not take orders from a woman. You are not your father's son, Camile. However much you wish it were so, however much you want to take Clint's place, you cannot. You make the men nervous now. It is not the same as when you were a little girl in braids. Forget this foolishness."

"They'll take orders from me same as they would Hank," Camile insisted, slipping into her buckskins. "I rope, ride, and brand better than most."

"Your father would be just as proud if you could cook a meal or darn a pair of socks. You have paid your debt, Camile. Give him what you can. Accept what you cannot change."

"I won't accept it!" Camile snatched a shirt from the floor. "Father will see that I can do as good as he did, as good as Clint would have done if I hadn't . . . " She caught herself, fighting the weakness that made her eyes water, her heart hurt. "You can't expect me to change after all this time. I'd go crazy following all the rules of being female. This body's been given to the wrong person."

When she immodestly pulled her nightdress over her head, standing before the housekeeper half-naked, Maria said, "That body will get you into trouble if you keep showing it off in those tight buckskins. Being a woman is not a curse. Someday, a man will come along to make you see there is more to life than sluggish cattle and headstrong horses."

After securing her hair with a leather thong, Camile retrieved a fringed jacket from her chaise longue. The longue was pink, like the rest of her room. A room that didn't match her personality. Everything about it was soft, delicate, feminine. Maria had lent a hand in the decor. A surprise gift for Camile's twentieth birthday.

"I wish Father would have bought me another horse, instead," she said, glancing around the room.

The remark sent Maria away, muttering Spanish under her breath. Camile watched her go, then studied the frilly decor surrounding her. Did her father want her to become a lady? Thomas Cordell didn't care one way or the other, Camile reminded herself. Since the accident, he hadn't cared about much of anything except his cattle and his financial ledgers.

His indifference hurt and angered her. She wanted his approval, his love, his forgiveness. Camile thought the only way to win those things was to become the son she'd taken from him. And she would. She'd speak to her father that very morning about letting her take over. Maria. What did she know anyway?

Certain her father would be pleased with her dedication to the ranch, Camile left her room and bounded down the stairs toward his study. She paused before reaching the bottom. Did Maria really think a man could change her? Make her want children? Strap her to household duties?

A face appeared inside her head. Wade Langtry, Hank said he called himself. The snake wasn't hard to look at, she'd give him that much. He possessed the devil's dark allure and a smile she supposed might turn a weaker female's knees to butter. The man had dimples. The kind that slashed deep grooves in his cheeks when he smiled.

His eyes were the color of spring grass. His hair, black

as midnight. He'd stood tall, broad at the shoulders and narrow at the hips. She supposed many a woman had sighed with pleasure over the mere sight of him. Camile sighed, then immediately straightened.

"Damn greenhorn," she muttered angrily. "Woman beater," she added, jumping the last three steps of the staircase. A few seconds later, Camile barged into Tom Cordell's study.

"Father, we need to talk about the ranch."

Tom Cordell's head turned in her direction. "Please knock before blowing into my study like a dust devil, Camile. I'm involved in a meeting."

She glanced across the room and froze. *Him.* The greenhorn. The woman beater. "What are you doing here?" she snapped.

"Have you met Mr. Langtry?" her father asked, his brows drawing together. "He only arrived an hour ago."

When Langtry opened his mouth, Camile quickly intervened. *"Of course not,"* she stressed, purposely narrowing her eyes on the man. "It took me off guard to find you had a guest is all. Mr. Langtry, is it?"

When Langtry smiled, she tried not to catch her breath too loudly. He pushed away from the mantel and approached her.

"And you must be the sweet Camile your father's been telling me about. I almost feel as if I know you."

Her stomach twisted. He had her at a disadvantage. Tom Cordell would lock her up and throw away the key if he knew she went into Rosie's every Saturday night.

"Mark my words, you don't," she warned.

"The sweet Camile to which I earlier referred was her

33

mother," Tom interjected. "This one is a little on the stickery side. Sit down, Camile. As long as you've barged in uninvited, you might as well stay."

Camile chose a seat with her back against the wall, scowling when Wade took one directly across from her.

"Mr. Langtry appeared out of nowhere to solve a problem of ours," Tom explained. "He worked the Tisdale spread out of Colorado. A good man, Martin. A shame he suffered a bad winter."

She snorted softly in response. "Tisdale ain't worth spit on a hay fire. He sold out to a group of money-hungry Easterners, and now they've come crawling around here. Tisdale should have sent them damned Yanks packing, the same as we did."

"Watch your mouth, Camile," Tom scolded her. He turned to Wade. "My daughter's rather outspoken. You'll have to excuse her unladylike mannerisms."

Langtry eyed her from head to toe. "Them damned Yanks, as she calls them, could polish her manners a bit. Miss Cordell might do well under the instruction of Margaret Pendergraft's school of charm in St. Louis. The woman's talents are known far and wide."

"I won't sit here and be insulted." Camile rose. "I'll speak with you later, Father. *Alone*. Finish your business so Mr. Langtry will go away."

Tom blushed. He rubbed his forehead. "Sit down, Camile. I'm sure Mr. Langtry only meant to suggest rather than insult. Besides, we may as well settle this now."

"Settle what?" Camile reseated herself. "Exactly what did Mr. Langtry miraculously appear to save us from?"

Her father straightened in his wheelchair. "I've hired Mr. Langtry to be our new foreman. Only a trial run to see if he works out, but Hank's been after me to replace him for over a year. Trouble was, I couldn't make a decision among our own men. Mr. Langtry will do the ranch good."

"Foreman?" Camile whispered, shocked. "But . . . I thought . . . *I* can run the ranch. We don't need him!"

"Calm down, missy," her father instructed her. "Hank hinted you might have that fool notion in your head. The men expect to take orders from another man, Camile."

"You won't give me a chance?" She jumped to her feet. "It was cruel, letting me work so hard to prove I could pull my weight, only to give a position rightfully mine to the first stranger who walked in here and asked for it!"

Tom squirmed under his daughter's fury. "This ranch has become your obsession, Camile. I can't bear the thought of you sinking your whole life into it and denying yourself a woman's needs. I want you to have a husband and children. I'd like to see you settled before I die. You should be wearing fine dresses and attending socials. Wait much longer and you'll be too old for marrying."

It was too much for Camile—Wade Langtry crumbling her dreams into dust and her father turning traitor. She must do something. Because of her, everything important had been taken from Tom Cordell. Camile meant to prove herself worthy of reclaiming his affections.

"I have a proposition," she said calmly, although her heart was about to beat out of her chest. "Mr. Langtry and I'll both run the ranch for the next month, and if I'm the better of the two, he goes."

"That's the most harebrained—"

"Hold up, Mr. Langtry," Tom said, interrupting. "What if you aren't better, Camile? What then?"

She shrugged. "He stays."

Ronda Thompson

"Not only will he stay, but you'll start wearing dresses and find yourself a husband," Tom said. "I swear I'll sell this place if I have to worry about you being here alone after I'm gone."

The stakes were high. Camile wasn't ready to find a husband. She wasn't ready for children, fancy dresses, or socials. Still, she took a deep breath and said, "All right, Father. It's a deal."

"I'll hold you to it, Camile," Tom promised. "You'd best think about it again."

"When do we start?"

He sighed. "Right now. I want each man to draw a mustang to break. The drive's coming up soon. We need horses for the remuda."

Camile crossed the study in her long-legged strides. "I'll get my chaps and meet you at the corral."

Tom wheeled his chair from behind the desk after her departure. "If she beats you, Mr. Langtry, I'll have to stand by my word."

"Call me Wade, Mr. Cordell, and no female is going to beat me."

"All right, Wade." He chuckled softly. "I'm counting on you being as good as Tisdale demands of his cowhands. I didn't figure Camile would take this sitting down. I've let her have her way too long. Camile's backward, and it didn't occur to me until Hank mentioned she had a notion of running this spread, that I've done her an injustice. I should have seen to it that she did female things, mixed with other ladies, learned about being a woman. I hope I didn't wait too long."

Given his short acquaintance with Camile Cordell,

36

Wade felt relatively certain that he had. Being privy to this recent conversation left him in an awkward situation. The decision to infiltrate had been reached after assuming father and daughter were two of a kind. Tom wasn't what he'd expected.

Middle-aged, with graying hair, and with a straight spine regardless of the wheelchair, Tom Cordell represented what society called a man's man. Tough, but not unreasonable, except maybe where Camile was concerned. Did Cordell actually believe a scrap of leather like Camile could run a ten-thousand-acre stretch of land and cattle? Would he sell if he had to own up to the possibility of his daughter running the ranch without benefit of a husband?

If Wade let Camile win, he could insure that Tom came to terms with that reality. But then again, if by some twist of fate Camile did prove herself capable, Tom might relent and give her control of the ranch.

It was as Wade expected, not as simple as Gregory Kline indicated it would be. "You wouldn't really consider selling, would you, Tom?" Wade asked, testing the waters. "They say Tisdale got a fair price."

"Worried about your job?" Tom smiled. "No, not as it stands. I don't see much point in keeping the place if Camile can't find a good man to help her run the ranch. She could have her pick of ranchers' sons in the area if she'd make an effort to be more . . . womanly. I deeded the Circle C to her after the accident. I didn't know if I'd pull through, but if she can't find a husband to help with the hard work, I might reconsider."

Damn, the place was in Camile's name. "Does she know?" Wade asked. It'd be better if Tom Cordell still had total control. Of course, deeds could be changed. Tom's concern over his daughter would work to Wade's advantage. He planned to show her up, make it clear to Tom she had no business owning a ranch.

Tom grinned at him. "Heaven forbid if she found out. I sleep easier knowing she won't come stealing in the night to slit my throat over the ranch. Camile loves this place, although it confuses me as to why she would. Men love the land; women usually only tolerate Texas because they have no choice. Her mother hated this life. Pretty pale thing, her mama. I shouldn't have brought her here; the land killed her."

Wade felt a stab of guilt for deciding on deceit to worm his way into the Cordell stronghold. This was necessary, he reminded himself. It was the Cordells or him.

"I need this position." The lie tasted bitter on his tongue. "I won't be easy on your daughter."

"Hell, I hope not," Tom grumbled. "That's what bothered me about deciding on Grady, or any other of my men for that matter. They've watched her lead Hank around too long not to be led themselves. You put Camile in her place, and we both get what we want."

"What about what *she* wants?" Wade hardly remembered his own father, but supposed most wanted their children to accomplish whatever they set out to do. It was one thing for Wade to use deceit in order to achieve his goals, but a father, that was different.

"This is best for Camile," Tom answered. "My daughter doesn't know what she wants, and it's up to me to convince her. Once we get past this silly dream of hers, and I find a nice rancher's son to make her his wife, she'll thank me for setting her straight."

"Out of curiosity, what if she does beat me?"

"You'll be out of a job," Tom said with the same steely glint he'd passed to his daughter. "And because I'm a man of my word, I'll give control of the Circle C to Camile. Then I'll watch the place go to hell because she can't manage the men or get them to work for her."

"She'd sell within a year," Wade considered out loud.

"Not in a hundred," Tom scoffed. "Camile inherited the Cordell stubbornness. Selling out is the same as admitting defeat in her book. She'd die first, and take the rest of us right along with her."

"More independents are selling every day. How do I know you won't do the same given the first opportunity? I'm already taking on more than the original agreement."

"You want better money." Tom nodded. "I'll double your pay if you make fast work of Camile. As for the other, nothing comes with a guarantee in these hard times. One bad winter can wipe a man out. I'll guarantee you a year, Langtry. If Camile hasn't got herself a husband by that time, I'm going to sell. Her mother would have wanted her to live a softer life."

A year was too long for Wade. Kline expected him back in three months. That left one option. Beat her fast, beat her good, and hope when Tom called her bluff, Camile would throw a temper tantrum the way she'd done the previous night and force Tom to rethink selling the ranch.

Reluctantly, Wade nodded. "Sounds like a fair deal."

"Well, let's get to it." Tom wheeled forward. "I've got to introduce you around and tell the men what's going on. Not everything, mind you. The extra pay for beating Camile is between us, Langtry."

Wade rose, following Tom from the study. If he felt less than respectful of the man's traitorous practices, he understood Cordell's motives. The female upstairs needed to be put in her place. He'd said it was time someone broke her. Wade guessed he was the someone.

Chapter Three

"About time," Wade grumbled when Camile joined him outside. "It's obvious you weren't up there primping. What took so long?"

She frowned up at him, already annoyed because Maria's cleaning had kept her searching long and hard for her chaps. She suspected the Mexican woman's claim of not knowing their whereabouts was a lie. Maria had been outraged when Camile told her about the upcoming contest. She'd also been too preoccupied with staring out the window at Wade Langtry to help search. The housekeeper had crooned and carried on about his handsome face and strong build until Camile thought she might throw up.

"I've been explaining the advantages of castration to our housekeeper," Camile answered under her breath. "Maria mistook you for a bull from the upstairs window. I'm about to prove you're only a steer in disguise."

Langtry smiled. "I've never seen a heifer get as nervous around a steer as you did last night. I think you know I've got all my parts."

Heat exploded in Camile's cheeks. She didn't want to think about last night. She didn't want to think about his lap, or her reaction to him. "You've already called me a whore and card cheat. Now you're calling me a heifer?"

"You two quit flapping your jaws and get this show under way," Hank shouted from the breaking pen.

The fact that Wade hadn't answered her, and from all appearances didn't intend to, further annoyed Camile. "Who goes first?"

"Normally, 'ladies first' is the rule, but all things considered . . ."

She stopped in her tracks, her anger growing by leaps and bounds. Langtry kept walking. Camile didn't care about being a lady, it was just the way he'd said it—the way he'd made her feel less than perfect—a whole lot less. She hurried to catch up with him. "What horse did you draw?"

"That black mare."

His misfortune pleased her. "Leonard Baker climbed on her last week. He ran off the next day. Where'd you say Leonard went, Hank?" she called.

The former foreman shoved his hat back on his head, then grinned. "We decided he went off to join one of them singing outfits!" he shouted across the breaking corral. "An opera, I think they call it. His voice was mighty high when that black filly finished with him."

An outburst of laughter followed. Wade climbed atop the fence and swung his tall frame over. "Singing's never been one of my strong suits." He ran a cool glance along

the men lining the breaking corral, his gaze settling upon
Camile. "Breaking hardheaded fillies, now there's a manly
chore. This one won't take long. Wait and watch. I'll show
you how it's done."

If Camile obeyed, it wasn't because he asked, but
because the moment he moved off, she noticed something
about him she hadn't noticed the previous night. Wade
Langtry looked good walking away. When he bent to dust
his hands with dirt, her gaze traveled the length of his muscled legs and settled on his tight behind.

"Bet he flattens his ass."

She snapped her head toward Hank. Camile thought
he'd caught her staring at what she shouldn't be staring at.
Hank had his gaze trained on the breaking corral. She
turned back to watch Wade. He climbed into the saddle,
pulled his Stetson lower over his eyes, and gave a nod.
When Grady released the horse's bridle, it became difficult
to keep her eyes focused on any particular part of Wade
Langtry.

"Hell, he ain't no greenhorn," Hank muttered. "Thought
he was too pretty to be good at much except getting
beneath a woman's skirts." The older man's cheeks turned
pink. His gaze slid in Camile's direction. "Sorry," he mumbled. "I wish you were still twelve."

"I'd have understood it at twelve, too," she countered
dryly, never glancing away from Wade.

The black squealed with outrage. The filly tried to get
her nose down, but Langtry took none of her nonsense. He
kept a firm grip on the reins to force her head up, foiling
her attempts to buck as hard as she could.

"Always was too smart for your own good." Hank held
the hat with the draw slips out to her.

He insulted her with pride, Camile noted. A pride Tom Cordell never indicated he felt toward his only child. As she withdrew the colored tag, she studied the five remaining mustangs in the holding pen. A tag had been attached to the halter of each horse. Her slip matched a scraggly buckskin. Looks, she knew, were deceptive when it came to horses. The scrawny ones were often the hardest to ride.

"Why didn't you tell me you gave notice?" she asked.

Hank sighed. "Your pa told me to keep quiet about it, that's why. Tom wanted to find a replacement first. Didn't figure Langtry for ranch foreman material last night. Something about him don't set right."

"Langtry won't be foreman," Camile assured him. "Are you behind me, or are you going to turn traitor like my father?"

"I'll go with whoever does the best job. If you care about this place as much as you claim, you'll understand the sense behind that decision."

"You don't think I can beat him," Camile accused Hank.

"I didn't say that, pumpkin." Hank tugged on her long ponytail. "If there's a female walking the earth who could out-hand a man, it's you."

The compliment, as well as the term of endearment, brought a warm feeling to her insides. Hank hadn't called her "pumpkin" since the age of nine. He'd taught her everything she knew about the physical aspects of running a ranch. Her father, unwillingly, had taught her the money end. "Will you stay with us?" she asked.

He nodded. "Where would I go? You and your pa are the only family I've ever known. Tom don't always see things the same as I do, but he's a good man. He'd never turn a man out just because he's too old to pull his weight."

"I'm glad you'll stay." Sudden tears burned the back of her eyes. "No one else is as easy to cheat at cards," she added to cover her soft feelings.

"Yeah, I got a bone to pick with you about that later," he warned her. "In the meantime, Langtry's brought the black around. Made fast work of her just like he said he would. Guess I was wrong about him."

"You're up, Cam!" Grady Finch shouted.

Camile pulled her gloves tighter and climbed the fence. Adjusting her hat, she watched Langtry give the black a pat on the rump before he ambled toward her.

"That buckskin looks pretty wiry. Sure you can handle him?"

"I cut my teeth on meaner horses than him," Camile assured him.

The mustang reared while being led into the breaking pen, earning Cam a skeptical glance.

"Why don't you forget this nonsense and go find yourself some needlework?" Wade said.

She smiled sweetly at him. "If I knew how to sew, the first thing I'd stitch shut would be that annoying mouth of yours."

Wade laughed when she walked away, then climbed the fence, jumping down next to Hank. The job with Martin Tisdale had paid off more than the original agreement. Tisdale had hired him seven years ago to ferret out those among his men tied to a rustling gang. It had taken him months of grueling labor to expose those involved. He'd learned a lot about ranch life—knew what it took to handle a half-loco horse. Wade hoped Camile did.

"Does she know what she's doing?" he asked, no longer smiling, but oddly concerned.

"She has a way with wild things. That jug-head will be eating out of her hand before she's through with him."

When the mustang pinned his ears back and nipped at the woman under discussion, Wade remained unconvinced. "The day I see that one cozy up to her, I'll do the bunkhouse laundry."

"I'm still acting foreman until one of you proves yourself the better man. I'll hold you to it, Langtry."

Despite the grin stealing over Hank's mouth, Wade didn't think he had much to worry about. Grady held the horse's halter as Camile eased her foot into the stirrup. She nodded, and hell with hooves came to Oldham County. The buckskin had more spunk than the black. He crow-hopped, tail-spun, and went down on his knees once, but Camile couldn't be thrown. Wade watched her, fascinated.

If he weren't seeing it, he'd have never believed she possessed the strength to hold the mustang. Unable to throw her, the horse tried to rub his rider off along the rough-edged boards of the corral.

"Get him away from the fence!" Wade shouted, having heard the tearing noise of her buckskins.

"Shut up, Langtry! You're breaking my concentration!" she shouted back. "I'm going to castrate you, you worthless pile of dung, then we'll see how smart you are!"

Wade assumed her threat had been directed toward the mustang. He breathed a sigh of relief when she pulled the horse to the center of the corral. Her mount was tiring. A cheer went up from the men lining the coral fence.

Sides heaving, coat lathered, the mustang gave up the battle. Wade grudgingly admitted Camile had proven herself a worthy opponent at breaking horses. She smiled smugly at him before removing her bandanna to wipe her forehead. Curiously, she then secured the rag around what appeared from his vantage point to be her leg.

Grady came forward and took the mustang's bridle. Camile eased her weight from the saddle. He thought she winced when her feet hit the ground; then she fumbled in her shirt and removed a sugar cube, extending her palm.

"He won't take it," Wade muttered.

Hank grinned broadly. "Our laundry ain't been done in two weeks. I hope your hands can take all that lye."

Sweat popped out on Wade's brow. Damn, he couldn't do a woman's job. He'd be a laughingstock. Uneasily, he glanced back at Camile.

"Come on," she said softly to the mustang. "You know you want it."

Her low, husky voice disturbed Wade. Everything about her unsettled him. He shouldn't respond to her the way he did—he was practically engaged. A real woman waited for him in St. Louis. Lilla Traften. Camile was the least feminine female he'd ever come across, and yet . . .

"Give it up, Camile," Tom instructed from his wheelchair. "The rest of you mount up and get to work. We need to get those spring calves branded before the drive."

A small burst of air left Wade's lips. He pushed away from the fence, headed toward his gelding. A shout from Grady Finch froze him in mid-stride.

"She's tamed him. The jug-head took it."

Slowly, Wade turned. The mustang chomped loudly, regarding Camile as if she were the salt of the earth.

"Christ," he said under his breath. It was loud enough for Hank Riley to hear.

"You should have done your praying right after you made that fool offer. Laundry's piled up at the bunkhouse door. Better get started. It'll take a while."

Twelve faces turned to gawk at him. Wade supposed if he were a female, he'd blush. Tom Cordell looked less than pleased his new man would spend his first day at the Circle C doing women's work. Accepting the circumstance seemed a more mature reaction than killing them all, if it was the less desirable option to him at the moment.

"I'll need the boiling pots and the lye," Wade said.

Easing through the coral fence, Camile asked, "What's going on?"

The foreman grinned at her. "Mr. Langtry offered to do the bunkhouse laundry if you got that jug-head to eat out of your hand. I'd say that was right friendly of him, wouldn't you, boys?"

Men snickered. A cold glare from Wade silenced them . . . all but one. A female.

Camile laughed so hard her eyes filled with tears. "Maria will be grateful to you, Langtry. We were thinking of hiring an extra woman to help out, but I guess that won't be necessary now."

"That'll be enough," Tom injected. "It takes a strong man to stand by his word, even if he didn't think too hard before making the pledge. The next man, or woman," he added, looking at Camile, "who finds Wade's predicament amusing, will work right along beside him."

She promptly straightened. The hard look Wade cast in her direction helped dissolve Camile's humor. It wasn't her fault he'd made that lame offer. Turning before her mouth bowed into a smile, she headed toward the barn. Her leg hurt like the dickens. She should have looked harder for the chaps. Thanks to the mustang, she had an ugly scrape on her thigh. A little doctoring would see her through the rest of the day; then she'd ask Maria to dig out the splinters.

"Wade, you'd best ask Maria to get you an apron," Tom instructed. "That lye will take the dye right out your clothes."

It started as rumble in her throat, then erupted from her mouth in the form of a loud snort. Camile kept walking, trying to control her shaking shoulders.

"I heard that, Camile," Tom said. "You were given a warning. Get an apron."

Camile choked, then wheeled around. "I couldn't help myself. It was that apron business that got to me. I don't know the first thing about washing clothes!"

"Temper tantrums are hardly the reaction a foreman would display when given a direct order," her father scolded. "You'd do well to follow Wade's example and take it like a man."

Having given her a proper set-down in front of everyone, Tom wheeled his chair toward the two-story boss house. Wade followed with the obvious purpose of asking Maria for an apron. Camile stood fast. Her father had never openly chastised her in front of the cowhands. His scolding both angered and embarrassed her.

"You can't win if you can't take orders," Hank muttered in passing.

As her gaze roamed the men waiting to see what she would do, Camile admitted he was right. This was no time for a temper tantrum. She would follow Wade's example. Lifting her chin a notch, Camile marched toward the house. She wouldn't wear an apron, but she'd help Langtry bring the pots and the lye. As it turned out, he

49

refused to wear an apron as well. They dragged the pots outside while Maria began piling the laundry on the porch.

Soon, the Texas sun became a fiery ball in the sky. Camile had trouble deciding if her shirt was soaked due to the heat, or her sloppy attempts at laundering.

"You scrub for a while, I'll hang," she insisted, rubbing her aching back.

"I've scrubbed twice as many pairs of longhandles as you already," Wade snarled, not turning from his task of spreading undergarments over a thin rope.

"My shirt's wet clear through, and my back hurts like the devil. Let me dry out for a while."

When he wheeled around to face her, Camile thought for a second he looked like a man drawing a gun. He pointed a clothes peg at her.

"Look at my hands," he ordered. "I can take cuts, calluses, open running sores, but dammit, my knuckles are raw with that lye. You pull your own weight."

She glared at his back when he resumed his clothes hanging. Unfinished laundry or not, she couldn't ignore the stinging in her thigh. The scrape needed tending. Camile rose, stretched her cramped muscles, and headed toward the barn.

The tack room held supplies for doctoring horses. Camile eased the door open and slipped inside, fumbling around in the dark. She knocked a jar of liniment from a shelf, swore loudly, and reached for the lantern. A match struck against wood behind her.

"We haven't finished the laundry."

Glancing over her shoulder, she eyed Wade coldly. "I

don't take orders from you. Go on about your business and let me tend to mine."

Rather than leave, he stepped inside the tack room. "Do you think because your daddy makes the rules, you don't have to follow them? If your back hurts or the sun's too hot, you can just walk off and do something easier?"

By God, but he was annoying. Her leg began to throb, deteriorating an already underdeveloped patience. "I hurt myself, all right?"

His brow lifted. "Let me see."

Camile tensed. "Do you think I'd purposely lie to get out of doing my share?"

"Any woman who'd cheat at cards would lie, too."

Ripping the bandanna off her thigh, Camile glared back at him. "There! Are you satisfied?"

He whistled softly. "That's a nasty scrape. Sit on the bench. I'll light the lantern."

"I don't need your help. It's not serious."

"You can't hold the lantern close, keep that torn buckskin out of the way, and dig splinters out at the same time," he countered, lighting the lamp and bathing the tack room in a soft glow.

Although it irked her to do so, Camile admitted he had a point. "All right. There's a pair of tweezers for plucking cactus from the horse's legs in that black bag. Jim Cummings stashes a bottle of whiskey behind those bandages on the top shelf. You'll find a mixture of prickly pear and coal oil in a tin container. That should take care of it for now."

"When you give in, you don't make any bones about it," Wade grumbled, searching for the requested items. "Have you always been the bossy type?"

51

"You offered," Camile reminded him. "I guess you're feeling a little testy about now. But then, washing's probably not what you had in mind for your first day on the Circle C."

"Too bad we aren't competing at women's work instead of men's."

"Meaning?"

"Meaning, you're lousy at laundry." He looked up at her. "It's a particular belief of mine that whatever you do, like it or not, pleasant or unpleasant, you should strive to do it well."

"I outrode you today," she grumbled. "Bet that stung your manly pride."

Wade smiled. "Not half as bad as this will sting yours."

When he poured the whiskey over her raw skin, Camile proceeded to impress him with every swear word she knew.

"Hasn't anyone ever taken a bar of soap to your mouth?" he asked flatly, going for the splinters.

"Hank tried it once. I told him if I had to eat soap for swearing, so did he and the others. After a while, Maria started to complain about the shortage. Seems there was always more cussing than soap to go around."

The indentations along his mouth deepened. Camile thought he'd smiled, but realized a second later he'd just been steeling himself to go after the last splinter, one lodged fairly deep beneath her skin.

"Gosh-dang, son-of-a-buck, hellfire almighty!" she swore, half-attempting to clean up her language. "Let me at least catch my breath between your clumsy attempts!"

He sighed, then sat back on his haunches. Camile supposed it was the sudden lack of pain that caused her to notice she had a man between her legs. One whose warm hand rested against the bare flesh of her thigh. She suddenly felt strange, nervous.

"Maybe you'd better go on and finish," she suggested. "Someone might come looking for us."

"What's the matter, hellcat? Afraid if your father finds out you've hurt yourself, he won't let you pretend you're a man anymore?"

"This isn't a game," she said. The tack room felt too small and too hot. "My father knows a meager scratch like this one won't slow me down. . . . " Her voice trailed away when his warm fingers smoothed liniment over her scrape. It took a few minutes to reclaim her thoughts. "I-I'll tell you what I think, Langtry. I think after seeing me ride this morning, you're afraid I'm more of a man than you."

For a moment he held her gaze; then he glanced down. Camile followed the direction of his eyes. The damp shirt she wore clung to the outline of her breasts, leaving little to the imagination.

"You might ride like a man, drink like one, and cuss worse, but you're definitely a woman."

Camile crossed her arms over her breasts. He laughed softly.

"Hiding them won't change anything. In fact, if you want to please your father and find a husband, showing them off might be to your advantage."

Instinctively, her hand shot out to slap him. He grabbed her wrist before her palm made contact.

"Don't do that," he warned. "I haven't given you a reason."

Camile tried to pull away. "You think I'll parade myself around like a prize sow for some man? I don't want a husband. I want the ranch!"

Wade held tight to the wrist she fought to release. Camile used the nails of her free hand to claw his fingers. She soon found that wrist captured as well.

"I heard you promise your father you'd find a husband if you lost the competition."

"If," she stressed, attempting to bring her leg up for the purpose of kicking him. "I don't plan on losing."

A jerk forward and Camile found herself straddling his lap, her hands twisted behind her. They were flush against one another—eye-to-eye, mouth-to-mouth, chest-to-breasts.

"You were bluffing, weren't you," he said.

She smiled smugly at him. He smiled back; then his gaze lowered to her mouth, the seemingly innocent gesture causing all kinds of unseemly things to go through her mind. Camile tried to wriggle off of his lap. His arms tightened around her.

"What's going to happen when I win?" he asked.

His breath sounded labored from their struggle. Camile tried to keep her eyes trained on his, but like his had done earlier, they lowered to his mouth.

"You won't," she replied.

"I will."

Something strange was happening. Camile squirmed uncomfortably. She felt odd. He felt . . . different. Or rather, his lap did. She tried to scoot backward.

"That won't help," he said, pulling her forward. "Stop moving around."

"Then let go!"

"Only if you promise to behave yourself."

She sighed. "All right. I won't try to slap you."

"Or bite, or kick."

"A show of greater strength doesn't make you the better man, Langtry."

"No," he agreed, staring her straight in the eye. "But the fact is, I *am* a man. And the fact that you're a woman is making me more and more aware of it."

Camile was very aware of his masculinity, as well. She suspected the strange emotions he stirred had something to do with her female side. She sensed they were dangerous—that he was dangerous—that allowing him to place her in this position was dangerous.

"Let go," she repeated.

Once more, his gaze lowered to her mouth before he released her. Camile scrambled up, regarding him warily. She wondered if their bodies pressed together had rattled him the way it had her. "You'd be wise to ride out," she said shakily. "Save yourself a lot of trouble and move on."

He rose and replaced the liniment. His movements were as graceful as a cat's when he strolled toward the door. "I knew you were trouble from the moment I laid eyes on you, but I don't spook easily." Wade turned, then winked at her. "You'll make a lovely bride."

Since she'd promised not to slap, bite, or kick him, Camile began searching for something to throw. She was no stranger to trouble, either. Wade Langtry was going to be a problem.

Chapter Four

The first week was hell. Camile's legs ached from count-less hours in the saddle. Regardless of the hat she wore, the skin on her neck and face was bright red. Her mouth tasted like dirt. To sum it all up, handing—serious handing—was miserable work.

In seven long days the hardship of running a ranch full-time became a reality. Wade Langtry was no greenhorn. He rode a horse as if he were born on one, threw a rope with amazing accuracy, and managed to look good even while wearing two layers of dirt. The men were starting to ask him questions—to follow his lead. Camile couldn't allow that to happen.

"Keep your attention trained on the ground ahead," Hank said beside her. "You can ruin a good horse by step-ping him into a snake hole."

Camile jerked her head forward. "I thought Langtry's

56

horse might be favoring his front foot," she mumbled in explanation.

Hank studied Wade's gelding for a moment before shaking his head. "He appears to be all right. I suspect Langtry knows enough to detect a limp. Thoughtful of you to be concerned for him, though," he added sarcastically.

"I'd hate to see his horse go lame. We're a long way from home."

"He's not limping," Hank argued. "Besides, it ain't the four-legged animal you been gawking at all day."

"Langtry, I think your horse has a rock in his foot!" Camile shouted before glaring at Hank.

Wade pulled up, dismounting as Camile and Hank reined to a halt beside him. "I don't think so," he said. He lifted the horse's right hoof. "No rock," he informed them, lowering the hoof.

"The other foot, you idiot," Camile insisted.

When he slid under his horse's neck to examine the left foot, much to her satisfaction, a small rock could clearly be seen lodged within the hoof's frog.

"You're right," he admitted, glancing up at her. "But the next time you call me an idiot, I'll smack your backside again. I'd give a man worse."

Camile's face grew hot. "Touch me, and I'll lay you out flat *again*."

"Try it without a man holding a gun for you, and we'll see what happens," he countered.

The reminder made her glare at Grady. He shifted in the saddle.

"Figured he should know we don't take to men manhandling our women in Texas," Grady said.

"Seems you prefer it the other way around," Wade drawled, remounting his horse.

"I'd consider that an insult, Finch," Jim Cummings, a cowhand who hadn't been with the ranch long, said. A slow grin stretched his mouth. He glanced between the two men, obviously hoping to see a scuffle.

"Is that right, Langtry?" Grady, hotheaded and hot-blooded, demanded. "Are you insulting my character?"

Nudging his horse closer, Wade met Grady's challenging stare. "Next time she gets herself into trouble, there might not be a man around to get her out."

"I told her she can't go in that place no more," Hank said defensively.

"Like hell I can't!" Camile exploded, making more than one horse dance nervously. "Langtry, I'm damned tired of you poking your nose in my business. As for the rest of you, the next man I catch pulling a gun behind my back will get a taste of my bullwhip. I don't need your protection. Hank, I'm grown now, you can't tell me what I can or can't do!"

Hank's face turned red. Several cowboys suddenly found the ground of interest, peeking from beneath their hats to see what the foreman would say. He said nothing.

"Appears to me, if she'd had her butt swatted more and kissed less, the lot of you wouldn't have to tiptoe around her temper," Wade offered.

"That does it!" Grady threw his hat on the ground. "Tom wouldn't like you talking about Cam's butt. Excuse me, Cam," he apologized before lunging for Wade.

Both landed in the dirt. Grady struck the first blow. It was his last. Wade quickly rolled from beneath him, gaining his feet. When Grady rushed forward, his nose met with a fist of steel. A face often described as handsome by the opposite gender, mostly those employed at Rosie's cantina, became sadly altered.

"Good God, hit him again, Grady," Hank swore. "You gonna let him take you out on the first punch?"

"I don't see you giving him any lip," Grady said, holding his bloody nose.

"Hell, I'm almost twice his age," Hank declared. "You're younger than him. Hit him again."

Wade lifted a brow, lifted his fists, and waited. "Every man has a right to his own opinion," he said to Grady. "You don't have to agree with me, but we don't have to argue with our fists. Give it up, boy."

"Hit him, Grady," Camile ordered.

The cowhand acted automatically, a charging bull up against a matador. Wade sidestepped, twisting Grady around before pinning his arms behind his back. "Surely you have more respect for your arm than you did your nose?"

"If you break his arm, you'll pull his weight," Hank warned.

Nothing earned a man honor among other men as much as knowing how to fight. Camile had opened her mouth to insist someone else step in when a distant spiral of dust drew her attention.

Hank took note of her discovery. "Look out yonder, boys. Something's headed this way."

"A herd," Camile said. "Can't be buffalo, they've all but disappeared. There are still a handful of wild mustangs roaming the territory." So saying, she removed a lariat from her saddle horn.

They came up over a slight rise. A wild herd, led by a

59

dappled gray. The stallion caught their scent and turned the mares.

"Look at him," Camile whispered reverently.

"That there is a killer stallion," Hank said. "He's got a price on his head for stealing mares. The gray has trampled more than one man who had a mind to catch him." He nodded toward the rope in her hand. "Best let him go."

Still at a disadvantage on the ground, Wade ran an appraising eye over the stallion. "I'd like to get my hands on a horse like that."

"He's mine, Langtry," Camile said, and to ensure herself a head start, she smartly slapped her quirt against his dun's hindquarters. Already excited by the scent of wild horses, the animal took off. Camile fought to keep her own horse under control.

"The mule-headed dun you ride couldn't catch that stallion, anyway," she said. "I'll bring the gray in or draw your bath and serve you tea. Even throw in a good cigar." She smiled, dug her heels into her mount's sides, and raced forward.

"Dammit," Wade swore softly. "Your paint can't catch him, either!"

"Cam, get back here!" Hank shouted. He glanced at Wade. "'Spect you're right. Diablo's fast, but he can't outrun the gray. I'd better follow her just the same. The rest of you go on back."

"I'll go," Wade decided. "Camile obviously believes roping the stallion will win her points in the competition. I have the right to try my hand."

Hank considered his request while watching Camile, wide open on the flat plains ahead. "Seems to me you've got a problem." He started to grin. "You ain't got a horse."

"You can use mine, Wade," a man offered, dismounting. "He's the fastest horse among us. We'll round up your dun. I'll ride him back."

Wade approached the man. "Thanks, Jake." He swung into the saddle.

"Mind your manners." Hank stared at him, a warning expression on his face. "Make sure Cam gets home safely."

"I'll see to her," Wade muttered, reining his mount around the men, then giving the horse his head.

Cam had veered off in a different direction, Wade noticed. The dust still spiraled ahead, identifying the path the mustangs took. What was she up to? He pulled up sharply, indecisive whether to pursue Camile or the horses. Knowing the shortest distance was always a straight line, he kicked Jake's horse out and continued forward.

The jagged canyon cut from the flat plains took him by surprise. A gaping hole that appeared from nowhere. Wade pulled the horse up, wondering how to find his way down. He scanned the area, spotting the telltale dust in the distance. The path the herd took.

His mount stumbled along the rocky trail as Wade moved deep into the canyon. The layered walls were tinged with shades of brown, orange, and yellow. Trees rose up from a small bit of heaven growing in the middle of hell.

Sounds of running water reached him in the tranquil silence. The canyon floor stretched ahead, green and alive. A soothing setting, but a deceiving one, he realized a moment later as a thundering herd of frightened mares came straight for him. Wade barely reined his startled mount aside before they raced past.

When the gray appeared, headed in his direction, he

reached for a lariat. He lifted his arm to swing, but noticed the horse already wore a rope around his neck. Attached to that rope was a body. One being dragged along the ground.

Instinctively, Wade reached for his gun. As the stallion raced past, a bullet severed the tie between horse and victim. Wade leapt from his mount's back and raced toward Camile. Gently, he flipped her onto her back, feeling her arms, legs, anything that might be broken. Her eyes were closed.

"Camile," he said, then shook her.

"Don't call me that, and get your hands off of me," she growled through tight lips. Her eyes opened, scorching him with blue fire. "Damn you, Langtry. I had him! Why did you shoot the rope?"

He narrowed his gaze on her. "You must have took a knock to the skull. He had *you*. You didn't have him, and you were about to get yourself killed!"

She pushed his hands aside and rose, brushing the dirt from her clothes. "As soon as he made it to that tall cottonwood up ahead, I intended to roll to the side and wrap him around the trunk."

Wade's heart still pounded inside his chest. She was loco. Plain and simple. "You'd have smashed your empty head in the process!"

"Now I'll never know, will I?" she shouted back.

"You're crazy." He stood, glaring at her the same way she regarded him. "You have no business out here if you don't have more sense than to let go when a horse starts to drag you. What makes you think you deserve a chance at running the ranch? You won't live long if you don't stop trying to outdo me."

"That should suit you. Then you can have my job. I'm surprised you severed the rope. I wouldn't have."

Wade grappled with the urge to throttle her as she walked toward a running stream ahead. He shouldn't have saved her. If she got herself killed, her father would sell out for sure. Maybe Wade would go ahead and accommodate her.

Camile bent on shaking legs, scooping water into her bleeding palms. She knew she'd gotten herself involved with too much horse again. When the stallion had begun to rear and paw, she'd frozen. That day years ago had come back to haunt her. The stallion had raced away, and she'd been too scared to do anything but hold on. Her insides were quaking with fear, her knees weak with relief. She couldn't let Langtry know. She had to be tough.

"You called me an idiot today," he said. "Got me into a fight and spooked my horse. I probably just saved your life. The least you can do is thank me."

Her spine stiffened. "Any fool should be able to tell when his horse is favoring a foot. You're none the worse for wear over that scuffle with Grady, and as for saving my life"—she rose, turning to look at him—"that's pure speculation on your part. If it wasn't for you, I'd have the stallion."

He shook his head, then laughed. "If it wasn't for me, you'd probably be dead. I should tell Hank about this. Let him decide if you're cut out to be foreman."

She felt the color drain from her face. "It'd be your word against mine. Which one of us do you think he'd believe?"

"You don't play fair, do you?"

"No."

His gaze softened on her. "Why is running the ranch so important to you? What do you have to prove?"

Tears stung her eyes. Camile blinked back the moisture and stiffened her spine. "That's none of your business, Langtry. Just keep in mind that running the ranch *is* important. It means everything to me. There's nothing I won't do to win."

The softness faded from his features, replaced by a twitching jaw and a steely stare. "Like I've said, if your butt had been busted more and kissed less, you wouldn't be such a spoiled brat."

His expression worried her, as did the underlying threat in his voice. He didn't have any fool notions about repeating the degrading episode in Rosie's, did he? To make certain he didn't, Camile reached down and retrieved her knife from her boot.

"If you touch me again, I'll hurt you. You know I can handle this knife."

His gaze rolled upward. "You took the drifter because you surprised him. You were lucky. I can wrestle that knife from you in a second."

"Not before I slice you up a little," she assured him.

Wade lifted a brow, then lunged for her. Camile went tumbling backward into the stream. Wade landed on top of her. The water wasn't deep, but the bottom was slippery. She thrashed and kicked at him, satisfied when her boot connected with his knee.

Scrambling from his reach, Camile headed for the opposite bank. She still had the knife. She'd barely made it out when a hand grabbed her ankle. In the slippery mud, she lost her traction and fell, instinctively turning on her back to kick out. Wade hoisted himself on top of her. His strong fingers fastened around her wrist. He pried the knife from her hand and brought it to her throat.

"Remember what happens when you pull a knife on someone stronger? They use it against you."

Camile wasn't afraid of him. He was making a point. Teaching her a lesson. "If you plan on spanking me again, you might as well kill me. I won't sit still for it."

He smiled. "You didn't sit still last time, either." In a lightning-fast motion, he threw the knife. It landed point-down in the soft mud. "I'm not going to kill you."

Camile began to feel strange again. His tall frame was stretched out on top of her. She felt his heart pounding. "And you're not going to spank me, right?" she asked breathlessly.

"I'm not going to kill you, and if I'd known you were a woman, I'd never have spanked you to begin with."

"Then why are you looking at me like that?" she demanded.

His gaze lowered to her mouth. "Because I'll be damned if I'm not going to kiss you."

For a moment, Camile was too shocked to react. A moment was all he needed. His lips brushed hers.

"Open your mouth," he instructed huskily.

"No," she had the bad sense to reply, granting his request.

Warmth flooded her. She shivered. Disgust, Camile told herself. She'd never been kissed before, never felt a man's tongue moving inside her mouth. It was horrible . . . well, maybe it wasn't too bad. She closed her eyes. Being that he was stronger than she was, she decided to let him have his way . . . this time, at least.

He deepened the kiss, and all kinds of strange things started happening inside her. Camile's arms crept up around his neck. Her limbs started to feel like churned butter. Suddenly, the kiss ended. Wade pulled away to stare down at her.

"Either you've never been kissed before, or whoever taught you was sorry at it."

It took Camile a second to realize he'd spoken to her. When his insult registered, she stiffened. "I've been kissed plenty, Langtry. It helps if I don't despise whoever's doing the kissing!"

"Maybe." He grinned. "Maybe not. Because of our first meeting, I assumed you were experienced in the ways between men and women. Now I'm wondering if the reason you're so busy trying to be a man is because no one's taught you to be a woman."

"Is this what being a woman is?" Camile hissed up at him. "Having a man I can't tolerate slobber all over me? I'm not saying it's so, but if it were, you damn sure won't be doing the teaching."

"You're right," he agreed, sliding off her. Wade regained his balance in the slippery mud, then reached down to give her a hand up. "I need a night in town."

Camile ignored the hand he offered, glaring up at him. "Figure on spending time with Rosie?"

He reached down and hauled her to her feet. "Maybe I do, and maybe I don't. Either way, it's none of your business."

Her skin began to itch beneath the mud coating her body. Some unidentified emotion began to knot her stomach. Camile didn't know why, but she had half a mind to retrieve the knife and go at him. She didn't much like the idea of him kissing Rosie the way he'd just kissed her.

Wade bent, retrieved the knife, and glanced over his shoulder at her. "I'll keep this until we reach the ranch." His dimples slashed deep grooves in the sides of his face. "It's not that I don't trust you, Camile."

"A stab in the back would be nothing compared to what my father would do to you if I told him about this. And don't call me that. Call me Cam the same as the rest of the men."

"I'll call you by your given name, just to remind you you're a woman." Wade didn't turn around. "And you won't tell your father. Otherwise, I'll have to mention our first meeting. Maybe tell him about watching the stallion drag you."

She cussed under her breath. "That lousy kiss wasn't worth stirring things up over. It wasn't anything a good dose of soda won't take care of." So saying, Camile stepped toward the stream. Her knees nearly buckled. She quickly disguised the fact that his kiss had affected her by acting as if she'd slipped in the mud. When Wade smiled slightly, she came close to tripping again. Damn those devil dimples of his.

Chapter Five

Wade watched Camile rinse mud from her hair and face beneath the pump. His gaze scanned her backside. Coated in slime, her clothes plastered to her skin, she might as well have been naked. He didn't know why he'd kissed her, but he doubted Rosie, or any of her girls, had a damn thing to do with it. Rarely, if ever, did Wade act impulsively. A man of his former profession plotted, planned, thought things through. His attraction to Camile didn't make sense.

His gaze roamed her slender body again. Then maybe again, it made perfect sense. She certainly wasn't hard to look at. Still, she was trouble—the only person standing between him and the deed to the Circle C. He couldn't afford to feel anything for her, lust or even dislike. His future depended on convincing Tom to sell.

"What happened to you two?" Hank Riley called, approaching them.

Camile groaned.

"We had a run-in with the stallion," Wade answered. "Camile got a rope on him but"—he paused, watching her gaze narrow on him— "the gray pulled us both into the stream and got away."

Hank frowned. "Well, you're lucky that horse didn't kill one of you. The pump's not gonna do much good with that sticky mud."

"As soon as I get most of it off, a bath's what I have in mind," Camile said, then pumped the handle harder.

A slow smile stole over Wade's lips. "I like my water hot. No tea. Whiskey."

Her hand froze on the handle. She glanced at him, her eyes growing wide. "You can't hold me to that!"

He turned toward the older man. "She said she'd bring in the stallion or draw my bath and serve me tea. Isn't that the way you heard it, Hank?"

"She sure as spit said so." Hank scratched his head. "But it wouldn't be proper for her—"

"If she was a man, she'd have to stand by her word," Wade said, interrupting. "I stood by mine when I did the laundry."

Hank nodded. "You did for a fact. I reckon the door swings both ways. Guess it'd be all right if you keep your clothes on until she gets the bath ready. Start boiling the water, Cam."

The bunkhouse was an adobe structure housing fifteen beds. Wade leaned against a bunk, removing his boots, as Camile entered. He'd placed a large wooden tub in the center of the room. The buckets she carried looked heavy. He didn't offer to help her. He did smile at her as she passed, sloshing water over the dirt floor.

"I figure one more bucket of hot water and one of cold will suit me," he said.

She glared at him in answer, emptied her buckets, and headed toward the door. When he pulled his shirt from his pants, Camile stumbled, then hurried out. It was none of his business, her innocence or lack of it, but he found himself curious. How did a woman raised around men all her life manage to remain innocent?

Maybe she was just a sorry kisser, he told himself. He should let it go. Whatever Camile was or wasn't had nothing to do with his job. Still, if she was innocent, she shouldn't go around pretending otherwise. She might get herself into trouble. Wade stripped, grabbed a blanket from his bunk, and wrapped it around his waist.

When she entered with the last buckets, Camile drew up short. "Y-You said you wouldn't undress," she stuttered.

"I said I wouldn't be naked," Wade countered. "And I'm not." He indicated the blanket with a nod.

Stiff-backed, she marched to the tub and emptied her buckets. "There. Your bath is ready."

"The whiskey, remember?"

"I'll bring you a glass," she mumbled.

"And one more bucket to rinse with. Oh, and a cigar."

She turned bright red. "I'll see to it," she huffed, then stormed from the bunkhouse.

Wade smiled at her retreating figure. He'd riled her temper, which wasn't difficult. Steam rose from his bath. He walked to the wooden tub, eyed the water thoughtfully, then let the blanket fall to the floor. Camile Cordell was getting ready to have her bluff called.

Whiskey sloshed over her hand. Camile swore, stuck the cigar behind her ear, transferred the glass to her other hand, and licked the liquor from her fingers. She wanted to get this degrading episode over with. She'd stood by her word, but seeing Wade Langtry wearing nothing but a blanket demanded a high price. His chest was broad and smooth, his arms muscled, and although she'd seen cowhands in various stages of undress over the years, no amount of skin had affected her like his.

Her female side responded to him. A side that Camile couldn't let compromise her dream of running the ranch. She needed her wits during this competition. Langtry wouldn't be easy to beat. Forgetting the feel of his lips on hers might prove distracting, as well as the sight of him half-naked, but Camile planned on putting those things out of her head. The ranch, and winning the position as foreman, should remain uppermost on her mind.

"Here's your whiskey," she said as she entered the bunkhouse, her attention trained on the brimming glass in her hand.

"Bring it to me."

She glanced at his bunk. He wasn't there. Her gaze darted toward the tub.

"I thought I'd enjoy the whiskey and the cigar while I soak."

"You weren't supposed to climb in until I brought your drink," she reminded him, cursing the quaver in her voice. "Hank said—"

"Hank rode out a few minutes ago with most of the ranch hands. I heard them leave."

He was right. They'd gone to string a rope corral for branding the spring calves. The tub wasn't big. His knees were drawn up against him. Camile didn't want Wade getting the notion she felt nervous around him. She walked toward the tub, but kept her eyes downcast.

"Here." She thrust the glass forward.

"I can't reach it. Come closer."

A peek from beneath her lashes made her groan in embarrassment. She stood more than an arm's length from the tub. Bolstering her courage, she closed the space between them. The moment he took the glass she turned to leave.

"The cigar," he reminded her.

Fumbling behind her ear, she removed the cigar and extended it in his direction.

"My hands are wet. Mind lighting it up for me?"

She sighed irritably. "Want me to scrub your back, too?"

"Since you can't bring yourself to look at me, that might prove interesting. No telling what you might scrub instead."

Her gaze lifted abruptly. "I've seen a naked man before, Langtry. I'm not looking because I'm not all that impressed."

He smiled. "You're as nervous as a preacher in a whorehouse. Admitting to being kissed plenty, along with seeing naked men, could get you into trouble. I'm wondering how you've managed to remain innocent."

Camile bit off the end of the cigar and spat, then dug a match from her pocket. Was innocence and ignorance the same thing? "I never said I was." She lit the cigar and blew a stream of smoke into his face.

"You don't have to." Wade accepted the cigar she handed him. "A man can tell."

Something in his tone annoyed her. He sounded almost as if he pitied her. Camile hadn't thought to consider why the cowhands so easily ignored her as a female, though they frequented Rosie's with dedication every Saturday night. She was one of the boys, a circumstance she'd never questioned. Not until Langtry had come along.

"Do you think no man would want me?" she asked angrily.

"Only that none have had you. There's nothing wrong with innocence, Camile. Just some serious consequences for pretending to be something you're not."

His lecturing further angered her. She felt like a child around him. An unattractive creature who hadn't managed to get herself kissed once in twenty years. Camile took a deep breath and lowered her gaze. She couldn't see much.

Skin, arms, legs. Enough to make her heart beat faster, but not enough to make her blush. Bravely, she went around behind him, dipped her hands in the water, and began washing him. The warm texture of his skin sent waves of pleasure racing up her arms. Camile traced soapy patterns across his back. Rather than relax, his muscles tensed.

"I feel a consequence coming on," he said. "You'd better go about your business."

Fascinated by his slopes and angles, she failed to heed his warning. "What happened here?" she asked, her finger circling a small, puckered hole.

"Bullet."

Ronda Thompson

"Did someone shoot you in the back?"

"It was an accident. A mistake for the man who shot me," he added quietly.

Her nails grazed a long slash along the side of his ribs. "How about here?"

"Knife," he answered, his voice husky.

"You sure have gotten into some scrapes."

"Get your hands off of me or you're going to get yourself into one."

Reluctantly, Camile ceased her explorations. She got to her feet, went around the tub, then placed her hands on her hips. "What do you think now?"

Wade snuffed the end of his cigar in what little remained of the whiskey. He set both cigar and glass beside him on the floor. "I think I'm finished."

When he rose, Camile stumbled back a step. Her gaze immediately flew to his face.

"Hand me that bucket of rinse water."

She was blushing; she felt the heat in her cheeks. Damn him for this underhanded trick. Bending, Camile scooped up the rinse water, her gaze quickly returning to his face while she handed him the bucket.

"You're wearing that preacher-in-a-whorehouse expression again. Why don't you just admit you've never seen a naked man?"

Purposely fixing her face into an indifferent mask, she shrugged. "I haven't looked because I thought you might be modest."

He grinned. "I'm not."

"You're bluffing," she decided. "You don't believe I'll look."

"You're the one bluffing. I'm calling you."

Their gazes locked. Camile wasn't the type to back down from a challenge. Maybe it was time she saw a naked man. Who knows what she might stumble upon once she became foreman? She didn't want to act shocked or ignorant. Bravely, she glanced down at his chest. Her gaze moved lower, past the flat plains of his stomach. His body was magnificent. Curiosity getting the best of her, Camile took a deep breath and looked.

"Gosh-dang, son-of-a-buck, hellfire almighty," she whispered. Her gaze shot up to his face.

He lifted a brow. "I'll take that as a compliment."

When he stepped from the tub and snatched up the blanket, Camile's shock receded. Turning tail, she ran. Deep laughter trailed her. Camile glanced over her shoulder and ran smack into something.

"Whoa there," Jim Cummings said, steadying her.

Camile tried to shrug his hands from her shoulders. "Sorry, Jim. I'm in a hurry."

His grip tightened. "Are you all right? Your face is as pale as a ghost."

Jim's breath smelled like liquor. He'd obviously snuck into the tack room for a drink. Camile didn't care for the cowhand. Something about him made her skin crawl.

"I guess the sun's gotten to me," she said, none too gently pulling from his embrace. "Why aren't you with the rest of the men?"

"Hank told me to muck out some stalls," he explained. "Said to have Wade give me a hand. Seen him?"

Her gaze slid toward the bunkhouse. "He's taking a bath."

"How'd you know that?" Jim asked, smiling.

"The bet, remember? I had to fill the tub for him." On shaky knees, she started for the house.

"Figure that ain't all you done for him."

She stopped.

"Tea. Didn't you throw that into the bargain?"

"Yes," she answered, then walked toward the house. She felt Cummings's gaze boring into her until she went inside. Camile leaned against the kitchen door, gulping in deep breaths of air.

Maria entered. She drew up short. "Good heavens. What has happened? You look as pale—"

"As a ghost," Camile finished. She didn't suppose Maria would appreciate hearing the real reason for her flustered state. "Could you fix me a bath?" she asked, pushing away from the door to go upstairs. "I guess the sun got to me."

Once out of Maria's hearing, she added, "And I think I just figured out why brood mares need to be hobbled, and how curiosity killed the cat."

Chapter Six

The spring calves were gathered in the rope corral. Wade watched Camile position herself over a bawling calf, smoking iron in hand. When she bent, pressing the heated tool against the calf's hide, he decided Hank shouldn't have given the job to a female. Especially not one wearing tight buckskins.

Hank sighed wearily beside him. "She's ready for another. Get this one. My arm's bothering me."

"You're showing your age, old man," Wade teased before turning to lasso a calf from the rope corral.

"I ain't that old," Hank grumbled. "Tom must have forgot to tell you the house rules."

A swinging lariat dropped to Wade's side. "House rules?"

"I strongly urge you to forget whatever it is about Cam you seem so damn interested in today. The first rule when hiring on with the Circle C is to keep your hands off Cam. That's the second one, too."

There it was—the reason Camile had managed to remain innocent despite her worldly facade. Hank Riley had obviously been riding roughshod over any man who cast an interested glance in her direction. That was all well and good, but surely he'd run up against a few who didn't spook. Wade knew of one in particular who watched Camile beneath the brim of his hat. Jim Cummings.

"Those tight buckskins she wears draw a man's eye easy," Wade said. "Men will be men. When she bends over, it's hard not to stare."

"She can't brand in a dress," Hank said defensively.

"That's my point. Camile shouldn't be branding calves or punching cows. Tom takes too much for granted. She's a woman whether she wants to be or not. One woman and too many men is bound to cause trouble."

"Reckon it will sooner or later," Hank agreed. "I'd like for Cam to get this ranch. To be able to run it. But I figure being female is always gonna get in her way. I've kept the men that come and go on this ranch in line up until now. A job I'm getting too old to handle. The job'll be yours if you beat her."

"If I win, the job will be her husband's," Wade reminded him.

Hank laughed. "Cam ain't the marrying kind. Figure if she ever does settle down, she'll choose a man she can cow, or one like you."

"I have a woman," Wade said.

"You married?" Hank asked.

"Not yet, but Camile isn't my type."

"That's good." Hank regarded him seriously. "Because

you ain't good enough for her. Tom has plans for his only daughter. She'll marry a rancher's son. One who brings land and cattle with him. Understand?"

"Sounds to me like Tom will do the choosing, and he'll use the Circle C as bait."

"This is a good ranch," Hank admitted. "Ralph Lamar has the adjoining land. He also has an unmarried son."

"How convenient," Wade drawled, not liking the information at all. He didn't want Tom planning a merger—he wanted him planning a sale.

"Are you going to get me a calf or flap your jaws with Hank all day, Langtry?"

Camile's impatient shout ended the disturbing conversation. Wade lassoed her a calf, concerned for her future and his. He didn't like the thought of Camile being roped into a wedding. Tom wouldn't sell if his daughter's marriage strengthened his cattle empire.

The Wagner Cattle Company wanted this ranch. Being a stockholder himself—Wade wanted it, too. He'd built a nice, respectable life in St. Louis. One far from killing for bounty. He wouldn't let anyone take that away from him. Not Gregory Kline. Not Tom Cordell, and not Camile.

She wasn't a problem he'd planned on. His foolish, but undeniable, attraction toward her wasn't anything he'd counted on. Maybe he'd played the respectable gentleman too long. It was Saturday. A night in town might put him back on track.

"Let's head for home, boys," Hank shouted. "It's Saturday!"

A chorus of whoops followed. Men scrambled for their mounts. The female among them approached her horse less enthusiastically. Wade knew Hank had forbidden her to accompany the men. That suited him. He had business to tend—business he didn't need Camile's presence distracting him from. She'd walked a wide path around him since the bunkhouse incident. He hadn't meant for things to go so far. Camile was stubborn. He'd learned that fact the first night he met her. Now he knew something else. She wasn't experienced.

"When you gonna put that bottle away and give Rosie what she wants?" Grady asked from across the table.

Wade looked up from his cards, glancing toward the brunette tending bar. She wasn't discreet about her desire to see him to a back room. He'd get there in his own good time. His plan to storm into the cantina, take Rosie by the arm, and go straight to bed had seemed less urgent once the ride relaxed his jumbled nerves. It wouldn't do any harm to build the tension a little longer. He had all night.

A slim arm dangled over his shoulder. Meg, one of Rosie's girls, pressed her breasts against the back of his neck. "Maybe Rosie's not to his liking."

"I got a notion he has a taste for cactus," Jim Cummings said.

Meg removed her arm. The woman served a tray of drinks, her gaze darting between the men before she returned to the bar.

"What's that supposed to mean, Cummings?" Wade asked.

The man slurped his beer, then belched. "It means, I think you got a stiff feeling for a certain firebrand. A gal whose daddy'd castrate you if he knew you'd been sniffing around what the rest of us have orders to leave be."

Silence fell over the table of four. Wade knew Jim's

problem. Cummings was the type to figure if he couldn't have Camile, no one else of his station should either.

"Not only are you compromising my position at the ranch, but you've slurred a certain firebrand's reputation. Since, lucky for you, Camile isn't here to defend herself, I'll have to beat some sense into you if you don't take that back."

"There won't be no fighting in my place tonight," Rosie informed the group, appearing at Wade's side. "Not over her. That scratchy scrap of a girl ain't woman enough for you, is she, Wade?"

In answer, he pulled her into his lap, never releasing Cummings from his hard stare. "I'll have an apology—not for me, I don't give a damn what you think—but for Camile."

Jim crumbled. "I-I, hell, I was just spouting off. Every man on the Circle C knows Cam's not that kind."

"What kind?"

A familiar voice snapped Wade's head in a new direction. He swore under his breath. "What are you doing here?"

"Whatever I please," Camile answered, running a cool gaze over Rosie. "I was headed toward Hank's table when I heard my name." She turned to Jim. "Well? What kind?"

"The kind to stay home like she's told," Wade answered.

"I'm not talking to you, Langtry," Camile ground out through her teeth. "Why don't you run along to the back, where you can pay someone to do what they're told."

Rosie stiffened in Wade's arms. "I find your barbs amusing as long as you direct 'em toward the cowhands under your thumb, Cactus. We provide an honest service for the men of this community." Her dark gaze strayed to Wade

81

before her sharpened nails stroked the strong shoulder they rested upon. "You run along and let me tend to women's business."

Camile decided she should have stayed home. She didn't like seeing Wade with another woman. To keep from saying as much, she moved away, intending to spend the evening with Hank and a few of the older cowhands. There was a problem when she reached the table. Hank had disappeared. She took his vacant chair, turning to Jinx Callahan.

"Where's Hank?"

Jinx, a hand who'd been with the ranch nearly as long as Hank, wouldn't meet her eyes. "He didn't see you come in. He's, ah . . . in the back."

In the back? Hank was surely too old for back rooms. The man had been like a father to her. Camile found his actions unsettling. Almost as disturbing as when Wade and Rosie left soon after. She wouldn't think about them together—wouldn't imagine him kissing Rosie or her hands moving over his magnificent body. Angrily, Camile snatched up the bottle of whiskey on the table. She poured herself a drink despite Jinx's disapproving frown.

The liquor burned a path all the way to her stomach. Camile coughed softly, glared at Jinx when he laughed, and poured herself another.

"You ain't supposed to be drinking," Meg, the barmaid, said, pausing before the table. "Rosie wouldn't like it, and neither would old Hank."

"Old Hank is busy," Camile snapped. "And so is Rosie."

The blonde sighed wistfully. "I wouldn't mind trading places with her."

"You might," Camile said softly. "If you'd seen what I've seen." Her voice sounded funny.

Meg eyed her thoughtfully, then frowned at the bottle on the table. "You'd better get on home. Hank would skin us alive if he knew we let you get yourself drunk."

"I'm not drunk," Camile argued, even as her head began to spin. "Well, maybe a little. I'm going. I don't feel well."

"You should have someone ride along with you," Meg suggested with a grin. "I bet you won't make it all the way home without losing your supper."

There wasn't a man in the room Camile would allow to witness that humiliation. She didn't want it spread around that Cam Cordell couldn't hold her liquor. Once she was on her feet, the spinning became worse. Her stomach lurched. Afraid she'd become ill in front of everyone, Camile bolted for the door.

Outside, she stumbled into the alley and did exactly what the barmaid had predicted. Then Camile wiped her mouth against the sleeve of her worn cotton shirt, leaning against the adobe walls for support. When she felt well enough to open her eyes, a figure loomed before her. Blurred vision, along with the darkness, made identification impossible.

"Wade?" she whispered, knowing the figure was too tall to be Hank.

"Sorry to disappoint you, Cam," Jim Cummings drawled, a significant slur to his own voice. "Langtry's too busy to take care of you tonight. You'll have to settle for me."

"I can take care of myself." Camile pushed away from the wall. She found herself shoved back, Jim's hands on her shoulders.

Ronda Thompson

"You know that ain't what I mean," he said. "I've seen the way you've been watching the back entrance. Your stud is servicing someone else."

Suspicion began to churn her already upset stomach. "You're drunk, Cummings. Let go, and I'll forget you had the bad sense to touch me."

Jim's eyes glowed in the dark. "You think you're too good for me, don't you? I figure Langtry's already had you, although he won't say so. If he's good enough, so am I."

"I don't know what you're saying, but you'd better let go of me."

"I'll explain it to you." Jim ripped the front of her shirt open. "You've got something I want. I'm stronger than you, and I'll take it."

Panic sobered Camile. She brought her knee up, intending to deliver a blow between Jim's legs, a tactic Hank had taught her. Either her reflexes were slow, or Jim wasn't as drunk as she thought. He grabbed her thigh, swept her feet up, and forced her to the ground.

"Fight me, Wildcat. You always do in my dreams."

She scratched his face. He swore, then struck her. The blow almost made Camile pass out. She heard the tearing noise of her cotton camisole and renewed her struggle. Her strength was no match for Jim's. When he fumbled with the fastening of her buckskins, Camile feared she might have gotten herself into something she couldn't get out of—not alone. She screamed.

"Ain't no one gonna hear you," Jim said, trailing a sloppy kiss down the side of her cheek. "Go ahead and holler."

Camile tried to twist her foot into a position where she could reach her knife. Cummings settled deeper between her parted legs. He threw his weight against her thigh and tore savagely at her buckskins. Camile screamed again. She bit, clawed, and twisted her body in an effort to escape.

The cowhand shook her. "I'm tired of fightin'. It's time to have what I've been wanting for too long."

"It's time to die."

Suddenly, Jim's weight no longer pressed Camile down into the dirt. She scrambled up, fumbling at her torn breeches with one hand and trying to pull a useless shirt across her breasts with the other. Wade, his bare chest glistening in the moonlight, had her attacker by the collar.

Rosie's arms settled around Camile protectively; then the sound of a fist connecting with flesh blended with lewd laughter spilling from the cantina. Camile trembled, a delayed reaction to the attack. Numbness spread through her. She watched Wade beat Cummings senseless through glazed eyes.

"You're gonna kill him, Wade," Rosie warned.

"That's the plan," he countered, wrestling Jim's limp body up.

"Leave him. We need to tend Cam," Rosie argued. "She looks bad."

Jim slumped to the ground. Wade approached the two women, tilting Camile's face upward. "Christ. I'll finish that bastard for this!"

Teeth chattering, heart pounding, Camile felt her shock receding. "Hold me, Wade," she whispered. "Get me away from here."

He lifted her into his arms, told Rosie to fetch water and bandages, then went around the back way. Camile didn't remember the short trip, but found herself being eased down upon a bed. When he tried to pull away, her arms tightened around his neck.

"I need to look at you," Wade insisted.

"Hold me."

He took a ragged breath and joined her. "How far did he get? Did he rape you?"

"No. He touched me and tried to get my clothes off, but he didn't . . . " Her voice caught on a sob.

Wade pulled her closer. "Go ahead and cry. You might feel better."

She sniffed. "I can't, Langtry. I gave that up years ago."

Smoothing the hair from her eyes, he said, "You don't always have to be so damned tough, Camile."

"I'm not," she whispered. "If you hadn't showed up . . . "

Bedsprings creaked when Wade shifted his weight, looking down at her. "Other than being in the wrong place at the wrong time, what happened wasn't your fault. I had a feeling about Jim. I should have stuck around and made sure your paths didn't cross tonight."

Her gaze darted around the room. Camile felt her face grow warm. "I guess it's lucky for me you're fast."

Confusion crossed his face. Then he smiled. "Lucky for you I'm slow. These walls are thin. I heard you scream before . . . well, before I got too distracted."

A silent pause followed. One in which Camile became aware of her bare breasts pressed against his naked chest. Her gaze settled on his mouth. Warmth flooded her veins. In light of what she'd just been through, the reaction puzzled her. Wade must have become of aware of her, also. He pulled back. Her arms tightened around his neck.

"Hold me a while longer. I feel dirty."

His jaw clenched. "Difficult as it might be for you to

believe, there's a gentler side to lust. You shouldn't judge future experiences by this one."

"I know all men aren't like Jim," she said. "You're not."

Wade suddenly had trouble meeting her eyes. "Not everyone is what they appear to be. Trust should be earned."

She frowned. "Are you saying I shouldn't trust you?"

"I'm saying you shouldn't be so comfortable lying half-naked beneath me. I may not be like Jim, but I'm still a man."

He was that. All hard muscle and smooth flesh. Camile felt protected and far from safe at the same time. It wasn't Wade she feared, but the emotions he stirred. Emotions she wasn't sure she should be feeling given the circumstances.

"Is this wrong?" she asked.

"What?"

"How I feel."

"Comfortable?"

Camile shook her head. "Strange. Hot. Expectant. Kind of shaky inside. If I wanted you to kiss me, would it be wrong?"

He groaned and tried to pull her arms from around his neck. Camile tightened her hold, aroused by the friction between their bodies.

"You didn't answer me," she said.

"What you're feeling isn't wrong. It's natural. Who you're feeling it for is wrong. I'm the enemy, remember?"

Her arms slid from around his neck. She *had* forgotten. What she felt had nothing to do with competition. She wanted him. Wanted him the way she supposed a woman wanted a man. And wanting him for no good reason didn't make sense.

"I guess I'm still upset," she said in explanation. "I don't know my own mind."

Wade was upset, too. Enraged over what had happened to Camile, and mad at himself for desiring her. He'd warned her—come as close as he could to telling her the truth. She was distracting him too much, compromising his future. He couldn't give in to his attraction to her. There'd be hell to pay.

"I'm not thinking too clearly, either," Wade said. "I'd better get the hell away from you while I still can."

He rose from the bed, walked over, and retrieved his shirt from the back of a chair. "Put that on. I'll see what's keeping Rosie."

"Wade?"

The quiver in her voice tore at his insides. He turned. She held his shirt clutched to her breasts. A dark bruise had begun to form along her jawline.

"You won't tell anyone about this, will you? If my father found out . . . "

Damn her, she'd just given him the ammunition he needed. Wade was sure he would have come up with it on his own. She had no business running a ranch by herself. Tonight proved what could happen without a man to protect her. He didn't answer, just walked to the door and opened it, glancing down the hallway to see Rosie rushing toward him.

"I've had so many damn fights in here I couldn't find any bandages," she complained, huffing when she reached him.

"Go in and clean her up," he said. "I'll get our horses and wait out back."

"Don't 'spect the Cactus wants anyone knowing about this. Is she all right?"

"She'll mend," he said, then shrugged into his duster and headed toward the back door. And he hoped she would. It was time to end the competition. Time to get on with his job. What he planned to do tomorrow would be for her own good, although he felt certain she wouldn't see it that way.

Chapter Seven

"Maria, have Camile come downstairs," Tom Cordell ordered.

"She is not feeling well this morning," Maria said. "Poor thing is huddled under her covers complaining of a headache."

"Sorry, Wade. I don't know what you have to discuss, but go ahead without her."

"She should be here." Wade turned to Maria. "Tell her if she won't come down, I'll come up and get her."

The housekeeper's eyes widened.

"Hold on a minute," Tom blustered. "Not only would it be indecent to go barging into Camile's bedroom, but as Maria said, she's not feeling well."

"Too much whiskey will do that to a person."

Tom's face turned roan red. "Are you suggesting Camile got herself drunk last night?"

"That and then some. Get her down here. I agreed to the competition, but I never agreed to get her out of trouble she shouldn't have gotten into. This is hard country, Tom. It's no place for woman trying to compete with men."

"Tell her to come down, Maria," Tom demanded. "I'd go myself if I could get this rickety chair up the stairs."

Maria paled. "She is testy this morning. Maybe we should wait until her ill effects wear off."

"Hell, I'm not afraid of her." Wade rose and walked toward the study door. He left an opened-mouth Maria and a helpless Tom Cordell in his wake. Knowing which room belonged to Camile by the few times he'd glanced up to see her staring down at him, Wade burst inside.

"Time to face the music, Camile."

A muffled curse sounded beneath the covers. Camile threw them back. She stared wide-eyed at him, wild hair tumbling around her shoulders, bruised features stunned.

"You can't barge in here! What do you think you're doing?"

"I'm taking you downstairs. I want you to tell your father what happened last night."

"He can't find out," she whispered. "If he knows I went into Rosie's—if he knows what Jim tried to do to me, it's over. He won't let me out of this house, much less run the ranch!"

Wade felt a stab of remorse. She looked so vulnerable, not something he imagined she did often. He'd seen her softer side. Exhausted, she'd almost fallen from her saddle the night before. He had taken her in his arms, settled her in front of him, and let her sleep the remainder of the ride home.

"You wouldn't do this to me. . . . "

It's a job, he told himself when his heart softened. A job that must be done in order to become the man he wanted to be. "You're not the only one who doesn't fight fair."

Her face drained of color, then just as fast, exploded with red. "You egg-sucking, belly-crawling, yellow-livered snitch!"

"It's best for you," Wade assured her. "For me and everyone. Cummings slipped off into the night like the snake he is. He might come back to get even. Tom's not going to risk letting you roam wild. Got anyone in mind you want to marry?"

"I don't see a wedding in my immediate future. I see a burial, though!"

She lunged from the bed. Her nails came within an inch of his face before Wade captured her wrists. He twisted her arms behind her back, pulling her up against his chest.

"Do you always sleep naked?"

Her gaze lowered. She groaned. "I was too tired to do anything but strip and crawl into bed last night." She struggled. "Let go of me and get out!"

He did release her, but Wade didn't leave. His gaze roamed her while she fumbled to remove a blanket from her bed.

"You're beautiful, Camile," he said, his voice a husky whisper. "You'd win more battles with those curves than you ever could with your fists."

Wrapping the blanket around herself, she glared at him. "You can go. Because of your back-stabbing, I have to tell my father what happened. You could have at least not looked while I'm at a disadvantage."

Wade walked away. "You've had an eyeful of *me*." He paused before leaving the room. "Now we're even."

The meeting with her father had been a horrible one. He'd yelled louder than Camile had heard him yell in her life. Maria had stood quietly in the corner, wringing her hands. When Hank had shown up, her father had yelled at him, too. Now Hank sat beside her, watching the men ride out to finish the last gathering of strays. The trail drive started next week. Camile wouldn't be going. Hank wouldn't be going. Wade Langtry had been given full charge.

"Look at him," Camile fumed. "He's eating this up. Strutting around like a rooster."

"He ain't showing off at all," Hank argued. "It's just 'cause you're fit to be tied that you see the worst in him. Langtry's better than I was at his age. Still, if he ain't careful, he's gonna talk himself right out of a job."

"What do you mean, Hank?"

"Last night he and Tom were chewing the fat on the porch. Langtry was going on about life back East, telling your pa about the fancy socials they have and so forth. I heard Tom ask him if it'd be a safe place for you."

"I'm not visiting them damned Yanks. Who cares what they have? They don't have wide-open spaces as far as you can see. I bet the stars don't look as if you could reach up and touch one. No, thank you, I wouldn't go if Father did say we could take a trip."

"I don't think your pa was considering a visit. I have a suspicion he was talking about a permanent move."

"No," Camile gasped. "Hank, he's not fool enough to sell the place?"

"I reckon that depends on you."

"Me?"

"On whether or not you find yourself a husband. I heard him tell Langtry if you don't cooperate, he might sell out after the drive. Pack up and cart you off to the East."

"It's Langtry's fault," she accused. "Ever since he set foot on my path, everything's gone to hell. He got himself in a pickle this time; he won't have a job if my father sells out."

"Sometimes they keep the younger hands on," Hank said. "Them Yanks only know how to buy land and cattle; they don't know what to do with it after they have it. Too bad Langtry's just a foreman, or I'd say Tom would be counting on him as a son-in-law."

"My father sounds desperate enough to take anyone. What difference does it make that Wade's only a foreman?"

"Not good enough for you." Hank spat a stream of tobacco. "Your pa's hoping you might take to Ralph Lamar's son. They've got a good ranch and the know-how to run both their spread and the Circle C."

"What his son has is knock-knees and buckteeth. I'd almost rather have Langtry."

Hank frowned. "I hope you ain't serious. That would sure stir things up. Your pa might like him, but he'd have Langtry horsewhipped and run off this ranch if he thought the two of you . . . "

"If the two of us what?" Camile urged him.

"Never you mind. Wade will be gone for a while come next week. I 'spect your pa is planning some shindig for you. I heard him tell Maria to press up all those pretty dresses you ain't never worn."

The auction block was already being prepared. Her

stomach pitched at the thought. But she wouldn't be around to attend any socials. Camile wouldn't be denied her right to go on the drive. She'd made plans. Now she had another one. If, once she proved herself capable of bossing her outfit on the drive, the men wouldn't accept her as foreman, she'd seduce Wade Langtry.

If he ruined her, what decent man would have her? After she rid herself not only of the possibility of marriage, but of Wade Langtry, as well, maybe her father would reconsider letting her run the ranch.

"What are you up to?"

Hank's voice made her jump. "W-what makes you think I'm up to something?" she stuttered.

"I know that look. It usually bodes ill for someone."

"Don't be silly." She laughed. "I was only wondering which dress to wear to the party."

"Yeah," he scoffed, rising from his position beside her on the porch. He ambled down the steps, then turned to look at her. "Your hell-raising days are over. Whatever you have in mind, you'd best forget."

Camile waited until he moved away before rising. She stared out over the flat plains before her. "I'm a Cordell. We don't forget, or forgive. We're not even yet, Langtry. Not by a far piece."

A week later, Camile sat at the very same spot on the porch again. Sounds of the cowhands' rowdy voices reached her. They were in high spirits for the coming drive. She wanted to ride out with them in a blaze of glory. Instead, she'd made plans to follow a couple of days later. The men would join up with four other outfits in Tascosa come morning. Three thousand cattle, over a hundred men, and four chuck wagons. The excitement was almost more than she could bear.

How she'd love to be swapping stories and readying her gear with the rest of the men. Instead, she sat alone, watching the sky melt from pink to purple. A gust of wind drifted across the yard. In the distance, a coyote called his lonesome song, squeezing at her heart. She loved this place. There wasn't anything she wouldn't do for the ranch—to regain her father's affections—to be released from the guilt.

"You look about like he sounds."

She jumped, then sighed. "Langtry."

"I need to go over a few things with Tom."

"He's in the study."

Wade started up the steps, paused, then sat down beside her. "I thought you'd come creeping in the night to slit my throat before now."

"Can't find my knife," she countered.

He laughed. "I knew there had to be a reason."

They sat in silence, staring out across the darkening plains.

"This is lonely country for a woman," Wade finally commented.

Camile stretched her long legs before her. "It's not so bad. This land can kill you. Beat you down. Make you old before your time, but it can't break your heart. Not like someone made of flesh and blood can do."

His head turned toward her. "Have you had your heart broken?"

For the briefest of seconds, she felt tears gathering behind her eyes. She blinded them back. "A long time ago. It's not a subject I want to discuss."

Although she felt his gaze studying her, Camile refused to look at him.

"Then let's talk about another subject," he said. "You plan on marrying that Lamar kid?"

She glanced up. "What's it to you, Langtry?"

He shrugged. "Just curious."

"No. Not if I can help it."

"You have another option."

Her brow lifted. "Are you proposing?"

"Hell, no." He flinched. "I meant, you can leave Texas. Go back East. Wearing a fancy dress, with your hair fixed up, you'd be something."

"I *am* something. Who I want to be. I'm just not who everyone else wants me to be."

Wade ran a hand over his whiskered cheeks. "You're too young to know that."

"I'm plenty old. Past marrying age. Maybe not much younger than you. How old are you?"

Wade began digging the toe of his boot in the dirt. "Near as I can figure, thirty."

"You don't know for sure?" she asked, surprised. "Didn't your folks throw you a party on your birthday?"

"My folks died when I was ten."

"Oh," she responded. "What about your relatives?"

"Had none."

"Then where did you live?"

He shifted uncomfortably. "It isn't a subject I care to discuss."

"But how did you live?" she persisted.

"Anyway I could." Wade rose. "I'd better speak with Tom."

Camile scrambled up. She wasn't ready to let him get

away. She found his past interesting. Sad, but intriguing. "How did your folks die?" She thought, by his rigid posture, he wouldn't answer. And he didn't for a moment.

"The war."

"Are you a Southerner?"

"Was."

Camile placed herself in front of the door. "I thought your drawl sounded different from the rest of us. Did you own slaves?"

Obviously annoyed by her questioning, he gently pushed her aside. Camile scrambled back.

"Well, did you?"

"My folks did," he answered sharply. "I was just a kid. I suppose I'd have owned them too if the war hadn't changed everything. We are what we're raised to be, Camile."

Her chin lifted a notch. "Yes. We are."

He stared at her, his tenseness gradually fading. A smile stole across his lips. "You must be part mule. Stay out of trouble while I'm gone."

"I never got into much before you came along."

His expression displayed skepticism. "You're too good at it to be a beginner."

Their gazes locked. For a moment, Camile thought he might lean down and kiss her. She wished he would—because she needed to know he could be tempted. Needed to know he found her attractive in case her plan to seduce him later became a necessary evil. They stood there for some time, their gazes locked, their lips mere inches apart. Wade broke the stare down first.

"Well, good night, and good-bye." He eased her from the doorway and went inside.

Disappointment was an emotion familiar to Camile. The

sudden emptiness she felt upon his departure was not. He'd resisted her. Walked away without a backward glance. Her spirits sank. In the past, the only things about her she'd hoped would appeal to a man were her roping and riding skills. In a few short weeks, Wade Langtry had managed to change that. Only because she needed him to think her pretty, Camile warned herself. Needed him to tie his own noose.

She sighed despondently, glancing over her shoulder. He'd kissed her once. He'd kiss her again. It wasn't over. Not by a far stretch. Camile smiled, feeling her spirits lift.

"Be seeing you, Langtry," she said under her breath. "Soon."

Chapter Eight

Camile spat the hardtack from her mouth. She cursed the dark, and the man responsible for her solitude. Without companionship, the Texas plains could be a lonely place— a dangerous place. Wood in the small fire she'd built popped. Camile jumped. Her nerves were as raw as her blistered face. For three days she'd been trailing the herd, hanging back, following the dust. She was damned tired of biding her time.

She was tempted to grab her blankets and head on in to surprise the boys—surprise Wade. Anticipating the look on his face kept her going. So what if the hardtack she'd packed became harder every day? Water was plentiful, at least. The herd followed the Canadian River through Texas. She'd even taken a dip to cool her sunburned skin, then braided her thick hair to keep it from her face.

Since her food supply consisted of hardtack, dried jerky,

and a dusty loaf of bread she'd snatched from the kitchen on her way out, Camile decided to get some sleep rather than wrestle with her food. Tomorrow, she promised herself. By then, it'd be too late to turn back. She spread one blanket on the ground, covered herself with another, and pulled her hat down low over her face.

From somewhere in the distance, an owl hooted. Camile tried to ignore the sounds around her. She'd spent her first night jumping up at every little noise. A twig snapped. She tensed. Maybe it had been the fire popping again. If she planned on camping with the men during the drive, she needed to accustom herself to hooting owls and crackling fires. Certain she couldn't peacefully drift off to sleep, she decided to try to identify different noises.

Rustling. The leaves on the trees lining the river. A soft whistle. The wind. Something cold against her neck. The barrel of a gun. Instinctively, she knocked the gun aside. She tried to roll, but her hat being shoved down hard against her face held her in place. She had trouble breathing. A weight settled on top of her, pushing what little air she had left out of her mouth with a loud whoosh. Her hand shot up, her nails swiping wildly.

A sharp intake of breath, along with the stickiness of blood on her fingers, said she'd made contact. Camile bucked wildly. When she managed to kick free of the blankets, she wrapped her legs around her attacker, intending to reverse their positions. Just as she thought to throw her weight to the side, the Stetson came away from her face. She recognized him immediately. Blood ran down the side of one darkly whiskered cheek. His green eyes caught the fire's glow.

"I'd know those damn long legs anywhere."

"Langtry," Camile gasped, then breathed a sigh of relief. "Thank goodness it's only you."

He wiped his hand down the side of his cheek, then glared at her. "Yeah, you're lucky it's only me. Something real bad can happen to a little girl in the middle of nowhere."

Camile squirmed. "I'm not a little girl. Get off me so I can breathe."

His features darkened. "Your body might be full grown, but your head isn't. What if it wasn't me who happened along? What if it was Jim Cummings?"

She sighed. "You'd worry about a drink before the well ran dry."

Wade rose, removed his bandanna, and wiped the blood from his cheek. "And you wouldn't give it a second thought until you'd drank the last drop. I thought you might have learned your lesson about roaming around alone."

"This might have ended worse than it did," she admitted. "I planned on catching up with the herd tomorrow. I've been careful."

A sarcastic snort sounded. "That's why for the past two nights you've built a fire anyone within fifty miles can see. Out here in the pitch dark, you're an easy target."

Her gaze darted around the area. Camile struggled to a sitting position. She couldn't tell Wade she'd been scared. "I got cold," she mumbled. "I don't see how one little fire could do any harm."

His brow lifted. Wade whistled. Six men crept from the shadows. All were Circle C.

"We figured you might be someone planning to lighten

our load," Wade said. "There's talk among the other outfits a gang is planning to rustle the herd."

"Cam?" Grady Finch inched closer to the fire. Upon seeing her, he swore softly. "Bet old Hank is hot on her heels."

"You'd lose," she countered smugly. "I ran what horses were left on the ranch out to pasture before I rode out. I imagine they've caught the scent of the wild mustangs and joined them."

"Smart move," Grady muttered.

The cowhand received a dirty look from Wade. "Don't encourage her," Wade said. "We have a problem."

When all eyes turned toward Camile, she scrambled up from the ground. "I'm going on the drive."

Wade beat the dust from his hat against his leg. "Like hell you are."

"We could send a man to take her back," Grady offered.

"Can't spare one," Wade said. "Maybe we could find somewhere to leave her and pick her up on the way home."

"I wouldn't stay put," Camile assured him. She placed her hands on her hips. "I'm coming with you, Langtry, and there's not a damn thing you can do about it."

The defiant tilt of her chin made him mad enough to cuss. Wade did, then turned to the men. "Ride back to camp. Straggle yourselves so no one notices how many there are of us. Camile and me will follow."

"But what'll we tell the other outfits tomorrow?" Grady asked. "They'll see we've got a woman with us."

Wade ran a thoughtful glance down Camile's body. "They'll see we have another cowhand with us. Cam got a late start. She's a boy, understand?"

Grady scratched his head. "Up close, she don't look like a boy."

"I couldn't tell the first time I saw her. If she keeps her hair out of the way and wears baggy clothes, no one will know the difference."

"You're the boss," Grady said. Then he and the other men disappeared into the shadows.

"I'd wipe that smug look off your face," Wade said to Camile. "You have no idea what you've gotten yourself into."

She bent, rolling her blankets into a lumpy roll. "You're mad because I outsmarted my father and Hank. You shouldn't underestimate me."

In three long strides, he joined her. Wade reached down and hauled her up. "I didn't. Figured you had horse dung for brains the first night I laid eyes on you. You've proven me right . . . again."

Her gaze narrowed on him. "You back-stabbed me. Did you think I'd let you get away with taking my rightful place?"

Patience fast fading, Wade removed his hat and ran a hand through his hair. "You don't know what you've done, do you?" When Camile stared blankly back at him, he continued. "I'm sure this latest stunt has pushed your father to the end of his rope. He won't trust you again. You can't even buy yourself time. He'll have that Lamar kid and a preacher waiting for you when you get home, either that or . . ."

"Or what?" she demanded shakily.

A bill of sale. Wade didn't complete his speculations aloud. He'd been so angry upon seeing her, he hadn't thought past what might have happened if the wrong men would have ridden into her camp. She'd played right into his hands. He shouldn't be scolding her; he should kiss her. And he wanted to—had wanted to the moment he pulled her hat from her face and saw those big blue eyes staring up at him.

"Or someone worse," he finished.

"There is no one worse."

He released his anger in one long breath. "What in the hell am I supposed to do with you?"

"I thought that was settled. I'm coming along. As a boy. You told Grady so."

"I meant that until I can think of something else."

"There is nothing else. If you leave me somewhere, I won't stay. You can't spare a man to take me back. You have no choice but to let me hand the drive."

Camile was right. She had furthered his own goals by rebelling against her father, but the trail was dangerous. Stampedes. Possible rustlers. Not to mention storms and renegade Indians. "It's dangerous," Wade said.

"I'm not scared."

"It's no place for a woman."

"I'm not your typical woman. I'm Cam, remember?"

His gaze lowered to her ripe breasts stretching the front of her shirt, then roamed her graceful hips encased in tight buckskin. "You're right about that. There's nothing typical about you. Why didn't you pull your knife when I attacked?"

She blushed in the firelight's glow. "I told you. I must have lost it the night . . . in the alley beside Rosie's."

Wade removed his knife from the side of his boot. "You need protection." When she reached for the weapon, he pulled her into his arms. "I'm going to remind you you're a woman, because after I do, you'd best forget it."

Camile's lips were warm and moist, slightly parted in surprise. She smelled womanly—felt womanly. Wade deepened the kiss, slanting his mouth over hers, then inching his tongue between her lips. She moaned softly, then slid her arms up around his neck. His hands were on her back, itching to slide around to cup her breasts.

Instead, he lowered them to her hips, pulling her against him. If the feel of his readiness for her alarmed Camile, he couldn't tell it. She snuggled closer and pressed back.

"Whoa." Wade ended the kiss.

Her lashes fluttered open. "Why did you kiss me?"

Good question, Wade thought, wondering the same thing. He quickly put distance between them lest he was tempted to repeat the mistake. "I told you. To remind you you're a woman."

"But I'm supposed to forget it now?"

"You and me both," he muttered. "From this point on, you're a boy. Remember that."

She cocked her head to one side. Camile pulled her thick braid over her shoulder and fiddled with it distractedly. "Don't suppose you'd kiss a boy like that."

"No," he assured her. His gaze settled on her braid. He frowned. "You have beautiful hair."

"Do you think so?" she asked, a pretty blush staining her cheeks in the fire's glow.

Wade sighed. "Unfortunately." In one fluid motion, he chopped off her treasure.

A hand flew to her hair. Camile's eyes widened. "You cut off my braid!"

"I had to," Wade explained. "You might have hidden it for a day, but—"

"You chopped off my hair!"

106

When her eyes narrowed on him, Wade anticipated her actions before Camile could complete them. He dropped the braid and the knife, then captured her wrists.

"I didn't figure you'd do it. Women are funny about their hair."

"Damn you, Langtry," she croaked. "You had no right—"

"I had every right!" he declared. "I'm the foreman on this drive. Get that through your thick skull here and now. I give the orders. You follow them."

"I'd as soon follow you into Hell!" She came down hard with her boot heel.

Pain exploded in his toe. Wade cussed, released her, and limped around the campfire. It wasn't as if he'd cut her hair for any malicious purpose. As usual, Camile didn't understand the seriousness of her situation.

"If just one man from another outfit realizes you're a woman, the game is up. I'll take you home myself. We've chased our hats plenty in the three days we've been driving. You can't be a boy and have a braid hanging down your back!"

Her gaze remained narrowed on him, her stance ready for attack. She glanced down. A small whimper left her throat.

Wade drew up sharply. "Are you going to cry?"

She lifted her chin. "No."

"I think you are," he countered, horrified by the notion.

Camile ran a hand across her nose and sniffed. "I'm not. You took me by surprise is all."

Wary, having come to know her temper too well, Wade remained alert. "I figured, to get that braid, I'd have to take you by surprise."

She looked at the ground again, a thoughtful expression

stealing over her features. "How'd you drop my braid and the knife and grab my wrists before I could claw you?"

It was his turn to be surprised. Even after five years of retirement, he couldn't seem to shake his natural instincts. Wade made a pretense of studying his injured foot. "We'd better get you packed up."

"You have fast hands, Langtry."

In answer, he shrugged, then moved to her saddle pack. "Did you bring bandages?"

"I didn't hurt your toe that bad," she scoffed.

"For your breasts. They need to be bound. Tight."

She pushed his hands aside. "I'll do it," she said.

"Have you anything with you besides . . . buckskins?" He looked at her. Really saw her since he cut her hair. "Damn."

"What?" she asked defensively.

"You have curls."

"I do?" she ran a hand through her hair.

A groan of frustration rose in his throat. "You look more feminine now than you did before."

"I do?" she repeated, smiling at him. Her grin faded. "Oh."

"Keep your hat on." He rose, grabbed a saddle blanket, and threw it over her horse's back. "Do you have any clothes that don't fit like a second skin?"

"What I wear is comfortable. Baggy clothes get in the way."

"Jake's not much bigger than you. I'll borrow something from him." He removed his duster and tossed it in her direction. "Wear that in the meantime."

Camile rose from her saddle pack, her hands brimming

with bandages. "Are you going to turn around while I bind myself?"

Wade thought that with her golden cap of curls framing her face, she looked like an angel. A deceptive picture if ever there was one. He was tempted to ask her if she needed help.

"I'll saddle your horse," he said instead. "As soon as you've finished, tell me. We'll get the fire put out." He led Diablo from the campsite, bending to scoop her saddle up on his way. "Camile." He turned back. "I was dead serious when I said I'm the boss of this drive. If you want to come along, you'll have to follow my orders."

Defiance flared in her eyes before she quickly lowered her gaze. "I'll try."

"You're damn right you will," Wade grumbled, leading the horse a short distance away. He busied himself with saddling the animal, fighting the urge to turn and watch Camile. Her body was a sight a man didn't easily forget. A sight a man didn't want to forget. But he must. She wasn't a woman from this point on. He had to remember, or place her in danger from the other men. Wade wondered how safe she was with him.

An ex-gunfighter? A man who'd been deceiving her from the moment they met? A man after her all-important ranch? Not very safe at all. More than the admission raised the hackles on the back of Wade's neck. He let the saddle cinch slither from his grasp. His hand strayed toward the Colt strapped to his hip. Something, or someone, watched them.

"Hurry," he called softly. "We have company."

"What?" Camile asked. "Who?"

"Might be wolves. Might be worse."

"I'm done."

"Kick out that fire while I finish saddling. Then let's get the hell out of here."

Attention trained on the distant darkness, Wade hurriedly slipped the cinch through the buckle and pulled it tight. He heard the scuffing sound of Camile dousing the fire. A low whistle brought his dun trotting into camp.

"Let's go," he ordered again, swinging into his saddle.

"Might be wolves," Sam Barton mimicked, his voice a throaty whisper.

"Wolves wantin' inside the henhouse," Lenny Holt added.

"That blond hen is mine," Jim Cummings warned. "Me and her go back a ways."

Sam scrambled up from his belly. He dusted off his knees. "Is she the reason me and my partner found you beat nearly dead outside of Tascosa?"

Jim didn't answer.

"Figure she didn't do the beating," Lenny speculated. He turned his scarred cheek toward the moonlight. "Although she's handy with a knife."

"Are you the one she cut up at Rosie's?" Jim asked, surprised.

"Yeah. Me and her go back a ways, too. You ain't the only man with a score to settle. Sam and me decided to ride into Tascosa before our meeting with Levi. Play cards. Have a woman. But that smart-mouthed girl got us into trouble. Her bastard protector shot me in the knee!"

"Wade Langtry. He's the one that gave you that limp,"

Jim said. "I've got some business to settle with him, too." He unconsciously ran a hand over his still-bruised face.

"He the one?" Sam asked.

"He's the one," Jim answered.

"Well, ain't this nice? You and Lenny got more interest in this drive than just cattle." Sam's gaze hardened. "Forget them. Levi sent us out to count men and to see what fool was stupid enough to build a lone fire out here in the middle of nowhere."

"Levi," Jim grumbled. "I say he ain't got enough men to take this herd. But if he does, he's got too damn many for us to get much of a split."

"Don't seem worth the trouble," Sam agreed.

"Are we gonna back out?" Lenny asked. "I'd trade my share for one night with that girlie."

"Too bad we didn't reach her camp before Langtry," Jim said. "She'd fetch us a pretty penny."

"What do you mean? Sell her?" Sam asked.

"Her daddy is Tom Cordell. Owner of the Circle C. Most of this herd is his. He'd pay plenty to get her back."

"Cordell, huh?" Sam scratched his whiskered face. "I said no female was worth the trouble that one cost us. I'd have to say I was wrong. Let's ride back and tell Levi there's too many of them to rustle this herd. I've got me a new plan."

Chapter Nine

Whatever kept prodding her shoulder was irritating. Camile tried to ignore it, snuggling deeper beneath her blankets.

"Get up. It's morning."

Was Wade in her room again? A dream, she decided. He barged into those often enough. Her eyelids felt stuck together. When she managed to pry them apart, a pair of boots took shape before her. Camile's nose wrinkled. One boot moved in the direction of her shoulder. She quickly scrambled up.

"Dang it, Langtry. Watch where you put your dirty feet."

"Get moving or I'll apply one to your backside. We've got cows to herd and dust to eat."

Camile blinked. The only light she saw came from a small campfire near a wagon. "It can't be morning," she grumbled. "I only went to sleep a few minutes ago. The sun's not even up."

"Wake-up on the trail comes with the morning star, not the rising sun. Hurry or miss breakfast."

The smell of bacon filled the campsite. Her stomach growled. Camile pulled on her boots, crammed her hat on her head, then shrugged into Wade's duster. "I'm starving," she said, taking a step toward the chuck wagon.

Wade gently took her arm. "Bedroll." He nodded toward the blankets. "Roll it up tight and pitch it in the hoodlum wagon. Any man who doesn't see to his gear, sleeps without it the next night."

She stooped and bunched the blankets into a ball, using leather straps to secure the lumpy roll. "Where's the hoodlum wagon?"

"Just ahead of the chuck wagon, but that bedroll's not ready. Try again. And smear some more dirt on your face," Wade instructed her before moving away.

Longingly, Camile watched him join the Circle C cowhands by the fire. The clanging of a metal spoon against a pot spurred her into action. After a few attempts, she managed to roll the blankets up tight. She approached a wagon sitting a few feet ahead of the cook's.

Inside, she made out the shape of bedrolls, dusters, slickers, and the like. She pitched her bedroll, smeared her face with dirt, then hurried toward the fire.

"Someone didn't throw their plate in the wreck pan yesterday," a thin-haired man with an ample girth complained. "If you boys want to eat . . . " His weasel gaze settled on Camile. "Who the Sam Hill is that?"

"This is Cam," Wade answered. "He joined us late. Cam, this is William T. Ferguson, the cook."

Camile paid the man little heed. Her attention was focused on the pan he held. "Nice to meet you," she mumbled.

"Well, it ain't nice to meet you. Do you think I don't know what you are?"

She glanced up, startled. Had she been found out so soon?

"You're a snot-nosed boy who'll most likely cry for your mama at night and eat my wagon dry every day. Don't come begging handouts to fatten those skinny legs, either. I fix three meals a day, that's all. You put your plate in the wreck pan or there'll be hell to pay, and if you complain about anything I fix, you go hungry. Understand?"

Relief over not being discovered wasn't exactly what she felt. Camile didn't much care for William T. Ferguson, and it was obvious from his scowl, the feeling was mutual. She swallowed her pride for the sake of breakfast, nodding reluctantly to his conditions.

While the cook dished up her plate, Camile studied the cowhands. She wasn't around the men often without Hank. They eyed her strangely—as if she were an intruder. Winning their respect might not be as easy as she'd thought. Most had finished eating. They drifted away from the fire.

"Hurry and meet me by the picketing string," Wade said under his breath. "I'll have those clothes for you."

She dug into breakfast. Maria insisted on manners at her table, but Camile figured she should cram the food into her mouth the same as a starving boy would. She did so with gusto, licking her fingers, smacking her lips, and thoroughly enjoying herself.

"Any left?" she asked, her mouth full.

114

The cook scowled at her, but emptied his pan. "Just like I thought. Them legs are hollow."

When his gaze lowered, Camile pulled her duster together. She didn't want William T. Ferguson staring at her legs for too long. Not without the baggy clothes Wade wanted her to wear. She finished breakfast, then handed the cook her plate. His beady gaze rolled upward.

"You wasn't listening. Follow me." The cook motioned her forward. "This here is the wreck pan. Put your dishes inside after every meal so I can wash them later. Firewood's hard to come by in this naked country. Anything you see that burns, you gather up and put in the—"

"Are you coming, Cam?" Wade called impatiently. "We need to get going."

"Bitch," William muttered.

Her head jerked in his direction. "Beg your pardon?"

"The bitch." He nodded toward a cowhide stretched beneath the chuck wagon. "Just pitch any wood or dried cow chips you find in there."

"Oh, that bitch." She laughed nervously.

"Bitch, cuma, cooney, cradle, whatever you want to call it. I can't cook without a fire."

"All right," she agreed, then started in Wade's direction.

"Hey, snot-nose!" the cook yelled. "You answer me with a 'yes, sir' when I tell you something, and thank me proper for the eats before you walk off."

She faced him with thin lips. A man usually showed a measure of respect when dealing with another man. Camile expected to be treated as an equal.

"Don't call me snot-nose, and don't push me around because you think I'm a kid. If you want respect, you'll have to do likewise. As for your cooking—"

"Problem?" Wade asked, joining them.

"This boy's too big for his britches," William said. "He's sassing me."

"Apologize to Mr. Ferguson, Cam."

A cocky smile stretched the cook's mouth. Camile found the order impossible to follow. The warning gleam in Wade's eyes insisted she obey.

"I'm sorry," she spat.

"You're sorry what?" William goaded.

You're a sorry son-of-a-bitch, Camile thought. "Sir."

William smiled. "That's better."

"Now, thank him for breakfast and let's go."

The greasy bacon inside Camile's stomach shifted. "Breakfast was good. Sir," she added quietly. "Bloated-up toad," she muttered when she and Wade put some distance between themselves and the chuck wagon.

He smiled at her. "Besides the boss, the cook's the most important man on this drive. His chuck wagon is sacred ground. No man treads too heavy on his territory or his feelings. He's allowed to cuss anyone he wants, including me. If you want to get on someone's wrong side, he's not the one. No matter how bad the meals are, they can always get worse."

"I don't like him."

"You don't have to, but you'd better compliment his cooking and follow his orders. I imagine he'll dish you short rations for a few days. Time enough to decide how to best deal with Sir Billy."

"Sir Billy?"

His grin stretched. "Not anything I'd call him within hearing distance. He looks like a billy goat."

When she laughed, Wade frowned.

"Don't do that around the other outfits," he said. "It calls attention to your mouth."

"What's wrong with my mouth?"

"Not a damn thing," he answered.

Thankful the dirt hid the blush of pleasure stinging her cheeks, Camile glanced away from him, then drew up short. "Where are we going?"

He nodded. "That wall of tumbleweeds ahead. I have your clothes in the saddle pack. As soon as you change, I want you to rope horses from the remuda."

Camile considered roping one of her more refined skills. It would be a perfect opportunity to show Wade up. Not that he wasn't accomplished in roping, as well. But she had to prove herself, and he didn't. Camile had more to lose if she couldn't convince the men her talents were worthy of a foreman's position.

After assuring herself they were alone, Camile slipped behind the wall of tumbleweeds. The sky had lightened. She felt nervous. Exposed.

"You will keep your distance, won't you, Langtry?"

"I kept it while you were binding your breasts, didn't I?"

"You also barged into my room and stared at me while I was naked."

"It'll be hard to forget you're a woman if you keep reminding me."

She slipped out of his duster and went for the buttons on her shirt. Camile didn't want Wade to forget. Seducing him might still become necessary if she couldn't change the Circle C men's attitudes. She wondered how difficult a chore that would be—either task. When she opened the saddle pack, her eyes immediately began to water. Her throat closed. She coughed. "Hellfire! What stinks?"

"That would be your clothes."

Holding her nose, Camile pulled a shirt and a pair of pants from the pack. "I can't wear these, Langtry. They're covered in—"

"Manure. I know."

Angrily, she threw the clothes on the ground and stuck her head from behind the tumbleweeds. "You know? And you expect me to wear them?"

Wade's dimples appeared. "Figure that'll keep the other men away from you."

The top of her head felt like it would explode. "I won't!"

His dimples disappeared. "You'll put them on or I'll put them on for you. I spent most of my sleep time trying to figure how to keep your secret during the drive. After one good whiff, I don't imagine anyone will hang around you long."

He'd figured right. Camile didn't think she could stand herself in Jake's clothes. "Couldn't you have thought of something else?"

"That's the best I could do. Get dressed."

Camile wanted to throw a temper tantrum, to flat out refuse. Seducing Langtry had to be easier than spending her days on the drive coated in manure. She took a deep breath . . . and held it while she dressed.

"Don't you figure the other men will wonder how I came to be coated in manure?" she asked, stepping from behind the tumbleweeds.

Langtry's eyes watered. He took a step backward. "Jake might've overdone it." He coughed, then cleared his throat. "I'm putting you on drag. After a couple of hours trailing the herd, no one will know for sure why you stink, only that you do. Don't wash those clothes first chance you get, either. Then we'll have to start all over."

"I can't move!" Camile stumbled toward him. "How am I supposed to rope and ride in clothes stiffer than a board?"

"They'll soften. But before they do, you should practice moving more like a man. You swing your hips too much when you walk."

"I do?"

He nodded. "Watch me." Wade turned and walked away.

Cocking her head to one side, Camile studied him. She liked the way he moved. The way his body filled out his clothes. His tight . . .

"See?"

Abruptly, her gaze lifted. He looked at her from over his shoulder, his expression questioning.

"I guess," she answered.

Wade motioned her forward. "Now, you try it."

It didn't take much effort to keep from swinging her hips. Her clothes were too coarse to allow freedom of movement. Stiff-legged, Camile reached his side. "Well?" she asked.

"Better. But once those clothes loosen up, you'll have to try harder. Study the men. Do what they do, especially in front of the other outfits. I'll put your old clothes in the saddle pack and meet you at the remuda."

She frowned before setting out. "Don't laugh at me behind my back. I'm not doing this because you told me to. I'm doing it for the Circle C."

"Maybe about now you're thinking that stretch of cactus and rattlesnakes isn't worth the trouble."

Awkward in the stiff clothing, she turned. "I still consider the competition on between us. I intend to win the hands' respect and take your job."

"The competition is over."

"You have a few days and nights to convince me of that."

His gaze narrowed on her back. He thought she'd come along to rile him. To prove she didn't tame easy. She obviously hadn't gotten the fool notion of running the ranch out of her head. Stubborn. Damn, but she was that.

The men wouldn't give her a chance. Wade didn't believe they took her seriously. But suppose she managed to change their minds? Angry as he imagined Tom was with his daughter, could a return with the men's respect make him reconsider giving her control of the ranch?

Nonsense, Wade assured himself. Camile was fighting a losing battle. A battle that had begun long before he'd ridden into her life. So what if a small part of him admired her determination? Admired her courage to pursue a goal regardless of the obstacles in her path? It didn't mean he considered his goal any less important. He'd sunk everything he had into the company. If he couldn't get the deed to the Cordell ranch, he'd lose everything. The secure life he'd built for himself. His respectability. His humanity.

Wade figured Kline might be a problem even if he returned with the deed. A blackmailer's word wasn't worth much. But Wade was gambling on the fact that the man was afraid of him. And Kline should be. He'd been there that night. That night in Atlanta. The night Wade had come face-to-face with what he'd become.

The sun moved behind a cloud. In Wade's mind, it was dark again. Pitch black. The kind of night when even shadows were swallowed. A cold sweat broke out on his forehead. Suddenly he was back in Atlanta. Suddenly he heard the click of a pistol being cocked, turned, and without thought, pulled his gun and fired. It had become a natural response. As natural as breathing. He was a killing machine. Something cold, hard, and dead inside. But that night, he'd been reborn. He'd finally seen what he'd let life make of him: a man as empty as the streets after dark.

Suddenly, the sun reappeared. Wade wiped his sleeve over his face, wishing the memory could be as easily erased. He'd been running from his past since that night. Running from those who wanted to test the speed of his gun. Running from himself. He squinted toward Camile's retreating figure. He figured anyone who wanted a dream bad enough, wanted it because they thought it could change something bad in their lives.

What was she running from? The restrictions of being a woman? The life her father wanted for her? Wade didn't know. He knew one thing as he watched her move stiff-legged toward the remuda where the other cowhands were throwing their ropes. By the end of the week, she'd be wondering why the hell she'd ever wanted to be a man.

Chapter Ten

Five days. Five days of hell. Eating dust. Swatting flies.
Short rations. Five days of stench. Camile could hardly
stand herself. Neither could anyone else. Wade's plan had
worked. Several men from various outfits had ridden up to
her over the past few days. The introductions were short.

"Hey, Stinky," Grady Finch called. "Ferguson wants to
know if you want more beans."

Camile shot him a dirty look and shook her head. "And
my name's Cam!" she yelled back.

"Stinky's what the other outfits call you," he said defensively. "You know it ain't nothing personal with us."

She didn't know that for a fact. She'd become a laughingstock because of Wade. How could she win the men's
respect under these unbearable circumstances? Her gaze
lowered to the plate of beans and sourdough biscuits she

held. The scent of her clothing ruined her appetite—not to mention the bellyful of dust she'd swallowed that morning.

Drag. The men who rode behind the cattle. The lowliest position on a drive. This adventure hadn't turned out the way she'd planned. No one paid her much notice. Not even her own outfit. Langtry kept his distance. Camile sniffed. She couldn't much blame him. William T. Ferguson had banned her from his chuck wagon, claiming her smell would sour the food.

The cook had at least filled her plate to brimming today. She guessed he didn't figure to starve her anymore. The old goat might even feel sorry for her. She'd been the butt of several jokes for the past five days.

"Langtry! Over here!"

Glancing up from her plate, Camile noticed the trail bosses gathered a short distance away. She sat beneath the only pitiful excuse for a tree she could find. They couldn't see her, but she was surprised they hadn't smelled her.

"Your turn to scout out a bedding ground for the night!" Wendell Cates, trail boss for the LC ranch, shouted.

Wade nodded, then turned his horse.

"Hold up a minute," Wendell called, motioning him closer.

If the group was unaware of her presence, Camile could hear them clearly. She had reason to be plenty mad at Langtry, but she still had trouble ignoring him. He cut a fine figure atop his horse. A man made for the hard life of cattle and dust.

"What is it?" she heard him ask.

The trail bosses appeared suddenly uneasy.

"It's about that kid you've got with your outfit," Wendell said. "Stinky."

"Cam," Wade corrected. "What about him?"

"Well, me and the bosses were wondering why you don't make him wash off with the rest of the men come evening? The kid has a good arm. Throws a rope well. He rides pretty fair, too. We figure it's your duty as his foreman to teach him the merits of bathing."

Camile was thankful she hadn't been eating. She might have choked.

"The way I see it, Cam is none of your business," Wade said. "He was raised to think bathing is unhealthy. I figure if he pulls his weight, he can believe whatever he wants."

"But—" Wendell started.

"That's the end of it," Wade stated. "Cam belongs to my outfit. Leave him be." He reined his mount from the men and galloped away.

Langtry had rubbed her temper raw over the past few days, but he'd defended her. Even said she'd pulled her weight so far. When Wade got that steely look in his eyes, not many men would stand up to him.

"So, now what?" she heard Wendell ask the other bosses.

"Langtry said to leave it be," one man answered.

"But I saw that kid scratching like the dickens today," Wendell argued. "I think he's got lice."

A strangled gasp lodged in Camile's throat.

"Lice?" one of the bosses asked. "If he's got bugs, probably so do the rest of the Circle C. Soon we'll all have them."

Abandoning her eavesdropping, Camile slipped behind the scraggly tree and scratched herself feverishly. Damn Langtry for this!

"Hey! Hey, kid!"

She stopped in mid-scratch. The bosses were moving toward her. Her gaze darted around the area. She wasn't close to the chuck wagon.

"Easy now," Wendell called. "We just want to talk to you."

"I heard what you were discussing. Langtry said to leave it be."

Wendell grinned. "Langtry ain't here."

Her hand shot up to ward them off. "I-I'll take a bath tonight."

"You'll have one now," the boss countered. "And we'll see to it you're good and clean."

"You won't be seeing anything," she warned him. "Grady!"

One of the bosses put his fingers between his lips and whistled loudly. Five men broke from the herd and sauntered toward them.

"What's up?" one shouted.

"We're gonna introduce Stinky to the river and hope it becomes a lasting friendship," Wendell answered.

The cowboys grinned.

Camile ran. Her path to the chuck wagon was quickly blocked by three men on horseback. She turned. Wendell Cates grabbed her.

"No need to make a fuss. You'll thank us after we're done."

A strong kick backwards into Wendell's shin won her freedom. Camile lunged forward. Another cowboy grabbed her around the waist.

"Let go of Cam."

A sigh of relief left her lips when she glanced up to see Grady and the Circle C hands.

"What's going on here?" Grady demanded.

"Stinky needs a bath," the cowboy who held her answered. "We're seeing that he gets one."

"The way we see it, a bath is Cam's own business," Grady said.

"We don't feel the same," the cowboy challenged him.

"No need to get your backs up," Wendell said. "The kid's got lice. That makes it our business."

"Mites?" Grady asked. "If Cam's bedroll has 'em, so do ours."

Unconsciously, he began to scratch his hatless head. Jake did likewise. A mass scratching among the Circle C hands followed. Even William T. Ferguson ran his fingers through his long, gray mustache.

"We don't take orders from anyone except Langtry," Camile reminded Wendell, sending the Circle C a message. Unless they stopped what was about to happen, she was in trouble.

"That's right." Grady straightened his tall frame. "We'll handle this ourselves. You'd best let go of Cam."

"I say we all see to it now and make sure the job gets done," the cowboy insisted.

The argument might have been settled more peacefully if Camile hadn't elbowed the cowboy holding her in the ribs. He slapped her lightly on the cheek. All hell broke loose. Fists flew. Caught up in the middle, Camile tried to wriggle her way clear. Someone grabbed the back of her shirt.

"You ain't sneaking off when you're the cause of this," Wendell said. "You'll have that bath while the others are busy."

Camile punched him. She swore loudly, then brought her stinging knuckles to her mouth. Wendell charged her like a bull.

"Help me with this wildcat!" he called to the other bosses.

Two men grabbed her feet, and with Wendell trapping Camile's arms at her sides, she had little choice but to accompany them to the river. She fought all the way. Her strength wasn't adequate to keep the men from tossing her into the water, but her squirming threw them off balance.

A tangle of bodies pushed her beneath the surface. If drowning wasn't uppermost on her mind, Camile might have died from sheer bliss. She broke the surface sputtering. Water gushed from the brim of her hat.

"I'll get his clothes off," Wendell said as the other bosses scrambled to climb out.

"No!"

He snorted. "Hell, you yelp like a girl. Settle down. You ain't got nothing the rest of us ain't got."

The loosening of her water-soaked bindings could provide an argument. Camile ducked down in the water. When Wendell reached for the buttons on her shirt, she slapped his hands away. His jaw tensed.

"Give me those clothes. They need to be scrubbed."

"I'll scrub them myself."

"You scrub *you*. I'll see to your clothes. Get them off."

"That boy giving you trouble?" one of the bosses called from the bank. "You need us to help you again?"

Camile cussed their meddling. If she could get them to leave, her secret might remain one. Wendell's face looked tense enough to crack.

"I can handle him," he assured the men. His eyes narrowed on her. "You look different without the dirt. Sort of . . . pretty."

While he stared at her, Camile made her move. She turned, then lunged into the water, hoping to outswim him. His weight came crashing down on her. When Camile tried to twist away, Wendell's hand closed over one breast. He let go quick. They both broke the surface, Wendell's gasp as loud as hers.

"You ain't no boy," he croaked.

"Hurry it up, Wendell," a boss called. "We're burning daylight."

Wendell blocked her from the other men's sight. "Does Langtry know?" he asked.

Clutching the edges of her shirt together, Camile matched him stare for stare. What was she supposed to say? What was she supposed to do?

"Stop!"

The boss glanced over his shoulder. Camile peeked around him. Grady Finch stood on the bank, a horrified expression on his face.

Wendell looked at Grady, looked at her, then swore. "Damn. They all know, don't they?"

"Yes, but—"

The boss turned, then trudged toward the bank. "Langtry will have hell to pay for this," he said in parting.

"Hey, they got the kid in the water!" she heard someone shout. "Let's have a look at him without the dirt."

The game was up. The water wasn't very deep. Camile ducked down, covering her breasts. She couldn't stay there forever. Nervously, her gaze scanned the men lining the bank.

"Hey," the cowboy who'd started the fight earlier said, squinting towards her. "He looks like a . . . she."

"He is a she," Wendell called.

"Stinky's a woman?" another man asked incredulously.

"Not just any woman."

A voice made all heads swing to the left. Wade kicked his horse into the water. "Cam . . . Camile is my wife."

Camile supposed her mouth fell open. She knew for a fact Grady Finch's did.

"We were married a few days before the drive began. I told her she couldn't come along, but she followed us. She wants a honeymoon in Dodge, isn't that right, Camile?"

She realized she was still standing gape-mouthed. Married? Her and Langtry? His steely gaze cut into her, sending her a message. She was supposed to play along. He obviously had a plan.

"He's right," she answered. "It was Wade's idea that I pretend to be a boy. And wear those smelly clothes," Camile added, wanting to assure all present she wasn't a filthy person by choice.

"That's all very sweet." Wendell sighed. "The problem is she can't stay, not being a woman and all. I can't trust these boys to remember she's a lady, and a married one at that."

"I'm no lady!" Camile inched forward. "I'm Cam Cordell . . . Langtry. And I won't be denied my right to be here because I'm a female."

"Cordell?" Wendell looked surprised. "Are you Tom's firebrand?"

"I am," she answered, lifting her chin.

The boss grinned. "Hell, this ain't no ordinary female, boys. This here's the Prickly Pear of the Panhandle. Old

129

Hank Riley has talked a blue streak about you from here to Kansas."

She stumbled back a step when Wendell entered the water. He extended his hand. Baffled, Camile stared at his offering.

"You've heard about me?" she asked.

"Any cowboy worth his salt has heard about Cam Cordell. Talk is, you took a bullwhip to one of them Yanks making offers for Panhandle land. Course, Hank didn't come this trip to tell the tale up right, but word got around all the same."

A shiver of delight raced up her spine. Camile clasped his outstretched palm. "It's a pleasure to meet a man who's not afraid to offer a woman his hand in friendship."

"Oh, I don't think of you as a woman," Wendell was quick to assure her. "You're more like a legend."

Stealing a glance at Wade, Camile smiled. He frowned in return.

"The way I see it, she's Langtry's problem," Wendell said. "I reckon he's man enough to keep the others in line where she's concerned."

A cowboy on the bank laughed. "Is he man enough to handle her is what I'm wondering."

"Thinking too much about her isn't a good idea," Wade warned. "The rest of you go on about your business. Let us tend to ours."

"Your whole outfit has business to tend," Wendell reminded. "Cam might have lice. Figure the lot of you should wash with yucca and boil your clothes and bedrolls."

Wade flinched. Unconsciously, he began to scratch. "Camile, you go first," he said. "Work the roots into a lather and cover yourself, then let it dry before you rinse. Grady, tell William to get a big pot of water boiling for our clothes."

"What the heck are we supposed to wear in the meantime?" Grady wanted to know.

"My outfit will chip in with some clothes until yours get dry," Wendell said.

When the men didn't move away, Wade said, "You boys can go now."

"You're coming with us, ain't you, Langtry?" Grady asked.

Camile watched a current pass between the two men.

"I mean, you ain't having yourself that honeymoon until you reach Dodge, right?"

Wade smiled at him. "Right. But I'll stay. Just to make sure Camile has privacy."

A short time later, Wade wondered why the hell he'd agreed to act as lookout. His gaze strayed toward Camile more often than it scanned the area for possible intruders. She had her back to him, but the smooth skin of her shoulders was enough to get him to thinking—pondering possibilities best left alone.

Good thing he'd hadn't ridden far when a feeling had come over him. A feeling that said the bosses might not leave well enough alone. The idea to say he and Camile were married had been a spur-of-the-moment decision. One he hoped he wouldn't regret.

"Don't suppose you'd bring me a shot of whiskey and a cigar?" she called.

He grinned. "No. But I'll scrub your back."

Camile glanced over her shoulder. "Would you?"

His smile faded. "Don't tempt me."

She ducked down in the water and turned. "Could I?"

The tops of her breasts teased him. He fought himself not to look below her face. "A smarter question would be why you'd want to."

Her shrug was almost his undoing. "I didn't say I wanted to. I'm just wondering if I could."

"You're a woman."

"So?"

"Sometimes that's all it takes."

Camile frowned. "Do you mean I wouldn't have to be pretty?"

"It helps."

"Are you saying when a man gets a hankering for a woman, any woman will do?"

As she bobbed in the water, Wade felt a hankering. He glanced away from her, pretending to do his job. "You ask a lot of questions."

"And you're slow with an answer. How am I supposed to learn if I don't ask?"

Wade rose from his squatting position and stretched his legs. "You should discuss men-and-women matters with another woman."

Lathering her skin with the yucca juice, Camile said, "I've never had one around to discuss them with. My mother died when I was two."

"What about Maria?"

She laughed. "Maria's an old spinster. What would she know? Besides, I figure you've had some experience."

"A little."

Camile glanced at him from beneath her lashes. "A woman should marry a man who knows his business if she doesn't."

A trickle of sweat slid down his temple. He wiped the side of his face with his shirt sleeve. "It's hot out here."

"The water's nice and cool."

Was she flirting with him? The coy look from beneath her lashes seemed a subtle invitation to join her. When did she learn these tricks? "You're borrowing trouble, Camile."

Her eyes widened innocently. "I'm not doing anything."

He had a painful argument taking place between his legs. Wade turned his back on her. "Hurry and finish. I imagine the others are growing impatient."

"I'm getting that way, too," he heard her mutter. "Give me the blanket Grady brought and I'll dry off."

His hand shook slightly as he retrieved the blanket from the ground. If she had a mind to practice her feminine wiles on a man, she should learn he wasn't the man. Camile had moved closer, but not close enough to expose herself. She held out her hand.

"Toss it here."

Wade tucked the blanket beneath his arm. "Come get it."

Her gaze locked with his. She smiled. "Do you think I won't?"

"I've called your bluff before."

The smile on her lips quivered. "It's not as if you haven't already seen me naked."

"That was different. We weren't alone in the middle of nowhere. Hank and your father can't protect you."

"And now you've taken on the job." She tilted her head to one side. "That's why you told the other outfits we're married, isn't it?"

"I suspected they'd think twice about messing with another man's wife," he answered, frowning. She'd pricked his conscience again. His current thoughts weren't those of a protector. Wade tossed the blanket on the ground next to the clothes Grady had scrounged up for Camile. "Come on out and get dressed. I'll move off a ways and stand guard."

She grinned at him. "Do you know what I think, Langtry? I think you're all talk."

His gaze roamed her in a manner that wiped the smile from her mouth. "When I stop talking is when you should start worrying. Every man has his limits. I'll stand between you and the other men, but there's no one standing between us."

Having warned her, he walked away. He allowed her privacy, but stood close enough to hear if she called out. She did say something under her breath. He wasn't certain, but he thought she'd muttered, "Who's gonna protect you, Langtry?"

Chapter Eleven

"A female," William growled once everyone had settled in for the night. "Why didn't you tell me, Langtry?"

"It was a secret," Wade reminded the cook for the fifth time.

William filled Wade's cup with coffee, then plopped down beside him. "She ain't got no business out here. It's dangerous. What if she's already breeding? You might have got your woman with child and she's been riding herd, sleeping on the hard ground, and I pretty near starved her!"

Wade almost laughed. William T. Ferguson was fussy about women. Who would have guessed? "I don't think you have anything to worry about," he said, unable to squelch his smile.

"My wife, Sarah, said that same thing to me eight times," William muttered. "Mark my words, pleasure always has a price."

"You have eight children?"

The cook nodded, his billy-goat mustache twitching. "Reckon there will be another one by time I get back. There always is."

"Sorry," Wade mumbled.

"It ain't so bad." The cook glanced around, then lowered his voice. "I got myself eight girls. You've never seen such a ruckus as when I drag my weary bones home after a drive. No cooking, no cleaning, and no doctoring until I get called out again. My girls take care of me like I was a king."

The picture wasn't one Wade could easily imagine. William T. Ferguson, lord of anything save a chuck wagon? A different vision flashed through his mind. Eight blond hellions cracking a whip over him while he did wifely chores. He shivered. "Camile lacks womanly instincts," he said more to himself than to William.

"That gal of yours can't cook?"

Wade didn't know for a fact Camile couldn't, but all things considered . . . "She throws a good rope," he offered dryly.

William's beady gaze darted toward her bedroll, then back to Wade. "Let me have her for a while. She needs to be learning to take care of you proper. I don't give a damn what Wendell says, the trail is no place for a woman."

Camile? A chuck wagon apprentice? Wade found the cook's offer tempting. If she were safely supervised by William, Wade wouldn't have to worry about her getting hurt. He drained his coffee cup, rose, and stretched his legs.

"You asked for it," he said to William in parting.

* * *

"Cook?" Camile paced, outraged. "I don't know how! I have no desire to learn! I won't!"

"I'm making it an order," Wade said. "Maybe Tom will be less likely to wring your neck if you learn something useful on this drive."

"Useful to whom?" Camile bent to retrieve her rope. "You've caused me enough humiliation! I won't do it, Langtry."

He noticed her ranting brought the Circle C bunch from the chuck wagon fire. Wade took her arm, steering her away from them. "You'll do this, Camile. At least long enough for the other outfits to get used to having a female with them."

"I hand. I don't cook!" She jerked free of him and stomped away.

Wade sighed, started to go after her, then noticed something in her path. He froze. "Stop. Don't move."

She didn't obey him. Instead, Camile wheeled around, placing her hands on her hips. "I—"

A rattling sound halted her words. Camile's gaze lowered, then abruptly lifted to him. A rattlesnake, coiled and ready to strike, lay at her feet. Wade didn't think, he drew and blew the snake's head off.

"My Lord!" Grady ran up to them, the Circle C cowboys hot on his heels. "Did you see Langtry draw?" he asked the others, his expression close to awe.

Wade ignored Grady. Camile was still staring at him, her eyes wide with shock. He went to her. "Are you all right?"

"Yes," she whispered.

"Damn, where'd you learn to draw like that, Langtry," Grady asked, joining them.

"You draw like a man who does it for a living," Camile said, her voice shaky.

He shrugged, hoping to make light of his talents. "Where I grew up, if you couldn't defend yourself, you didn't live long. Time to get moving." He dismissed the subject, walking toward the picketing string.

"Who taught you?" Camile demanded, falling into step beside him.

"Living on the streets taught me," he answered. "A respectful fear of death. Hunger, squalor, things you know nothing about."

"Was it awful?"

"I told you once, I don't like to talk about it."

Gently, she touched his arm. "You can tell me."

His gaze roamed her features. "Why?"

She glanced down. "I know all about stolen childhoods."

Tilting her face upward, Wade forced her to look him in the eye. He saw pain there—a deep, dark pain. "What happened?"

The torment reflected in her gaze vanished. She pulled away from him. "We aren't talking about me, remember?"

"We're not talking about me, either." He continued toward the picketing string. She'd touched him a moment ago. Not just physically. He had lived with his own pain for years. The loneliness. The fear. When he'd seen the same suffering that was in his own eyes staring back at him from Camile's, he'd wanted to hold her—wanted to erase whatever had happened to put it there.

"I still don't understand how you learned to shoot like that," Camile said. "I mean, if you were alone, if you were just a kid—"

Annoyed by her stubbornness, Wade stopped. "I found a

gun on a dead man one night. Didn't figure he needed it anymore. I was twelve by then, and damned tired of bigger men stealing what little I could scrounge for myself. I didn't have bullets, so I learned to draw fast. Whoever was trying to steal from me didn't know the gun wasn't loaded."

Her gaze widened. "Damn, Langtry. They could have called your bluff."

"That came later," he muttered, walking away. "I need to mount up. Good thing the herd's up farther; otherwise, that shot could have started a stampede."

She grabbed his arm again when he threw the reins over his horse's neck. "Teach me to draw and shoot."

He glanced at her, then rolled his gaze upward. "No way in hell, Camile."

"Why not?"

Wade laughed. "You're dangerous enough."

"I know how to shoot a rifle," she argued. "I'm just asking you to teach me to use a six-shooter."

"Give me one reason worth spit why I should?"

"I should learn to defend myself."

"You should learn to cook," he scoffed, easing his foot into the stirrup.

"I'll learn to cook. No complaining. I promise. Just teach me to draw and fire that Colt."

Swinging up into the saddle, Wade regarded her thoughtfully. What harm would it do? Camile didn't own a six-shooter of her own. The only time she'd handle the weapon would be under his supervision. He found her offer tempting. Camile accepting her new position without a fuss?

"All right. But you don't touch a gun unless it's mine, and only if I give you permission. Understand?"

"Whatever you say," she answered, a smile lighting up her face.

"You're damn agreeable when you want something," he muttered. "Go help William. Don't irritate him."

She appeared offended. "Have you ever known me to get on anyone's wrong side?"

"I've never seen you on the right side of anyone," he countered dryly. "Who knows, you might take to cooking as easy as you took to riding, roping, cussing, and God knows what else."

Camile opened her mouth to respond, but quickly closed it. She shrugged, then turned away.

His gaze lowered to her hips as she walked toward the chuck wagon. The Circle C cowhands shifted his attention from what he had no business appreciating.

"Where's Cam going?" Grady asked.

"I put her on chuck wagon duty for a few days."

Grady glanced from Wade to her retreating figure. "And she's not pitching a fit?"

"I can handle her."

"Then you're more than just the fastest damn draw I've ever seen." Grady snorted. "I never thought I'd see the day Cam put on an apron and did something a normal woman would do. I know you're the boss and all, Langtry, but I ain't sure Tom and Hank would like you telling the other outfits you and Cam are married. The boys and me . . . well . . . " Grady paused, glancing at the Colt strapped to Wade's thigh.

"The boys and you what?"

"We trust you ain't got any notions about carrying that pretense too far. We respect your leadership, but we owe Tom our loyalty. And Cam, she ain't for the likes of us.

Cowboy justice strikes swift and hard in these parts. For Tom, we'd feel obligated to kill any man who took advantage of Cam as a female. Understand?"

Wade matched his steady stare. "Seems to me she should do the choosing, but you have nothing to worry about."

"Hope not," Grady said. "I wouldn't want to go up against you, but I would. We all would."

The warning received, Wade nodded toward their horses tied to the picketing string. "Let's go. Maybe Camile will have us something tasty fixed for dinner."

Grady laughed, the tension broken. He mounted his horse. "Guess she didn't tell you the last time Maria tried to teach her to cook, she burned down the kitchen. We spent that winter rebuilding it."

"What is it?" Wade eyed his plate that evening skeptically.

"I think it's a biscuit," Harley Tims offered.

Grady's lip curled in disgust. "Looks like a cow turd left to dry two weeks in the sun."

"No, turds are softer than this," Jake argued. "Hell, tie this thing to the end of a rope and you could kill someone with it."

"Quiet," Wade said. "She's coming."

A hush fell over the group as Camile seated herself. Wade thought she looked lovely, damp tendrils clinging to the sides of her face, a smudge of flour on her cheek. William muttered in the background, banging pots and pans with a vengeance.

Wade nodded toward his plate. "Did you make this?"

"Just the biscuits," she admitted shyly.

"Well, they look good," he lied. "Eat up, boys."

141

Grady frowned. "You first, Langtry."

Casting him a dark look, Wade lifted the hard, black ball in question to his lips. Although he'd been blessed with strong teeth, the advantage was sorely lost upon the biscuit. No amount of chiseling would loosen the granite coating. Knowing any criticism would set Camile off like a spark to dry brush, he increased his efforts. Finally he cracked the surface . . . of his tooth.

"Damn!" he swore, rising. "What the hell did you put in these?"

"I knew it!" Camile jumped to her feet. "I knew you'd find something to complain about. Nothing I do suits you, Langtry. You insist I cook, then insult my efforts!" She threw her plate in his face.

Her biscuit bounced off Wade's forehead, leaving a stinging welt. He cussed as Camile stomped off. "Bury them while she's gone. And tell her they were good after I bring her back."

It took only a minute to catch up with Camile. Her legs were long, but his were longer. When he turned her around, the apology on his tongue died. Tears streamed down her cheeks.

"What are you staring at?" she demanded.

"The damnedest woman I've ever met," he said softly. "You didn't cry when the stallion dragged you. Not when Cummings nearly raped you, and not when you almost got yourself snake-bit. A biscuit? You're crying over a biscuit?"

"If you tell anyone, I'll kill you. I'll slit your throat while you sleep."

He fought the urge to laugh. "I'd hate to die over one bad attempt at dough rolling."

"I suppose you know how to cook, too?" she huffed.

"Only because I wanted to eat."

"Maria tried to teach me once," Camile admitted quietly. "I—"

"I know. You burned down the kitchen. Maybe I'll forget the bargain we struck. Rolling out biscuits must be harder than breaking a horse or drawing a gun."

"I had help learning to break a horse," Camile said. "Sir Billy refused to believe I didn't know the first thing about cooking. Any idiot can make biscuits, he claimed. What was I supposed to do?"

Wade ran his tongue over the small chip at the base of his front tooth. "What did you do?"

"Poured everything he set out into a bowl and mixed it up."

"You didn't knead it?"

"How was I supposed to know what I needed or didn't need?"

He sighed, started to explain, then shook his head. "Come along." Wade turned her toward camp. "First thing tomorrow morning, you learn to tame a rolling pin."

Chapter Twelve

Wade Langtry had his sleeves rolled up, a flour-sack apron tied around his waist, and his arms up to the elbows in dough. William Ferguson wasn't much for letting another man intrude upon his sacred territory, but when Camile explained she had no notion on how to make biscuits, he'd buckled, claiming he had too many things to do to teach her proper. Camile glanced at Wade. She doubted there was another man alive who could look as masculine under the circumstances.

"Knead, don't pound," he said. "Understand?"

Although she didn't understand at all, Camile nodded.

"I've got the Dutch oven heated up for you," William said from his position against the water barrel. "I'll be inside preparing one of my specialties. Camile, come help after you've finished there."

She grumbled under her breath. "You should be helping William. You're much better at cooking than I am."

"And if you tell anyone, I'll kill you." Wade's tone was teasing.

He placed her hands beneath his, showing her how to knead the dough. The feel of him pressed so snugly against her was distracting. The motion of his body moving with the rhythm of his hands stirred primitive feelings. She wondered if he felt excited by their close proximity, by the friction between their bodies.

Could she get him to admit he wanted her? Did she dare admit she might want him, and not only for her future plans of revenge? Again and again his body pressed against hers. A trickle of moisture traced a path between her breasts. The Dutch oven close by didn't help matters.

"It's hot," she complained quietly.

"It is," Wade agreed, his breath stirring the damp tendrils at her neck.

"How long you figure this will take?"

"Longer than I can stand."

He released her hands and moved away. Camile watched him wipe his face with a bandanna. She continued to knead the dough as he'd instructed, noting the rapid rise and fall of his chest—and the heated look in his eyes.

"I thought you said you could cook," she teased.

"I'm used to doing for myself. By myself," he stressed.

"I'm surprised you don't have a woman to take care of you." Camile realized the oddity of that for the first time. Wade Langtry was a handsome man. Why hadn't some woman staked a claim on him by now?

"I never said I didn't."

She felt as if a mule had just kicked her in the stomach. Her knees nearly buckled. She straightened, pretending an interest in the task at hand, hoping to hide the confusing feelings his simple statement brought to the surface. "You're married?"

"Not yet."

Camile glanced at him. "But you're figuring on it?"

"Someday."

Her throat closed. Damn, she thought she might cry. Instead, Camile laughed. "Well, where is she?"

"St. Louis."

"Oh." The dough began to stick to her fingers. Considering her raw emotions concerning the subject, Camile knew she should leave the questions rolling around in her unsaid. It took five seconds for curiosity to get the best of her. "Is she one of them fancy women? The kind who wears silk and holds her pinky out when she drinks tea?"

Wade joined her, studied the sticky dough, and added more flour. "Now that you mention it, I think she does do that when she drinks tea."

"Do you love her?"

He seemed to have trouble looking Camile in the eye. "I admire her. What she represents."

"But you don't love her."

An answer from him wasn't quick in coming. Wade removed the flour-sack apron and snatched up his hat. "Love is something that's taught. I don't know much about it. I'd better get going. You can handle the biscuits from here."

Her heart began to pound inside her chest. She couldn't let him leave. Not when she needed to know for certain how he felt about the woman he intended to marry.

146

"Didn't your parents teach you about love before they . . . well, before?"

Again, he wouldn't look at her. "Funny thing about the good and bad in a person's life. The bad is usually the easiest to remember."

"You survived," she said softly.

His gaze met hers. His eyes were too old for a man of thirty. "Do you know the first thing I learned to cook? Grubs I dug from the ground. I'd eaten them raw before I found a pan and figured out how to build a fire. You call that survival? I called it a living Hell."

Camile had no witty remarks for him. She felt sick—enraged that any children should have to fend for themselves, should be forced to live on the streets alone. "You grew into a fine man," she said to ease the pain evident on his face. He flinched as if she might have struck a blow.

"You have no idea what I grew into," he said quietly, then walked away.

Confused by his last remark, she watched him move toward his horse. Did Wade not see the good in himself? As much as she didn't want to, she did. Anything he'd said or done to her, Camile believed he'd done with her best interests in mind. Competition aside, Wade was a fair man. Instead of flat-out refusals, he'd given her trade-offs. Which reminded her of one in particular.

"Don't forget, you promised to teach me to shoot the Colt," she called.

"Yeah, yeah," he called back, swinging up onto his horse. "Later."

After he'd ridden from sight, Camile slumped against the crude table. Wade's brief insight into his past had her thinking about her own. He was right. The bad was the easiest to remember. Camile didn't want to remember. She should be thinking about the future. About how she would make amends and win her father's love and forgiveness. Wade occupied her thoughts too often.

He had a woman. One he greatly admired. One who probably knew how to fix biscuits without his help. She reached inside her shirt and pulled out her braid, then ran a hand through her short curls.

"Heaven sakes! Did you scalp someone?"

William startled her. Camile quickly tried to hide the braid.

"What's that?" he demanded, moving closer, although cautiously.

She sighed. "It's my hair. Wade cut it off."

The cook frowned. "Why?"

"Because I was supposed to be a boy and all."

"Don't know why you're down in the mouth about it," William said. "You're pretty enough without that braid."

Blinking back tears, she glanced up at him. "Do you think so?"

He smiled. "Sure do. And I bet Langtry thinks so, too."

"Wade said I was beautiful once. But that was before, and he hasn't . . . "

"He hasn't what?" William prompted.

"He hasn't so much as kissed me since he chopped it off!"

"Oh." William scratched his scraggly mustache. "Hurt your feelings, has he?"

Embarrassed, Camile stuffed her braid inside her shirt and turned toward the dough. "I don't know how he expects me to get something in the oven without his help."

"That does present a problem. Tell you what. You cut these biscuits with that tin cup, and leave patching up your marriage to me." William winked, then scrambled inside the chuck wagon.

Camile stared after him, confused. What did biscuits and marriage have to do with each other?

Later, as promised, she held Wade's revolver in her hand. The walnut handle was worn smooth. The trigger was wired back. She stared at the weapon thoughtfully. "Have you killed anyone with this gun?"

The lazy smile Wade wore faded. He shrugged away from his horse. "Just a few nosy, curly-headed blondes. If you have the feel of my Colt, I'll load it."

She handed him the weapon. He loaded the gun efficiently. Quickly, like a man used to preparing for trouble in a hurry. Curious, his familiarity with that Colt. There were no notches. She'd looked. He was a man of many surprises, the latest one having caused her much deliberation throughout the day.

"I can't see it," she said matter-of-factly.

He lifted a brow. "See what?"

"You with some pale-skinned, silk-swishing, finger-crooking woman."

A slight smile shaped his lips. "I'm sure she'd appreciate that string of compliments."

"Would she appreciate her intended kissing another woman?"

His gaze met hers. "I doubt it, but we're not officially engaged."

"So that makes it all right?"

Wade handed her the gun. "I thought you wanted to learn to shoot."

"I do," Camile assured him. "I told you, I figure I should learn about men-and-women things, as well."

149

"And I've told you, I'm not the man to teach you."

"You taught me to kiss."

"No. I showed you how to be kissed."

"What's the difference?"

Eyeing her reproachfully, he put distance between them. "Never mind. Steady your aim."

Camile raised the gun, but refused to be sidetracked. Having decided she needed to focus more on her goal of running the ranch, she needed to know if Wade's woman would get in the way of her plans to seduce him. "What about Rosie? Would your woman understand about her?"

He sighed. "Nothing happened between me and Rosie."

"Only because you were interrupted."

"Choose a target," he ground out.

You, Camile thought. "That tumbleweed up ahead," she said instead.

"There's fifty tumbleweeds up ahead. Pick something else."

"How about that steer skull directly to the left?"

"Fine. First you learn to hit the target, then you practice your draw."

"Sort of the same as first you have all the women you can, then you settle down?" She shifted her gaze in his direction.

His rolled upward. "Drop it, Camile."

She dropped the gun to her side. "I'm just trying to understand what's between us."

"Nothing. Nothing *can* be between us."

The backs of her eyes started stinging. Before Langtry had come along, she hadn't known a man could make a person feel so weepy . . . unless she counted her father.

"Because I'm not like her?"

"Because I've been told to stay away from you."

"You have?" she asked, surprised. "Who told you to keep your distance?"

Wade walked over, lifted her arm, and steadied her aim. "Hank and Grady. You're not for just anyone. If a man doesn't bring land and cattle with him, he's not good enough for Tom Cordell's daughter."

Those cursed tears welled up in her eyes. She was thankful Langtry stood behind her. "I'm breeding stock. That's the only way my father sees me, unless I make him see me differently."

"Is that why you've tried so hard not to be a woman?"

His breath felt warm against her neck. His body molded to hers the way it had been while kneading biscuit dough. Trying had been easier before Wade Langtry had stumbled into her life.

"I never saw much to be gained by being one," she answered, then turned her head. His mouth was only inches away. Her gaze lifted and met with his. There was something between them. She knew it, and he knew it, but he wouldn't admit to the truth. More than the possibility of Wade's woman in St. Louis getting in the way of her plans suddenly bothered Camile.

"How does a simple cowhand win a fancy lady's interest?" she asked. "I'm not too educated about the ways between men and women, but even I'm expected to make the right match."

Her speculations obviously took him off guard. Camile saw wariness cross his face before he quickly masked the emotion.

"I don't plan on being a cowhand for the rest of my life," he said casually. "I'm building a stake, hoping to buy into a prosperous gold mine and strike it rich."

"She won't have you unless you're wealthy. Isn't that right?"

His jaw tensed. "I suppose it is. Lilla Traften is used to the finer things in life."

Camile had more than one reason to resent the woman. Men's money had never interested her. Men in general had never interested her. Not until she'd had her first run-in with Wade. It seemed to her, in the short space of time she'd come to know him, that money or position shouldn't figure into what was natural between a man and woman.

The spark was there or it wasn't. It suddenly became important to her that Wade acknowledge the attraction between them. She told herself that what she intended to do next was solely for the sake of her future plans. So what if the thought of his fancy lady making unfair demands had angered her?

Was she any different? She wanted something from him, too. She wanted to get rid of him so she could run the ranch. With those thoughts in mind, Camile bravely closed the distance between their lips.

Their mouths fit perfectly together, only his wasn't responding. From beneath her lashes, she saw him staring at her. He'd said she'd never kissed him, only been kissed by him. With the tip of her tongue, she traced the outline of his lips. They parted.

Her mouth slanted over his, her tongue delving deeper into his mouth. He made a sound in his throat, a low animal sound, then pulled her around and into his arms. The gun made a thud as it hit the ground. Her hands were in his hair. His were on her back, sliding over her hips. Camile melted into him. She wanted to get closer, although she couldn't feel a single place where their bodies didn't touch.

"Dammit, Camile," he swore, then gently pushed her away.

She staggered back a step, feeling as if she'd drunk too much whiskey. Her breathing sounded ragged. She ached all over. Hurt with a need she didn't understand.

"That didn't feel like nothing," she whispered.

He ran a hand through his hair. "No," he agreed. "Keep tempting me and I'm liable to tumble you in the dirt like a common trollop."

"You will?" she asked, nearly pleased by the prospect.

His green gaze narrowed on her. "Don't sound so hopeful." He walked to the gun, stooped, and picked it up. "You worry me, Camile. Kissing a man that way will get you into trouble."

"It will?" She knew she sounded hopeful again. Camile bit her lip.

Wade approached her. "Hasn't anyone warned you about men like me?" Tilting her chin up to make her look at him, he said, "We're dangerous. Don't offer what you can't afford to lose. My kind will take it and never look back."

There wasn't a teasing glint in his eye. He was dead serious. "Are you trying to tell me something?" she asked.

He released her chin, then slapped the Colt in her hand. "I've been trying to tell you something for a while now. You're playing with fire."

"Fire?" She lifted the Colt, took aim, and squeezed the trigger. The skull shattered. Camile sauntered toward him, slapped the gun in his hand, and said, "How about we bet your job I can do that again?"

153

"I can't offer what I can't afford to lose," he answered, placing the gun in his holster.

"You said you didn't spook easy. Are you afraid to go up against me again?"

With a disbelieving shake of his head, Wade asked, "Don't you ever give up, Camile?"

"Don't worry. I won't."

"Those weren't words of encouragement. Let me rephrase them. Give up. You've been beat. The contest no longer rages. I'm sorry, but the men won't take orders from you. They'll never consider you one of them. Why can't you accept that and move on?"

Camile took a deep breath. "I'm asking for another chance. Let me ride the herd again—be one of the Circle C hands—"

"Why?" he demanded. "What do you expect to gain?"

A lump formed in her throat. She couldn't tell him the truth. What would he think of her if he knew she'd crippled her father and killed her brother? Camile lifted her chin. "My rightful place. I have to prove myself worthy."

"Worthy of what?"

My father's love and forgiveness. Instead, she said, "Worthy of more than keeping house and tending children. It's important to me, Langtry."

He sighed. "It's dangerous out there. I-I don't want you to get hurt."

A warm feeling spread through her. "You don't?"

His gaze lowered. He scooped his hat from his saddle horn and placed it on his head, pulling the brim down low. "Tom and Hank would skin me alive."

"Oh." Camile hoped she hid her disappointment. "Sorry

to be such a damn burden." Angrily, she trudged toward camp.

"Three days," he said to her back. "I'm giving you three days to change their minds. Three days to show me up. If you can, you finish out the drive with the men. If you can't, you go back to the chuck wagon and mind your manners until we reach Dodge."

"Three days?" She wheeled around. "I can't do anything in three days."

He shrugged. "That depends on how determined you are."

She considered his offer for a moment. It wasn't much of one. He'd given her three days to perform a miracle. If she failed, he wouldn't give her another chance to win her rightful place among the men. If she failed, she'd have no choice but to move on to her next plan. Seducing Wade. His response to her a few minutes earlier boosted her confidence.

"I'll take it," she said softly. "You just offered something you can't afford to lose."

Chapter Thirteen

The night felt eerie. Days of sweltering heat, and now the air felt heavy, sticky. Wade scanned the bedded-down herd. Their horns glowed green in the dark, an occurrence he'd seen very few times. The gates of Hell were fixing to split wide open.

"I don't like it," Wendell Cates said.

"Trouble," Wade mumbled. "Smell it coming?"

Wendell inhaled deeply. "All I smell is cows," he said, then laughed nervously. "Ever seen fire dance on a steer's horns that way, Langtry?"

"Right before a storm hits. A bad one."

The trail boss glanced up. "Ain't a cloud in the sky."

"I figure it's rolling in behind us. It should be here before long."

"You sure?" Wendell asked. "Thunderstorms and stampedes go hand in hand."

Wade didn't answer. He waited. In the distance, an angry roar rumbled across the plains.

A whistle slithered through the space between Wendell's teeth. "Sounds like a mean one. We'd better roust every available hand. The situation could get ugly."

"It will," Wade assured him. "Real ugly. Real fast. Let's move."

All was quiet when Wade rode into camp. He dismounted, moving toward the sleeping men. Most stirred without having to roust them. Their instincts were sharp. Silently, they pulled on boots and reached for hats and rifles. Camile scrambled up. Wade cussed softly, then approached her.

"Stay with the chuck wagon."

She began shoving her feet into her boots. "Not a chance, Langtry."

"That's an order."

"An unfair one and you know it." She grabbed her hat. "If you've come for everyone, something is going on."

He stilled the motion of her hand when she reached for her saddle. Wade pulled her away from the others. "A storm is blowing in. The herd might run. It's no place for you."

"Stampede?" she whispered. "I can't miss this. This is my chance. If I don't ride with the rest of the men, what will they think?"

"That you finally have a lick of sense," he answered angrily. "This isn't a game. It's dangerous. Many good men, experienced men, have been trampled to death during a stampede. I won't be out there worrying about you when I need my head clear."

"Your concern is touching," Camile drawled. "Forget

157

what Hank or my father would say. If the herd runs, you need every available hand. That includes me."

"I said no."

She pulled free of his grasp. "I'm going. You can't stop me."

Wade removed his hat and ran a hand through his hair. The defiant tilt of her chin made his blood boil. "I've never punched a woman in my life, but you're pushing me. If I have to knock you out cold to keep you from getting hurt, possibly killed, then I'll do it."

A jagged streak of lightning split the sky. Her eyes were huge.

"You'd hit me?"

"If you give me no choice."

Camile frowned. "Didn't figure you for that sort."

"I'm not," he muttered darkly. "I don't know what else to do."

"Kiss me."

"What?" He shook his head, thinking he hadn't heard her correctly.

"When you ride out, I may never see you again. You just told me how dangerous a stampede can be. Kiss me once before you go. In case . . . "

His mind had trouble galloping off into a different direction. Wade wasn't sure he could hit her if drastic measures became necessary. He'd sworn he wouldn't kiss her again—vowed to keep his distance and concentrate on the reason he'd come to Texas.

"Langtry!" Grady Finch shouted from the campsite. "Come on. The storm will be over us any minute!"

The others were standing by the campfire. They had saddled the night horses and donned their slickers. Wade knew they couldn't see him in the darkness, although the occasional bursts of light from the sky had intensified. He glanced toward Camile. She could be right. He might not see her again.

"Here's a little something to remember me by . . . just in case."

Pulling her into his arms, Wade took her lips without ceremony. There wasn't time for tender explorations or gentle persuasion. Their tongues clashed, their wills merged. They melted into each other. Desire, red hot and rampant, coursed through him. He felt singed by the heat—insane to surrender so completely to what he'd been fighting so diligently to resist. Lilla Traften couldn't make him feel this way—not her, or any other woman.

The admission scared the hell out of him. The ground trembled beneath his feet. Startled by her power over him, Wade ended the kiss. The sky lit up. Their gazes locked, but the earth still moved.

"Christ," he swore. "The herd." Wade started to turn, but his feet were suddenly knocked from beneath him. He landed with a jar. Camile raced toward camp.

"Not everyone fights fair," she called. "Be seeing you, Langtry."

He struggled to his feet. "Dammit! Come back here!"

She didn't. Camile ran up to William Ferguson, snatched a slicker from the cook's arms, and raced toward the picketing string. The men stood gape-mouthed, staring at Camile, then squinting toward the darkness. Wade clenched his jaw and followed her.

"Mount up!" he barked to the waiting men. "Grady, you

159

go after Camile and I don't care if you have to hog-tie her, bring her back to the chuck wagon and see that she stays put!"

"How'd she get the jump on you?" the cowboy asked.

"She tricked me," he grumbled. "Let's move!"

The men ran for their horses. William fell into step beside Wade, handing him a slicker. "That wife of yours sure has some strange notions in her head. What's a female doing riding stampede?"

Wade didn't answer. He shrugged into his slicker. Their regular horses were grazing the remuda. Only one night horse remained. A half-loco black mare no one wanted to ride.

"Seems to me if you gave her more to occupy herself with, she wouldn't be searching for trouble to get into," William suggested. "A baby or two would settle her down."

The suggestion caused him to stumble. He couldn't picture Camile settling down, two babies or six. Her "kiss me because I might never see you again" act had been a smart move. She'd only wanted to lower his guard. She had.

"That woman's gonna be the death of me." Wade swung up into the saddle, then dug his spurs into the black's sides.

The mare didn't have much horse sense, but she had speed. Wade quickly closed the distance between him and the Circle C cowboys. He tried to find Camile among the dark shapes, but the sky opened up. The rain fell hard. The ground turned to mud. His horse slipped, then recovered, plunging forward.

Flashes of light exploded all around him. Ahead, a thousand candles lit the plains. The glow of horns. Wade urged his mount onward, hoping to get ahead of the herd and turn

Thrill to the most sensual, adventure-filled Historical Romances on the market today…

FROM  LEISURE BOOKS

As a home subscriber to the Leisure Historical Romance Book Club, you'll enjoy the best in today's BRAND-NEW Historical Romance fiction. For over twenty-five years, Leisure Books has brought you the award-winning, high-quality authors you know and love to read. Each Leisure Historical Romance will sweep you away to a world of high adventure…and intimate romance. Discover for yourself all the passion and excitement millions of readers thrill to each and every month.

SAVE AT LEAST *$5.00* EACH TIME YOU BUY!

Each month, the Leisure Historical Romance Book Club brings you four brand-new titles from Leisure Books, America's foremost publisher of Historical Romances. EACH PACKAGE WILL SAVE YOU AT LEAST $5.00 FROM THE BOOKSTORE PRICE! And you'll never miss a new title with our convenient home delivery service.

Here's how we do it. Each package will carry a 10-DAY EXAMINATION privilege. At the end of that time, if you decide to keep your books, simply pay the low invoice price of $16.96 ($17.75 US in Canada), no shipping or handling charges added*. HOME DELIVERY IS ALWAYS FREE*. With today's top Historical Romance novels selling for $5.99 and higher, our price SAVES YOU AT LEAST $5.00 with each shipment.

AND YOUR FIRST FOUR-BOOK SHIPMENT IS TOTALLY FREE!*

IT'S A BARGAIN YOU CAN'T BEAT! A Super $21.96 Value!

LEISURE BOOKS A Division of Dorchester Publishing Co., Inc.

GET YOUR 4 FREE* BOOKS NOW—
A $21.96 VALUE!

Mail the Free* Book
Certificate
Today!

---

4 FREE* BOOKS 🌹 A $21.96 VALUE

Free Books Certificate*

YES! I want to subscribe to the Leisure Historical Romance Book Club. Please send me my 4 FREE* BOOKS. Then each month I'll receive the four newest Leisure Historical Romance selections to Preview for 10 days. If I decide to keep them, I will pay the Special Member's Only discounted price of just $4.24 each, a total of $16.96 ($17.75 US in Canada). This is a SAVINGS OF AT LEAST $5.00 off the bookstore price. There are no shipping, handling, or other charges*. There is no minimum number of books I must buy and I may cancel the program at any time. In any case, the 4 FREE* BOOKS are mine to keep—A BIG $21.96 Value!

*In Canada, add $5.00 shipping and handling per order for first shipment. For all subsequent shipments to Canada, the cost of membership is $17.75 US, which includes $7.75 shipping and handling per month. [All payments must be made in US dollars]

Name _____

Address _____

City _____

State _____ *Country* _____ *Zip* _____

Telephone _____

Signature _____

If under 18, Parent or Guardian must sign. Terms, prices and conditions subject to change. Subscription subject to acceptance. Leisure Books reserves the right to reject any order or cancel any subscription.

(Tear Here and Mail Your FREE* Book Card Today!)

Get Four Books Totally
F R E E* —
A $21.96 Value!

PLEASE RUSH
MY FOUR FREE*
BOOKS TO ME
RIGHT AWAY!

Leisure Historical Romance Book Club
P.O. Box 6613
Edison, NJ 08818-6613

AFFIX
STAMP
HERE

them back. The scent of danger filled his nostrils, his throat, his lungs.

Wade knew the smell. If he were totally honest with himself, he'd admit he sometimes yearned for that fragrance. His life had been one long brush with death, and yet, here he was, in the middle of Oklahoma territory, riding like a madman after a bunch of dim-witted cows. The worst of it being, he liked it.

But not enough to let go of his dream. To forget he had another life waiting for him in St. Louis. A peaceful, respectable, secure life. Something he'd never had until five years ago. Something he'd yearned for since his parents' deaths. His thoughts sobered him. He didn't have to take chances. Hell, lose all the damned cattle and Tom would take a beating. A bad one. A financial loss like that would surely convince him to sell.

Another flash of lightning gave Wade an advantage. He had almost reached the front of the herd. To his surprise, he was also very much alone. A second flash froze his blood. A shadow loomed ahead. A bluff. Fate had played right into his hands. He didn't pull up the reins, allowing the steers to race foolishly to their deaths.

Camile had already done Wade's dirty work for him. Her father should be more than willing to sell after her defiant action. Tom needed the profit from this drive, as well as a fair price for the ranch, which Wade had every intention of seeing he received. Still, he couldn't let him suffer the setback of losing the herd. The black picked up speed. Wade got ahead of the cattle, drew his gun, and fired. The steers turned. All but one.

The black went after the straggler. Wade pulled up hard

on the reins, but the horse fought the bit and plowed ahead. In the darkness, Wade couldn't calculate the distance to the drop-off, but he knew it wasn't far. The wisest thing to do when a mustang wouldn't obey was to get off. Wade tried to stand. The slippery soles of his boots made the task impossible. His foot slipped through one of the stirrups. He was trapped. The fool horse mistook the jerking of his foot as encouragement.

Wade dropped the reins and leaned low, trying to free himself. The lightning flashed. He glanced up. It was too late. The steer veered away from the bluff at the last second, but the horse dug in her hooves. They slid toward the chasm. Wade felt his foot pull free from the trapped boot, then he was flying. Over the horse's head, straight to Hell.

He fell, his arms squeezed against his sides, his breath trapped in his throat. His body jerked. A hard, rocky surface slammed into his shoulder. He twirled, suspended in midair.

"Langtry!"

He'd died and gone to Hell. Camile was there. It figured.

"Dammit! Answer me, Langtry?"

Her voice came from above. Wade glanced up. Nothing but darkness and rain. Rain? It didn't make sense that it would rain in Hell. He didn't imagine they'd allow Camile to cuss in Heaven, either.

"What happened?" he shouted.

"Hold on. The ground's slippery, but I'll try to back my horse and pull you up."

A rope? That was what squeezed his chest and trapped his arms. Camile had obviously roped him before he'd gone over the edge.

"I'll be damned," he mumbled. His gaze shot skyward. "Sorry."

* * *

Camile thought she'd backed all the way to Texas before Wade wriggled his way over the top. The air left her lungs in a relieved rush. It'd been a long shot, a miracle really, considering the distance between them when she'd thrown the rope.

Her limbs shook. Her heart pounded. Wade had almost gone and got himself killed! She'd shoot him if she had a gun. The fizzling storm outlined his form as he walked toward her. Camile noticed his limp. She supposed the polite thing to do would be to ride forward and spare him a few steps. The closer he got, the angrier she became.

She slid off her horse before he reached her. Wade stopped. He stared at her. She stared back. Something funny happened inside her. A burst of joy bubbled up through her anger. Tears burned the backs of her eyes.

Langtry was a problem she'd been trying to rid herself of from the moment he'd set foot on the Circle C. So why had the thought of losing him been unbearable? Why had the thought of never seeing him again made her risk her own life for his?

Roping Wade hadn't been wise. She might have missed and lassoed the mare. If the horse had gone over with him, Camile and her mount would have been pulled down with them. Her safety hadn't mattered. He mattered. The realization was unwelcome. She could find him attractive, enjoy his kisses, but she mustn't allow herself to care for him. The Circle C, winning her father's love and approval, making amends for her past mistakes, all were too important. She couldn't allow Langtry to compromise those as well as her heart.

Although she itched to throw her arms around him as he drew closer, longed to weep with relief that fate had spared him, she did neither. Camile blinked away her tears. She placed her hands on her hips.

"You idiot! Why didn't you jump?"

Wade stumbled. He cussed and hopped a few steps toward her. "My foot got hung up," he snapped, regaining his balance. "Glad to see you, too, Camile."

The breath she drew was a shaky one. "I reckon so. I just saved your life."

Their gazes locked. His jaw clenched for a moment; then he glanced around. "Did anyone see you?"

"I don't think so." She frowned. "Why? Are you going to say I didn't?"

Ignoring her question, he gathered the reins of her mount as if preparing to swing into the saddle. Camile grabbed his shoulder.

"Are you?" she demanded.

"It'd be my word against yours."

"And telling the truth might win me respect from the others, isn't that so?"

Slowly, he faced her, his expression hard. "Is that why you risked your fool neck for me? For that damn stretch of dust and cactus you call home?"

Burning sensations began behind her eyes again. The ranch wasn't the reason she'd saved him. She supposed she could say she would have done the same for anyone, and maybe that was true, but bravery, or the Circle C, hadn't entered her mind. Camile didn't want to think about what had.

"Truth is, I was aiming for the horse," she said.

His mouth became a tight line. "Why doesn't that surprise me?" He tried to slide his bootless foot into the stirrup and groaned softly. "Lucky you missed. If that loco black went over, so would you."

"I'd have jumped off before that happened."

Wade swung up into the saddle. He extended a hand. "Maybe. And maybe you'd have panicked like you did when the stallion dragged you. Froze up. Then we'd both be dead, wouldn't we?"

"But I didn't freeze up and we're not dead!"

He opened his mouth, but whatever he might have said was drowned out by the pounding of hooves and Grady's shout.

"Langtry? Cam? Is that you?"

Before either of them could answer, the Circle C riders, along with men from two other outfits, rode up. Grady sighed upon seeing Camile.

"Someone said they saw a rider go over the bluff. We figured it might have been Cam."

Camile tensed. Why must men always assume that if a man and woman got themselves into trouble, it would be the female who needed rescuing?

"You were supposed to take her to the chuck wagon," Wade reminded him, casting a dark glance in Grady's direction.

The cowboy shrugged. "Couldn't catch her. Damn, she rides better than any man I know . . . besides you, Boss," he quickly added.

Grady's compliment took the sting out of his earlier assumption. Camile said nothing, waiting to see what lie Wade would tell.

He glanced at her, seemed to grow an inch taller in the saddle, and said, "Actually, *I* went over the bluff. Cam

165

roped me at what had to be an impossible distance and saved my life."

Silence. Heads turned toward Camile, then back to Wade, until she thought the men would grow dizzy and fall from their horses. Grady whistled softly.

"You don't say? Gosh, how far away was you when you threw, Cam?"

"A ways," she answered, stunned. Wade had told the truth. He'd given her the ammunition to defeat him. Or at least to unseat him for the night. Why?

"Show us how far away you was," a voice insisted.

"Yeah, Cam, tell us the whole story."

Her gaze roamed the men's expectant faces. The storm had passed, and now a full moon lit the plains. They wanted to hear the story. Not from Wade. From her.

"Let's look for the spot your horse started digging in," Grady said, dismounting.

The other men followed suit. Camile suddenly found herself surrounded, a lasso shoved in her hand.

"Bet she can't do it again," a man from Wendell's outfit said. The same one who'd once slapped her lightly and caused all hell to break loose.

"Bet she can," Grady countered. "Cam's got the best damn ropin' arm on the Circle C."

"She can spit a far piece, too," Jake added. "Plays a mean hand of poker. Cool as a north wind as she steals you blind."

"Saw her cut up a man," Grady said low, as if telling a scary story. "Prickly Pear of the Panhandle. She didn't get that name for no good reason."

"Drinks whiskey like it was water," another Circle C

hand piped up. "Knows swear words that'd make the devil blush."

Their boasts grew wilder, more outrageous as the seconds passed. Camile wasn't listening. She watched Wade ride away. On her horse, no less. He took something with him. A part of her. The part that should be pleased, proud her outfit was singing her praises. She didn't imagine Wade's fancy woman in St. Louis could spit a far piece or make the devil blush.

That silk-swishing, finger-crooking woman didn't have anything Camile didn't have . . . except him.

Grady slapped her on the back. Camile flinched. It stung.

"Come on, Cam. Throw your rope. Don't make us look like liars."

Distractedly, she began loosening her wrist. She continued to stare at a lone figure fading into the night. Camile told herself Wade and his preferences in women shouldn't bother her. She should press the advantage he gave her. Show off. Become one of the boys. The problem was, the longer she spent in Wade's company, the less she wanted to be one of the boys. Something strange and unfamiliar was happening inside her. Something she couldn't let happen.

Chapter Fourteen

Every muscle in his body ached. Wade limped toward the chuck wagon, blessing Sir Billy when he spotted a pot of coffee resting on the warming rocks next to the fire. He bent, grabbed up a tin cup, and poured. His shoulder throbbed. His foot hurt like the dickens. Neither bothered him as much as what he'd just done.

He knew he should be thankful Camile had tricked him. If she hadn't come along, he'd be dead, but Wade didn't feel beholden. He felt like a softhearted fool. Why had he allowed her a victory tonight? He'd given her a heady taste of acceptance among the men—a charitable act he had a feeling he would regret.

"Is everyone all right?" The cook's head protruded from the back of the chuck wagon.

"As far as I know," Wade answered. "Coffee's good."

"Figured I'd better have some ready. Coffee and my doctoring bag."

William left the wagon. He scratched his ample belly as he approached. "Where's the others?"

"Coming."

"How about that spirited filly of yours? I don't see her."

"She'll be along."

"She had no business out there," William grumbled. "I'm telling you if you'd give her the attention a new wife deserves, you wouldn't have these problems. She'd be docile as a lamb."

Wade nearly choked on his coffee. Docile was a word as far from describing Camile as one could get.

"When you figure on taking care of the deed?" William demanded.

The cup in Wade's hand stopped midway to his mouth. "The deed?"

"Your husbandly duty. Guess if I have to spell it out, there is a problem."

"I don't think my personal life is any of your concern," Wade said, taking a sip.

William lifted the coffeepot, swirled the contents, then replaced the pot on the fire. "That gal of yours has made it my business. She's lower than a snake's belly on account of you. Why don't you give her what she needs?"

"Which is?"

"A night of romancing. Since you bed down a far piece from her every night, I'm beginning to wonder if you know where young'uns come from."

The trail boss cast the cook a dark glance. "This"—he indicated the campsite—"is no place for that. Sleeping with fifteen other men every night doesn't help."

169

"Oh." William distractedly scratched his belly again. "I see what you mean. Can't very well rut around on the ground with every man listening and wishing he was in your place."

Wade nodded, uncomfortable with the conversation. He wanted the other outfits to believe Camile was his wife for her protection. He figured if Sir Billy didn't know otherwise, there'd be one less man to keep her secret.

"We're waiting until we reach Dodge for the honeymoon," he said. "I don't think it'd be right to have comforts the other men are denied. They might get to thinking on it too much."

" 'Spect so," the cook agreed, although he sounded reluctant. "Still, she ain't of a mind to wait, and I figure tomorrow night—"

"Did she say that?" Wade asked.

Sir Billy grinned. "Didn't have to. I know what's eating on the two of you. Any fool can see the way you feel about one another."

"They can?"

The cook sighed wistfully. "Love. Ain't nothing like it."

Again, Wade nearly choked on his coffee. He set the cup down and stretched to his full height, wincing slightly with the effort.

"Are you hurt?" the cook asked.

"Just sore. I cut my foot."

"Where the heck's your boot?"

"In the stirrup of a saddle strapped to that loco mare, wherever she might be."

William stepped forward. "The boys will round her up. Let me tend to you."

"I'm fine."

"Sit down," William ordered, his beady eyes saying he'd brook no argument.

Sitting caused Wade discomfort. He rubbed his throbbing shoulder. The cook pushed his slicker aside.

"You're bleeding. Shuck that slicker and your shirt so I can have a look."

"It's only a scrape."

"Do as I say, Langtry. I'm the boss around my chuck wagon."

Wade shrugged from his slicker. While he removed his shirt, the cook doctored his heel. When Sir Billy poured a stinging concoction over the cut, Wade let loose with a string of swear words. William bandaged the heel, then began to clean the ugly scrape along his shoulder.

"You know, there's a rough-and-tumble town not too far from here," William said. "Thought the bosses would let the men have a night in town."

"We discussed it." Wade unconsciously glanced toward the darkness beyond the campfire. "But now with the herd spread out all over the countryside, I don't imagine we can spare anyone. We'll be rounding up strays for a while."

"Damn," William swore. "If most of the men were off seeing to their own needs—"

Voices interrupted. Laughter and loud jibes as the cowboys returned.

"You shouldn't have made that bet. No one who belongs to the Circle C would," Grady Finch said.

He and a cowboy from Wendell Cates's outfit were the first to reach the fire.

171

"I didn't think she could do it again," the cowboy mumbled.

"You owe us a day's pay," Grady reminded him.

"Where's Cam?" Wade asked, squinting into the darkness.

"Don't worry about her." Grady's fingers stretched toward the fire. "She can take care of herself. We found that black mare. And your boot," he added with a chuckle.

"Wendell sent me in to tell you our outfit is securing the herd tonight," the cowboy said. "We told him you were beat up a bit. Said your outfit can relieve us come morning. Also said to tell you if you don't feel up to riding tomorrow, that pretty wife of yours can boss." The cowboy grinned.

Wade did not. He narrowed his gaze on the man. "I can ride. Get back to your outfit."

No longer grinning, the cowboy nodded respectfully and slipped off into the night. Other faces appeared around the campfire. Wade didn't breathe a sigh of relief until he saw a familiar blond head. Camile stopped in front of him and dropped his boot.

"Missing something?" she asked.

A few men snickered. Wade pushed William's fumbling hands from his shoulder and pulled on his boot, grinding his teeth together in an effort not to groan. "Anyone else hurt?"

"We're all fit as a fiddle," Grady answered, smiling broadly.

"Then spread your bedrolls. We've got morning shift and the night's nearly gone."

The men grumbled, but broke away from the fire. All but Camile. She was staring at his shoulder.

"It's just a scratch," he said.

She glanced up. She'd been admiring his naked chest. Unthinking, she reached to touch him. He caught her hand, turning it palm up.

"You forgot to wear gloves."

"I was in a hurry."

"Do you have any liniment?" Wade asked the cook.

William fished a small tin from his doctoring bag. Wade took it from him, then said, "Good night."

"But I need to—"

"Good night."

The cook glanced between them. He winked. "Save it for tomorrow. I've got a plan."

Camile waited until the man scurried into the chuck wagon before lifting a brow. "What was that about?" she asked.

He opened the tin and reached for her hand. "I'm not sure. William has a notion you're anxious to be bedded."

Her hand jerked slightly. The liniment stung. "Where did he get that fool idea?"

His green gaze locked with hers. "Near as I can tell, from you."

In response, she laughed. "William is a strange man. I have trouble understanding what he's saying most of the time."

Wade said nothing, just stared at Camile thoughtfully. The firelight dancing on his flesh mesmerized her. His shoulders were broad. She couldn't see an inch of fat on him anywhere. Lean, muscled, and handsome. She swallowed loudly. Her thoughts were headed into dangerous territory. When Wade released her doctored palms, her

173

hands stung from rope burn, or from the desire to touch him, she wasn't sure which.

"Are you finished?" she asked.

"With your hands. Not with you."

Lumbering to his feet, he grabbed his shirt and slicker, then nodded past the men settling in for the night. "Let's take a walk."

She wasn't certain following him was a wise idea. Camile suspected that beneath his cool exterior, something mean and ugly festered. She had tricked him, figuring a kiss might distract him and allow her to take him by surprise. But if he was angry with her, why hadn't he lied earlier? Surely he knew what a coup like that could win her . . . what it *had* won her.

For the first time in her life, she felt accepted by the Circle C hands. More than accepted. Respected. What was he up to? She followed, intending to find out.

Once they reached the outskirts of camp, Wade turned to her. "Don't ever disobey my orders again," he said quietly.

Camile huffed up. "You don't own me, Langtry."

"No. But I'm responsible for you." He shrugged into his shirt. "I didn't ask for the job, either."

"Taking care of me isn't part of the job. I've proven I can take care of myself."

"In the past, you've also proven you can't. You could have gotten yourself killed tonight!"

"And you almost did," she shot back. "If not for me, you wouldn't be here. That's what you're all fired up about, isn't it? That a woman rescued you?"

"A woman? Hell, Camile, a woman can't throw a rope like you. She doesn't spit, drink, and swear. Or maybe I should say a lady doesn't."

He might as well have hit her. Camile stumbled back a step. "I never said I was a lady. I don't care about being one. You must have me mixed up with someone else."

"I'm confused, all right." Wade removed his hat and ran a hand through his hair. "I don't understand you. I don't understand what spurs you to take the risks you take, to try so hard at doing a man's job. Tell me greed isn't the reason. Tell me it isn't because you can't stand the thought of giving control of the ranch to someone else. Tell me you aren't just being spoiled and hardheaded. Tell me something!"

His questions made the backs of her eyes sting. Camile turned away. Could she tell him? A vision assaulted her. She almost felt the jarring of her small body when she hit the dirt—almost heard her brother shouting her name. The stallion had loomed above her, his nostrils flaring, his eyes wild. Then he'd reared, his sharp hooves pawing the air.

She'd been frozen on the ground, too frightened to move. Her brother, Clint, had charged into the corral, waving his hands at the horse. Camile had crawled from harm's way, but the enraged stallion had struck a blow to her brother's temple and knocked him down. She'd screamed for her father. Screamed as the horse continued to paw her brother's still form, then screamed while she watched her father become the next victim. Camile shuddered, then stuffed her fist into her mouth to keep from screaming again.

It was her stubbornness that had killed her brother and crippled her father. That and a need to be accepted and loved by Tom Cordell. As much as he seemed to love her brother.

Tell Wade? Tell him she was a murderer? Tell him that unless she proved herself worthy of winning her father's love, became the son she'd taken from him, she could never be free from guilt? She couldn't bear the disgust in Wade's eyes if he knew the truth. Better he believed she was greedy, spoiled, and stubborn.

"I'm all of those things," she said. "You played right into my hands tonight by telling the men I rescued you." Blinking back her tears, Camile turned to face him. "What was your reason?"

He replaced his hat and pulled the brim down low. "Stupidity. I keep thinking there's more to you than meets the eye. Guess I'm wrong."

No, he wasn't, she thought as he walked away. There *was* more to her than he knew. There was a soft side. A side that wanted to tell Wade the truth. A side that wanted to be loved and accepted by more than the father she'd crippled. If she didn't watch herself, Wade would compromise her goal. He confused her. Made her feel things she'd never felt. Made her long for things she thought she never would.

"Better turn in," he called. "After you impressed everyone with your roping skills tonight, I figure they'll hang me if I don't move you up to swing tomorrow."

Swing? He'd given her a promotion. Pride should have filled her chest. Instead, Camile's shoulders drooped. She might be too good at making Wade see her as a man. If drastic measures became necessary—and who knows if the men would treat her differently tomorrow—she'd be forced to seduce him.

Chapter Fifteen

Swing, Camile discovered the next day, wasn't much of an improvement over drag. Both positions were hot, dusty, and for the most part, uneventful. The men had acted differently toward her today, treating her with more respect than usual; however, not one had suggested she replace Wade as boss during the drive. She gratefully rode toward the picketing string beside her outfit, then noticed a strange occurrence.

All of the chuck wagons, with the exception of William T. Ferguson's, were pulled up close together. The cook and Wendell Cates had gone into a nearby town for supplies. It appeared as if tonight something special was in the works. Camile assumed fresh rations might be the reason for the festivities. She tied her horse to the picketing string and turned toward Grady Finch.

"What's going on?" she asked.

He shrugged. "Don't know. Looks like we're having a get-together." He glanced around. "You'd better stay close."

"I can take care of myself," she reminded him.

"Even so, Langtry told us to keep an eye on you. He's a lot like old Hank, ain't he?"

The man under discussion was still mounted, speaking with the other bosses. All but Wendell, who hadn't returned from town. In her opinion, Wade wasn't like old Hank in the least. The mere sight of the old foreman didn't make her heart skip a beat.

"I'll be damned," Grady muttered. "Looky yonder what's coming."

Four wagons lumbered toward camp. Wendell and Sir Billy led them.

"What do you reckon it is?" she asked.

Grady drew a deep breath. He grinned. "Take a whiff. Wind's out of the south. That'll tell you."

Camile sniffed. "Smells sweet." Her nose wrinkled. "Too sweet."

"It's perfume, Cam." Grady rubbed his hands together. "Female companionship. We're gonna have a good time tonight." His head jerked in her direction. He blushed. "Ah, sorry, Cam. I meant the men. I forgot."

Finch forgot she was a woman? She might have been pleased another time. This wasn't one of them. As the wagons drew closer, a cheer went up. The lead wagon had reached the mounted bosses, and one woman, her hair a bright shade of red, nearly fell out while trying to get a better look at Wade.

The big breasts her low-cut gown exposed nearly fell out, as well. Wade smiled. The woman waved, then blew him a kiss. Grady hurried with the rest of the men to welcome the wagons. Camile stood rooted to the spot. She hadn't counted on competing for Wade's attention.

Not with anyone but his fancy lady in St. Louis, and Lily or Lilla, whatever he'd called her, wasn't around to fight for him. Not that Camile imagined the finger-crooking woman would. She supposed ladies didn't fight.

Her hands clenched into balls when the bosses followed along beside the wagons. The redhead was still ogling Wade. When he dismounted, she jumped down and approached him. Camile figured he needed to be reminded he was a married man.

Pushing her way through the crush of men gathered around the wagons took some doing. Camile had been elbowed in the ribs more than once by the time she reached Wade. He stood next to one of the wagons, the woman about to spill from the front of her dress beside him. Wade looked as if he intended to catch her if she did. Camile silently cursed her own bound breasts.

Although it was no longer necessary to play the part of a boy, Wade had insisted she wear the binding. He didn't want her bouncing around while she rode with the other men—a constant reminder she wasn't the same as everyone else on the drive.

"I'll tidy up a bit," the woman was saying as Camile stepped up. "Wash the dust from me. Then I won't mind spending some time with you."

When Camile cleared her throat loudly, Wade glanced at her. He frowned.

"Who's this?" The woman smiled seductively. She sashayed toward Camile, then ran a finger down the side of her cheek. "This boy ain't even got whiskers yet. You're a

179

mite young to be taking on a man's job, but after I've finished with this handsome feller, I'll—"

Camile jerked away. "I'm not a feller," she said through tight lips.

The redhead's painted mouth shaped an O. "You could have fooled me." She eyed Camile's baggy clothes. "Are you telling me there's a girl under there somewhere?"

"A woman," Camile said, then glared at Wade because he had a silly grin on his face.

"Then I ain't got nothing for you," the redhead said. She smiled at Wade. "But I sure have something for you."

"I have something for him, too." Camile took his arm and pulled him from the wagon.

"I'll be seeing you as soon as I've tidied up," the redhead called.

Wade didn't answer, but the smile he flashed in her direction made Camile's blood boil. It didn't appear discouraging. He tugged loose from Camile's hold.

"What have *you* got for me?" he asked dryly.

"A reminder. In case you've forgotten, you're a married man."

His gaze rolled skyward. "Only as far as the other outfits are concerned."

"And how's it going to look if they see you sniffing around another woman?"

"I guess I'll have to be discreet."

Her mouth dropped open. "Are telling me you mean to—"

"Camile," he said, cutting her off, saying her name with a sigh. "A man has needs. It's an exchange. Nothing more."

She didn't want Wade exchanging anything with another

180

woman—touching her, doing what Camile could only speculate about.

"You'd better run along," he said. "Stay clear of this situation. The men might be less inclined to remember you're . . . different." His gaze ran her length. "Despite how well those clothes and that dirt on your face manage to hide the fact."

"And what will you be doing?" she demanded.

He shrugged. "Whatever comes natural."

Their gazes met and held in a showdown.

"There you two are," William called, ambling toward them. The cook grinned upon reaching the couple. "Well, what do you think of my diversion?"

"Was this your idea?" Camile asked, her gaze swinging toward the cook.

His grin broadened. "I figured if the other men were busy, they wouldn't give a hoot about what the two of you were doing in my chuck wagon. I got it all fixed up, and away from the rest of the wagons so you'll have privacy."

"You brought these women here for us?" Wade asked.

"So you can work on putting something in her oven." William winked at Camile, then focused his attention on Wade. "The other bosses will expect you to help keep things under control for a while. It'd be better if the two of you commenced with the honeymooning after the men get good and distracted. Then, well, enjoy yourselves." The cook waggled his eyebrows suggestively and left.

"I was talking about biscuits," Camile mumbled.

Wade frowned. "Sir Billy is a romantic fool."

"He's also not going to understand if you keep hanging around that redhead instead of—"

"I'll show up later. Rock the wagon a little. He won't know the difference."

But she would. Camile couldn't tell him her insides were tied in knots. She couldn't tell him her heart was hurting. What would he think if she threw a temper tantrum and told him he couldn't be with another woman? He'd believe she loved him or something. She couldn't love him. He'd set his sights on another woman.

"What would your fancy lady think about you and that redhead swapping slobber?" she asked.

His mouth turned up slightly. "I don't know."

"And don't care," she predicted. "I'm not sure you should marry her."

"Lilla is a lady. Since ladies aren't free with their charms, I figure they expect a man to make do the best he can until after the wedding."

"You and her haven't . . . "

He laughed softly. "No. Haven't even come close."

A ray of sunshine broke through the dark clouds gathering inside her head. Wade wasn't in love with his fancy lady. From near as she could tell, he didn't much like her. "What about after the wedding? Do you plan to carry on with other women?"

"There won't be any reason." He pulled his hat down tighter. "And it's none of your business. Go to the chuck wagon."

"In case some man forgets I'm different?" she huffed.

Wade turned to her, his eyes softening. "You're not like Lilla, and you're not like that redhead. I'm not sure what to make of you, but this"—he indicated the campsite with a sweep of his hand—"is no place for you tonight."

It was no place for him, either. Camile ground her teeth

together when he walked away. She wasn't like his fancy woman, she wasn't a light-skirt, and he didn't know what to make of her. Maybe it was time she started trying to be more one way or the other. Camile was certain she couldn't be a lady. That left the other.

Her gaze strayed toward the wagons. Wade had laughed when the redhead had mistaken her for a boy. He wouldn't be laughing when she showed him just how much of a woman she could be.

The men had settled down. There hadn't been a fight for better than an hour. Trail bosses were the law on a drive, and Wade was damned tired of riding roughshod over the group. He had other things on his mind. The redhead. It wasn't that he found her so all-fire irresistible, but the woman his body hungered for was forbidden fruit.

Wade figured that for Camile's sake, he should release some of the frustration building in him. Whatever she was, Camile Cordell was tempting. Next time she decided to practice her womanly wiles on him, he might not be able to resist. Not if he didn't feed his male appetite.

He glanced around in search of the redhead. Strange, but he hadn't seen her since she'd disappeared earlier. He supposed a few of the women might be entertaining inside the wagons, but most had slipped off into the night with their customers. Wade made his way through the cowboys, headed toward the wagons.

It was as he suspected. Men stood in a semblance of a line behind three of the wagons. The fourth, the one he'd seen the redhead enter, appeared all but deserted, except he noticed a lantern burning inside.

"Langtry!" Grady Finch moved from the front of the line at the next wagon. "She said she was waiting for you."

Wade lifted a brow. "Then why the hell didn't you come get me, Finch?"

"Because I wasn't gonna lose my place in line for one thing, and for another, you can't go in there." The cowboy lowered his voice. "How's it gonna look to the other outfits?"

He opened his mouth to answer, but the flap of the wagon was suddenly thrown back. The silhouette of a woman stood before him. A very womanly woman. His gaze started at her feet, then traveled upward. The tight red dress she wore had a slit up the front, exposing a long, slender leg. The spit in his mouth dried up. Material stretched tight over her slightly flaring hips, accented her small waist, and all but disappeared when it tried to cover her breasts.

Where once there had been no spit, he now had an abundance. Wade distractedly wiped the drool from the corner of his mouth. He swallowed loudly. Her nipples were poking through the fabric of the dress, and likewise, he felt himself growing hard. They looked vaguely familiar, those perfect mounds of smooth flesh.

Reluctantly, he pried his gaze from them, admiring the slim column of her throat. Her mouth was painted a deep red. Full and delicious. Her eyelids were darkened with whatever women used to paint their faces. He could see their color, but suddenly, he realized they were blue. Blue as a Texas sky. The rest of him tensed.

"Do you like what you see?"

"Damn," he swore softly. "What the hell do you think you're doing?"

"Isn't it obvious?"

"Get those clothes off!"

"Ah, L-Langtry," Grady managed to stammer beside him. "I don't blame you for wanting to hurry, but as I said, you can't—"

"Finch! Are you taking your turn or not?" a man called from the next wagon.

"I think I'll stand behind this one instead," he answered.

Wade's head snapped in Grady's direction. His eyes hadn't even made it to her face.

"Move on," he ordered. "This one is going to be busy for a while."

"Who's she?" the same man standing behind the next wagon called. "I ain't seen that one." He left his place in line and approached them.

"Get inside, Camile," Wade growled.

"Cam," Grady croaked. His gaze shot up; then he turned bright red. "I didn't recognize her."

She smiled. Wade took a threatening step toward her.

"Hey, Langtry! Go find your own woman and leave that one to us," the man from the next line said, joining the group. He whistled loudly. "Hey, boys! Come take a look at this!"

A crowd had gathered. The smug smile on Camile's face melted away. She crossed her arms over her breasts and backed into the wagon. Wade started in after her, but someone grabbed his arm.

"Like we said, see to your wife and leave her to us."

He glanced at the man's hand resting on his shoulder. "That woman's gonna be the death of me," Wade muttered, then punched him.

Fists flew. In a matter of seconds, the whole camp joined the ruckus. Wade took two good jabs before he broke free and stumbled up into the wagon. Camile was worrying her lower lip. The redhead sat on a makeshift bunk along one side. Her face looked pale by the lantern light.

"S-She made me fix her up," she stuttered. "Said she'd cut me up if I didn't."

He glared at Camile, trying not to notice what too many men already had. "Grab your clothes. I'll try to get you out of this mess."

For once, she didn't argue with him. Camile snatched up her clothes, then started to put on her shirt.

"We don't have time. We need to make the chuck wagon while they're fighting."

"Fighting?" she whispered. "Over me?" She grinned proudly.

His gaze rolled upward. Wade took her arm and turned toward the wagon flap.

"Them clothes ain't hers," the redhead reminded. "Although I told her if she wants a job, I'll sure give her one."

"She has a job," he countered flatly. Wade dug in his pocket and tossed the redhead a few bills. "That should pay for the dress she's almost wearing."

"I was hoping to get more than your money." She looked him up and down, then sighed.

"Maybe another time." He wondered how many women he'd say that to before he parted company with Camile Cordell. And they might part company soon, because he wasn't sure he wouldn't kill her if they managed to reach William T. Ferguson's chuck wagon.

They didn't get far. About two feet from the wagon, someone yelled, "Langtry's trying to steal the goods!"

186

The fight came to an immediate halt. A circle of men formed around them. Wade pulled his six-shooter.

"Back off," he ordered.

"What's going on?" Wendell Cates demanded.

"Langtry ain't satisfied with one woman. He wants this one, too," a cowboy said.

Wendell shook his head. "Don't tell me William's fool romantic notions have gone up in smoke, Langtry."

"We told him to see to his own woman," the same fellow explained.

"This *is* my woman," Wade ground out.

More than one mouth fell open.

"It *is* Cam," someone finally muttered. "Didn't know she was hiding all that beneath them baggy clothes."

"And now you'd best forget it," Wade instructed. His gaze roamed the men. "All of you."

"Get her out of here," Wendell suggested.

Wade pulled Camile from the circle of men. Grady Finch was close on his heels.

"What you figure on doing about this, Boss?"

He pushed Camile ahead of him, watching as she ran to the chuck wagon, then turned to Grady.

"I'll stand guard over her tonight. Go back to your socializing, Finch. I'll handle Camile."

The cowboy's eyes narrowed. "Watch what you handle, Langtry. I'll spell you in a while."

"It'll be a long while," Wade commented, craning to see over the men. "You've lost your place."

"Damn," Grady swore. "Best remember who she is," he warned over his shoulder, racing away to reclaim a position in line.

187

"I know who she is," he muttered, setting off for the chuck wagon. "Trouble."

She was in the process of changing when he entered. The dress had been discarded, her baggy pants replaced. Camile wheeled around, her shirt clutched to her breasts.

"There can't be a damn good explanation for this," he growled. "What the hell were you trying to prove?"

Her chin lifted a notch. "You laughed when that redhead thought I was a boy. I wanted you to see me as woman."

He removed his hat and threw it on William's cot. "I've always seen you as a woman. You're the one who demanded I see you otherwise. Now everyone sees you as a woman. Too much of one!"

"I didn't think—"

"No. You didn't," he declared, storming toward her. "You've just undone everything you've tried to accomplish on this drive. The men were starting to accept you—to treat you like an equal. Tomorrow, they'll see you altogether different."

She supposed he had every right to be angry. As usual, the consequences of her actions hadn't been considered. All she'd wanted was . . . Camile had trouble completing her thoughts. Getting back at Wade for laughing at her wasn't the real reason she'd fixed herself up. She wanted Wade to desire her more than his fancy lady, or the redhead. He'd done the worst thing he could do to her. Wade Langtry had made her a woman, inside and out.

"This is your fault," she suddenly decided.

Wade blinked. "What?"

"You goaded me into it."

"Like hell I did. I never asked you to put on that sorry

excuse for a dress and show everything you've got—and to anyone who'd look, I might add."

She glanced down at the wadded puddle at her feet. "You didn't like the dress?"

With a sigh, he untied his bandanna and wiped the paint from her face. "No, but I like what was in it."

A warm sensation curled around her.

"So did everyone else," he added. "You're going to have to leave, Camile. I can't let you stay. Not now."

The warm sensation quickly became a blazing ball of anger. "And just what do you plan to do with me?"

"I'm not sure." His gaze lowered to her bare shoulders. "But the longer you stand there half-naked, the more ideas I get. You'd better put on your shirt."

His green gaze filled with heat. The small confines inside the chuck wagon suddenly shrank. Camile became acutely aware of him. Of his masculine scent, of the purple bruise forming beneath his eye. She supposed he'd rescued her again. Angry as she was at the thought of being banned from the drive, she should be beholden to him.

Camile moistened her lips. "I guess you got me out of trouble again."

"Out of one fix and into another," he countered. "When a woman gives a man an eyeful, next thing you know, he wants a handful to go with it, then a mouthful, and so on and so forth."

She'd never thought of that—about his mouth doing more than kissing her. Her gaze automatically lowered. His lips were nicely shaped. Not too full, not too thin . . . perfect. Camile quickly looked up. She wasn't supposed to be thinking about his mouth, or all the things he might do with it. The drive, her dream—he intended to sabotage her plans.

"I'm not going home," she assured him.

"Yes, you are. Finch can take you. He's due to come by in a while. I'll tell him then."

A soft snort was her response. "Finch couldn't catch me during the stampede. I figure it'll take all of five minutes to lose him."

Red crept into Wade's face. "Then, I'll take you myself!"

"You can't." She smiled smugly. "You're the boss."

"Finch can boss the drive."

Her smile faded. There was only one man who worked for her father she might not be able to outsmart. Langtry. She quickly weighed her options. There didn't seem to be any. Any but one.

"You say Grady's due to come by?" she asked, allowing her shirt to slide lower.

Wade's gaze slid lower, as well. "He can't help you. Finch answers to me."

She took a deep breath, using the ploy to expose more of her breasts. "I should have considered the consequences."

"Then, and now. I just told you what happens when you give a man an eyeful."

Camile widened her eyes innocently. "Something about hands and mouths. I didn't understand it."

"I'll explain." He unbuckled his gun belt, removed it, and placed it aside. Wade stared into her eyes for a moment; then he lowered his mouth to hers.

Should she resist? Pretend she didn't want him to do exactly what he'd done? But then he might stop, and Camile didn't want that . . . because of her plan. With Wade out of the way, no man would have the nerve to send her home. With Wade gone, she might convince them to let her boss in his place. Without Wade . . . she wouldn't feel the delicious feelings stirring to life inside of her.

Her arms crept up around his neck. He groaned, and she realized she'd dropped her shirt. Her nipples hardened against the rough fabric of Wade's shirt. Slowly, his fingers slid down her back, sending ripples of sensation up her spine. He moved his hands around to cup her breasts, then rubbed his thumbs across the sensitive peaks. Her knees nearly buckled.

They stood there for a minute; then Camile found herself being eased down onto William's cot. She supposed what was happening between them wasn't proper. But he felt right stretched out on top of her. His mouth did wonderful things to hers, then broke from her to travel a hot trail down her neck. She arched against him, offering the full bounty of her breasts.

He fastened on one hard nipple, sucking gently, then tracing lazy circles that nearly drove her insane. Her insides had a rope around them, squeezing, tightening, until she felt his hardness pressing against her. Camile pressed back. He groaned, then tried to pull away. Her fingers were in his hair. She refused to surrender him.

"Camile," he warned, his breath raspy in her ear. "I shouldn't have started this."

"Why?" she whispered.

"Because it's not right."

"It feels right," she argued, then tried to bring his lips to hers.

Wade resisted. "You deserve better."

"It gets better?" she asked dreamily.

191

A smile stole over his mouth. "You say the damnedest things."

"And you're always starting something you can't finish. Don't you want me?"

An expression close to pain crossed his handsome features. "The answer to that is obvious, but it's not that simple. There are reasons I should get up and walk away. Reasons you should let me."

His lady in St. Louis, she realized. Camile might have started out to seduce Wade in hopes of removing an obstacle from her path, but what he made her feel had nothing to do with revenge, or her future position on the Circle C. It had to do with her heart. She knew, because it was breaking.

"I know the reason," she said through tight lips.

"There's more than one." His hands captured her face. "You don't know—"

A soft thud sounded. He stopped speaking. His eyes took on a glazed look; then his head dropped. Camile's fingers returned to his hair. Her hands were sticky. She lifted one. It was covered in blood.

"Dammit, Grady," she swore. "You might have hurt him!"

Camile wriggled from beneath Wade's limp body. She turned her back so Grady couldn't see her nakedness, snatched up her shirt, shrugged into it, and scrambled to the cot.

"Wade?" She shook him, then turned murderous eyes on Grady. "You . . . " Her heart slammed against her chest. It wasn't Grady Finch standing before her with a gun butt poised in his hand. Her gaze darted from the gun to his face. She recognized him and the two men standing at the back of the wagon. A scream rose in her throat. It never made it past her lips.

Chapter Sixteen

For three days the nightmare continued. Camile's head still hurt. She had a goose egg the size of a silver dollar. Her abductors rode day and night to put distance between them and the drive. They hadn't said much to her, and she'd spoken less to them. Not that there weren't questions bothering her. She wasn't sure she wanted to know the answers. What they intended to do with her was a worry, but not as big a one as what had happened to Wade.

She told herself they'd only knocked him unconscious and left him on William's cot. He was alive. To imagine anything else would send her over the edge of sanity, and she was barely hanging on.

"When you gonna ask?"

Lenny spoke. He rode to her left, Jim Cummings to her right, and Sam sat behind her, his arms holding her before him on his horse. They followed the trodden ground the herd had torn up. She saw familiar landmarks. They were headed back toward Texas.

"Don't you want to know about your man?"

Camile stared straight ahead.

"Maybe she wasn't all that sweet on Langtry," Jim said. "Maybe she'd roll around naked with anyone."

"Anyone but you, Cummings," Lenny countered. His grin stretched the puckered scar across his cheek.

His face sickened her. The man repulsed her, but it had nothing to do with his scar, only with his character. Camile had a feeling she wouldn't have to ask, Lenny was itching to tell her.

He squinted an eye on her. "You ain't gonna ask, are you?"

She didn't respond.

"Told you she was tough," Jim said. "Too much woman for the likes of Langtry."

"Too much of one for you." Lenny laughed. "Bet I could tame her quick."

Jim nodded toward his scar. "The same as you did last time?"

"She took me by surprise," Lenny said. "She ain't got a knife now. But I've got one I'd like to slip her."

"Ain't neither of you slipping her nothing. Not until I give you permission."

Sam's voice made her jump. If it wasn't for his smell, she might forget he sat behind her. He said little, but he bossed this particular outfit. Lenny and Jim walked a wide path around him.

"Hell, we've been riding for three days straight," Jim complained. "I say we stop a while and stretch our . . . legs."

"Your neck is gonna stretch if any of her friends catch

up with us. Good thing Lenny saw to that fast gun. It'll take the rest a while to figure out what happened."

"Maybe they'll think she killed him," Jim said. "No one from the Circle C would put it past her."

Her hands shook. Camile wanted to clamp them over her ears. Deep down, she knew they'd never let Wade live, but she wasn't ready to face the truth. She wasn't certain she could.

"You *did* make sure he was dead, didn't you?" Sam asked.

A tinge of guilt flushed Lenny's features. "You told me to take care of him. Well, hell, I took care of him. What kind of satisfaction could I get from killin' a man who was unconscious?"

"The kind that comes from knowing he won't be trailing us," Sam answered, his hot breath tickling the hairs on Camile's neck. "If the rest of her outfit manage to track us through this cattle-torn ground, we can handle them. Langtry was different. He was dangerous."

"Lenny got to do him, I get to do *her*," Jim declared.

"We draw for her, same as we did for Langtry," Lenny argued.

Camile wasn't listening to their bickering. Shock claimed her first; then the realization that Lenny had killed Wade set in. Anger began to build. She turned toward the scar-marked man, and without thought, leapt. Lenny's face registered a moment of surprise before she tumbled him from his horse. They landed in the dirt.

"I'll kill you," she vowed, then went for his face with her nails. He quickly caught her wrists, reversing their positions.

"You're a feisty little piece, ain't you, girlie?"

His rancid breath made her gag. "Ugly bastard," she snarled. "You weren't brave enough to take him on man to man!"

"Think I'm ugly?" he whispered, then laughed. "I wish you could have seen that pretty-boy face of his after my knife finished with him!"

The fire racing through her blood froze. Tears gathered in her eyes. A sob escaped her throat.

"Ain't so feisty now, are you?" Lenny glanced up at Sam. "Let me take her."

"I get her first," Jim growled.

"Shut up. Both of you," Sam ordered. He dismounted, then glanced around the area. "I figure we've ridden hard enough to stop for a spell. I'm gonna backtrack and make sure no one is following us. I'll tie her to that scrawny tree. You both get some sleep."

Lenny scrambled up, then pulled Camile roughly to her feet. "I could use some shut-eye."

"Me, too," Jim said. "Ain't had any for a long while."

When his gaze raked her body, Camile figured Jim wasn't referring to rest. Surely Sam wouldn't leave her with these two. They'd be on her like wolves the minute he left.

"Take me with you," she said to Sam quietly.

"Can't. You'll slow me down. Besides, Jim and Lenny know to do as they're told. They'll mind their manners, - won't you, boys?"

Neither answered.

Finally, Lenny nodded. "You're the one with the brains, Sam. Hell, Jim and me can't write no ransom note. We ain't got the brains to have figured on getting the money from her pa, then selling her in Mexico."

"Sell me?" Camile shook her head. She'd been forced to deal with too much. Kidnapped. Wade . . . she couldn't complete the thought. "You can't sell me! I'm not an animal!"

"No," Sam agreed, then smiled. "You're a woman. And

women, especially blue-eyed, light-skinned, blondes, fetch a high price in Mexico. More than some stupid animal would."

Part of her had died when Lenny admitted to killing Wade. The other part, the part of her that wanted to survive, sent her racing for Sam's horse. She almost made it into the saddle before he grabbed her leg and pulled her down. Camile kicked, clawed, and bit, but he twisted her arms around her back.

"There's that spirit," Sam said against her ear. "Some men find that appealing in a woman. Them men you take between your legs in Mexico will just pound it out of you."

"Maybe we should settle her down for them," Jim suggested, rubbing his hands together. "If she's biting and scratching, she might not bring a good price."

"Maybe," Sam agreed, then shoved her toward the tree.

It took all three of them to secure her. Camile felt hands where they had no business being, places that weren't necessary to grope while securing her wrists above her head. A mixture of emotions battled within her. Helpless rage. Overwhelming fear. Bitter resentment.

A man should have a woman only at the mercy of her own desires. She'd once foolishly believed her body could be traded for the price of cattle and land. Now she knew better. In William's wagon, she would have given herself to Wade out of love and for no other reason.

Since the day he'd trespassed on her sacred domain, he'd been intruding upon her heart—working his way beneath her skin—into her blood. Wade was a good man. Tough when he had to be, tender at times, and all male. She'd met her match. Camile more than loved him; she respected him. What these men planned had nothing to do with love or even respect. She wouldn't let them take what she would have easily given to another.

"I'd rather die than feel your filthy hands on me," she said, running a cold glance over the men.

"That ain't an option," Sam drawled. He removed a knife from his boot and stuck it point-down into the ground before addressing Lenny and Jim. "I figure one of you is gonna kill the other over her, anyway. Whoever is left standing can have her, at least until I get back." He walked toward his horse. "Have fun, boys, and whoever ain't dead, don't be too rough on her. She'll bring more in Mexico without bruises."

"Hey!" Lenny called. "I thought we was partners."

"I ain't splitting with two men," Sam said over his shoulder. "The knife'll decide which of you is my partner. I figure you can take him, Lenny. Besides helping us trail the herd, he ain't been much use."

Lenny glanced at Jim. He grinned. Both men lunged for the knife. Camile watched helplessly as they scrambled in the dirt. The way she saw it, there was no lesser of two evils where Lenny and Jim were concerned. If she got lucky, they'd both seriously hurt each other.

Luck was not on her side. Jim was tall and heavy, Lenny short and quick. The scar-faced man quickly gained the upper hand. Jim's eyes widened, and his expression turned to one of surprise. He lowered his gaze to the knife buried in his chest.

Camile looked away. Cummings was an animal. He'd attacked her outside of Rosie's—would have had his way with her if Wade hadn't rescued her. But despite her feelings toward him, the sight of Jim's blood spilling down the front of his shirt brought her no pleasure. She choked down the bile rising in her throat.

"Guess it's just you and me, girlie."

She kept her lids tightly closed, cursing the moisture dammed up behind them. Lenny would enjoy her fear. His kind preyed on the weakness of others. She blinked back her tears and glared at him.

"You're next," she said softly.

He grinned. "I know." Lenny wiped the bloody knife on his leg, placed the blade between his teeth, and fumbled with the fastenings of his pants.

"I meant you'll be the next man to die."

Lenny took the knife from between his teeth. "Because you're gonna kill me, right?"

"No. Sam is."

His gaze narrowed on her. "I'm his partner."

"You did his dirty work for him. Jim's dead. I'm betting he won't split the money with you, either."

A frown replaced his cocky grin. "Me and Sam go back a ways. We've been running together for a year."

"You've been running together? Or have you just been tagging along behind him?"

"Shut up!" Lenny snapped. "You're trying to distract me. Confuse me. You're stalling for time. Time's up, girlie."

Instinctively, she flinched as he raised the knife. He brought the sharp point to her throat, then lowered the blade, cutting open her shirt. Lenny whistled softly.

"Reckon a man would pay plenty to put his hands on those."

She recoiled when he cupped her breasts. Camile bit back a scream. No one would hear her. No one could help her. Wade was dead, and the pain that sliced through her over his loss was worse than anything Lenny could do. The rough fondling of one man brought memories of another's touch. Wade had been gentle. She'd come alive beneath his hands, hungered for him as she'd hungered for no other. Lenny's touch made her feel defiled.

To blot out the ugly present, she sought solace in the past. Three days ago she'd been in Wade's arms. What she wouldn't give to be there again. To see his smile. To hear the low timbre of his voice. His name left her lips in a sob. Lenny jerked away from her. He wheeled around, the knife held out in front of him. Warily, he searched the area.

"Why'd you turn around?" she demanded, her voice shaky. "You thought he was here, didn't you?"

"Spooked me is all," he answered, returning to her.

"Are you afraid of his ghost? Or of him?"

"I ain't scared of no man," Lenny muttered. "I proved it, too."

The pounding in her chest was so loud she thought Lenny could hear it. "You didn't kill him, did you?"

"Now, why wouldn't I? Sam told me to."

"You wanted another chance. Wanted to get even when he wasn't out cold. Otherwise, you wouldn't get satisfaction. You admitted as much to Sam."

"I think you're dreaming with your eyes open, girlie. If you want to pretend he's alive, picture him watching us." Lenny fondled her roughly again.

To keep from screaming, Camile bit her bottom lip. To keep the tiny flare of hope alive inside of her, she said, "If you didn't kill Wade, it will be the biggest mistake you ever made. He'll come after me."

Distracted, Lenny muttered, "He can't track us. Not in that torn-up ground. He'll figure we went the other direction."

"Sounds like you're dreaming with your eyes open," a deep voice responded.

Lenny froze. Camile's heart leapt into her throat. Her knees buckled. The ropes cut into her wrists, but she didn't care about the pain. Wade stepped from behind a clump of mesquite trees. She sucked in her breath at the sight of his face.

"Told you he wasn't so pretty anymore," Lenny said under his breath. "Smarter than I counted on, too."

Wade lifted his revolver. "Move away from her."

The pockmarked man grinned, although his lips twitched nervously. He quickly lifted his knife to Camile's throat. "Seems we've played this hand before. It'll end up different this time."

"Yeah. You'll end up dead." Wade motioned with his revolver. "Step away from her and I'll kill you fast. Otherwise, I'll make you die slow."

"I ain't wearing my gun, Langtry. This knife and her pretty throat are the only things between me and a bullet."

To her horror, Wade tossed his gun to the ground. Camile swallowed with difficulty, the knife pricking her skin.

"I'm giving you a fair chance. Are you going to hide behind a woman's skirts?"

Lenny laughed, but lowered the knife. "She don't wear skirts. But she sure is a woman." He slid his free hand inside her shirt.

A muscle in Wade's jaw twitched, then he was in motion. He dropped to the ground, rolled, and came up with his gun. A shot exploded. The knife flew from Lenny's grasp. He howled, clutching his bloody hand.

"Go for your gun," Wade said coldly.

Still doubled over in pain, Lenny glanced toward his gun belt a short distance away. "You ain't gonna let me near my gun."

Wade replaced his Colt in the holster strapped to his hip. "I won't kill a man I didn't give a fair chance."

Lenny bolted toward his gun.

"Shoot him, Wade!" Camile screamed.

He didn't obey. She watched, disbelieving, as he allowed Lenny to reach his gun belt. Camile stopped breathing when the pockmarred man fumbled with his weapon, then took aim.

"You're a damn fool," Lenny called, then grinned, cocking his pistol.

She looked at Wade. He moved so fast her vision blurred. A burst of fire exploded from his gun. Camile's head jerked toward Lenny. He stood, the gun still aimed at Wade, a blank look in his eyes. He had a hole between them. Slowly, he crumpled to the ground.

"No. Not a damn fool. Just a fast one."

Camile sobbed with relief at the sound of Wade's voice. She sagged against the ropes securing her wrists, wanting for all the world to cry her heart out. She was safe. Wade was alive.

"Where's the other one?" he asked.

Slowly, she lifted her face. Wade held Lenny's knife. After he sliced the ropes securing her wrists, Camile threw herself into his arms.

"They told me you were dead."

He took her by the shoulders. "The other one, Camile. Where is he?"

"I'm right behind you. Don't turn around or I'll shoot you where you stand. Should have known Lenny wouldn't do as he was told. He was stupid. Thanks for killing him for me."

From over Wade's shoulder, Camile watched Sam walk forward, his pistol trained on them.

"Will you give me a fair chance like I gave your partner, or shoot me in the back?" Wade asked.

"What do you think, Langtry? I ain't got no morals. Step away from him, girl. You're money in the bank."

"Do what he says," Wade instructed her quietly. "As soon as the shooting starts, make a run for the horses and keep running. Understand?"

She understood. Wade was about to get himself killed again. He was fast, quicker than anyone she'd seen draw and fire a gun, but she wasn't certain he could beat a man already holding a pistol on him. Not without a diversion. Camile stepped around him, placing herself between the men.

"I'd rather die than be at your mercy," she declared to Sam.

"Move!" Both men shouted at the same time.

Camile hit the ground. A bullet whizzed overhead. Another shot was fired. She didn't think she could lift her head and see who still stood. Losing Wade twice in one day would be too much to endure.

"You're gonna be the death of me. Next time you want to create a diversion, do what I tell you to do and run!"

Wade was among the living. Her relief was almost painful. He was also as annoying as ever. He would berate her actions instead of thanking her for, once again, probably saving his life.

The past three days suddenly caught up with her. Camile was too tired to snap back at him. Instead, she sighed, glanced up, and said, "I liked you better when you were dead, Langtry."

Chapter Seventeen

Shadowy figures stalked her. Camile knew who they were—demons disguised as men. She tried to run. Her feet wouldn't move. Hands slithered up from beneath the ground, grabbing her ankles, crawling up her legs, lashing her arms to her sides. She must escape.

"No," she moaned. The hands were on her shoulders, shaking her. She sat up abruptly, gasping for breath. A dark figure sat beside her. Jim? Lenny? Sam? Camile bolted. He was on her in a second, holding her still.

"It's me, Camile. You're safe."

The air left her lungs in a long sigh. "Wade?"

"You were dreaming."

"They were after me," she whispered. "Their hands were on me."

Wade pulled her into the safety of his arms. "It's over."

"Where are we? I don't remember—"

"You almost fell out of the saddle right after you climbed on a horse. I put some distance between us and . . . well, then I stopped and put you to bed."

"Did you bury them?"

"No. You were more important. Nature will see to them."

She shuddered, either from the night chill or the thought of the grizzly scene they'd left behind. "How did you find me?"

"Tracked them."

"But—"

"You need your rest. Go back to sleep."

Her hand reached up to touch his cheek. "I'm sorry Lenny did that to your face."

"He gave me an invitation to come after you. Not that I needed one."

"Why didn't you bring the others with you? If you'd had help—"

"Did I need help?"

"No," she admitted quietly.

"I left after William stitched my cheek closed. I didn't tell anyone else. I gave William instructions to turn the drive over to Grady, though I imagine Finch didn't obey and is looking for us."

A coyote howled. Camile shivered again. "If you hadn't found me—"

"I should have found you the first night. I lost a lot of blood with the cut. Passed out about an hour into the chase and didn't wake up until the next day."

"I'm all right," she assured him.

His body tensed. "I have to ask. It's eating me alive. Did they—"

"No," she said. "Lenny and Jim were fighting over me. Lenny won. He would have forced me if you hadn't stopped him."

"I should have killed him slower. Made him suffer."

Camile couldn't honestly say she wished the threesome weren't dead, but she'd had all the violence she could stomach in one day. "I want to forget." Exhaustion drained her strength. "Hold me while I sleep. Keep the nightmares away."

He eased her down onto the blankets, pulled her into his arms, and covered them both up. Camile listened to the steady beat of his heart. She felt safe in his arms. Safe, but guilty. She'd dragged Wade into her own troubles. First with Sam and Lenny, then with Jim, and finally with all three of them. She was just as responsible for the cut across his cheek as Lenny. If he'd died at their hands, that would have been her fault, as well.

"I guess you're thinking I'm more trouble than I'm worth," she mumbled into his chest.

"That's what I should be thinking."

She lifted her head. "What *are* you thinking?"

"Things I shouldn't. Go to sleep."

"What shouldn't you be thinking?" she persisted.

Distractedly, he ran his thumb along her jawline. "I'm wondering if those three have killed what's natural inside of you. Women aren't meant to be handled roughly."

"You're worried that because of what Jim tried to do me outside of Rosie's, and what Lenny would have done if you hadn't showed up, I might never want a man?"

He tilted her face up, staring intently into her eyes. "One day you'll meet someone worth giving your heart to. He'll take it quick enough, but he'll want more in the bargain.

206

Prickly Pear

There's a difference between what he wants from you and what they wanted."

"How will I know the difference?" she whispered.

His thumb moved up her chin to tease her lips. "If he treats you right, respects you for who you are. If he cares about your feelings. If he'd die for you, then you'll know."

"Someone like you?" she asked softly.

The movement of his thumb across her lips stopped. "I didn't say that."

With a sigh, she lowered her head to his chest. "You know you don't love your fancy woman, don't you?"

For a moment, she thought he wouldn't answer. Wouldn't confess to what she felt in her heart. Finally, he sighed.

"It isn't because I don't want to love Lilla. I'm not sure I know how."

"But you did once," she said. "Before the war." Her eyelids suddenly felt weighted down. "Why won't you tell me about your past? About your life?"

The soft touch of his thumb against her mouth resumed. "It's not a pretty story."

"Everyone has at least one ugly story in their past," she countered tiredly. "Do you think that makes you different?"

"It made me different. It made me into someone I didn't want to be." His hand moved to her hair, gently stroking her short curls. "I never took to the thought of owning other people, even as a child. Slavery was wrong, but what I wouldn't give to have grown up the Southern gentleman, far from the stinking gutters where I slept. Far from the fear that churned my stomach as much as hunger. From the lessons I learned in order to survive."

"I like who you are," Camile whispered, on the edge of

sleep. She nestled closer to him. "Maybe to learn to love again, you'll have to learn to like yourself better."

His hands ceased stroking her hair. He didn't like himself at that moment. Why couldn't he tell her? He wanted to—she deserved the truth.

For three days he'd been riding around with his gut twisted into knots. He'd imagined the worst being done to Camile, imagined finding her bloody and bruised, her spirit crushed. Wade had never imagined her dead. He couldn't. He'd have gone crazy. For the first time in a long time, someone had mattered more than himself.

He hadn't thought about schemes, dreams, or his all-important need to live a respectable, peaceful life. He hadn't thought about Atlanta and the night that changed everything. All he'd thought about was Camile. The blue of her eyes. The sweetness of her lips. The softness inside her that she rarely showed to anyone.

Lilla was whispering silk, rosewater, marble-white skin, and manners. Lilla was only part of a dream, nothing more. Camile—she meant more to him than any woman. He had feelings for her. Feelings he strongly suspected were proof that he didn't have to like himself to love someone else. Camile deserved better than a man who'd lied to her from the beginning, who lied to her still. Not telling her the truth was the same thing.

Her breathing became steady. She slept. Trusting. Believing the man who held her was different than the scum he'd rescued her from. And maybe he was different. Because of Camile, he'd changed. Wade had made a decision over the past three days. He'd promised himself no one would hurt her again. Not even him. Tomorrow, he'd take Camile home.

Tomorrow, he'd slit his own throat, and Gregory Kline be damned. He would place Camile in the safe hands of her father and ride away. She had won, and she'd done it in a way he would have never guessed possible. She'd stolen his heart.

Morning held an unnatural chill. Camile glanced up from rolling the blankets to watch Wade saddle the horses. He seemed different. Had this cold man held her in his arms last night? Had he played with her hair? Worried her kidnapping might have tainted her ability to love a man? To trust one? To give herself completely? He had nothing to fear. She did love a man—trust him—want to give herself completely.

"How long will it take us to catch up with the drive?" she called.

He stuck his foot in the horse's side to keep the animal from swelling while he cinched him, but didn't answer.

"I said how long—"

"I heard you." Wade finished cinching his horse and moved to the sorrel Jim once rode. The horse belonged to the Circle C. "We're not returning to the drive."

She halted in her task. "We're not?"

Wade turned to her. He had a no-nonsense glint in his eyes to match his attitude. "I'm taking you home."

Camile was on her feet in a second. "Like hell you are. I didn't go through what I've been through to turn tail and go home!"

"You're going if I have to hog-tie you and drag you there. Good God, when is enough enough? Don't you ever give up or give in?"

In answer, she placed her hands on her hips and glared at him.

"Don't turn this into a contest," he warned. "We can reach the ranch quicker than we can catch up with the herd. It's over, Camile. Let's count our losses and call it quits."

Over? Losses? Call it quits? Camile felt her heart sinking. There were things left unsaid between them. Things left undone.

"Bring the bedrolls," he instructed gruffly. "If we ride hard, we can reach the ranch within four days."

Four days? That didn't leave her much time. Time she needed to explore the feelings she had for Wade, to discover if he had feelings for her. Maybe she should speed things up. Let him know his fears the previous night were unfounded. Camile moistened her lips, took a deep breath, and blurted, "I want you to make me a woman."

Still in the process of saddling her horse, Wade seemed not to hear her.

"I said—"

"I know what you said."

A frown settled over her lips. "Well, are you going to or not?"

"Want me to just drop my pants and have at it? Or would it be all right to ask why?"

Her frown deepened. She didn't count on him asking questions. She couldn't tell him the truth. He might not love his fancy lady, but he'd never said he loved her, either. "Seems to me some man's going to do it whether I ask or not. I want the choice to be mine."

He visibly tensed, but continued with his work. "Why me?"

His voice sounded odd. Almost angry. Camile couldn't imagine what she'd done to offend him. "I figure you're the best man for the job."

Wade muttered something under his breath and turned around. "How'd you figure that?"

She felt foolish. This wasn't going well. "B-because women seem to like you. You've been with lots of them, haven't you?"

A muscle in his jaw began to twitch as he approached her. "Before I became a full-grown man, I discovered a whore's bed was a cheap place to spend the night. I've spent plenty of them there."

She felt her face growing hot. Imagining Wade with other women wasn't her objective. "Then you should know what to do."

"I know exactly what to do," Wade assured her, snatching up the bedrolls before returning to the horses. "Forget you asked."

Camile stomped her foot, frustrated. "And what if I just keep asking?"

He muttered something again, slung his bedroll across the back of his saddle, then motioned her forward. "I don't think you know what you're getting yourself into."

Her brow lifted. Camile walked forward and mounted her horse. "I know what goes where, Langtry."

It was Wade turn to regard her smugly. "But you don't know why."

"That's what I figured you'd show me."

The muttering began again. Wade mounted his horse. "You're asking for trouble, Camile. You don't want to dance with the devil. You'll have to pay the fiddler. When the right man comes along, he'll show you what you need to know."

"Who? Ralph Lamar's homely son? Him or some other man my father chooses for me?"

His jaw muscle clenched; then he gave his horse a nudge and started forward. "Damn you for putting that picture in my head. I hope it doesn't come to that. I imagine once Tom settles down, he'll let you make your own choice."

She had made her choice. Camile wasn't certain what her father would demand of her, but knew she couldn't give herself to a man she didn't love. Not without first giving herself to one she did. Four days. Before they were up, she'd dance with the devil, and the fiddler be damned.

Chapter Eighteen

The rain started the second day and fell into the third. It was a dreary downpour that turned the trail slippery and made traveling miserable. As they sat before the Canadian River, watching the water churn, Camile glanced longingly across to the other side. There was an abandoned line shack not far from where they'd planned to hole up for night. Not only a chance to dry out, but an opportunity to see if the devil would dance.

"It might be down by tomorrow," Wade said.

"It might not," Camile muttered. "I'd give anything to get out of this miserable rain. I say we cross over."

He glanced skeptically at the fast-moving river. "We're a day's ride from the ranch. We've come this far without getting ourselves killed. I say we wait."

Camile had waited long enough. Tomorrow night she would be sleeping in her own bed, probably under lock and key. Who knew how long she had until her father demanded she marry. If she refused, would her father sell out and cart her off somewhere she didn't belong? These were possibilities Camile didn't want to face.

From beneath her lashes, she studied Wade. Rain dripped from the brim of his hat. He was soaked through. The nasty cut on his cheek gave his handsome face character. Her heart swelled with love. There were things in life worth dying for. One night. It wasn't too much to ask. She closed her eyes, dug her heels into the sorrel's sides, and plunged headlong into disaster.

She knew immediately she'd made a mistake. The current pulled her horse under the water's surface. They bobbed back up, Camile gasping for the breath the icy water stole.

"Camile!"

Glancing over her shoulder, she saw Wade jump into the water. He disappeared beneath the surface. A choked cry sprang from her lips. Her gaze searched the rolling water.

"Wade!" she shouted.

He broke the surface coughing. The current carried the weight of a man much easier than that of a horse. With the swiftness with which it might twirl a stick on a calmer day, the rushing river sent him careening toward her. Camile reached for her rope.

With one hand, she fought to keep the sorrel directed toward the opposite bank; with the other, she swung the lariat overhead. When he came even with her, Camile threw. She missed. Frantically, she gathered the rope back.

"Go!" Wade shouted at her. "Get out!"

Camile wasn't about to abandon him. She tried to turn the sorrel toward Wade. The horse fought the bit, struggling to make the bank. She realized roping Wade and controlling the horse couldn't be achieved at the same time. A decision had to be reached.

Quickly, she wrapped the rope around the saddle horn, pulled it tight, and gave the line added security by weaving the rawhide together twice more. Camile slipped the loop over her head, settled it around her waist, then jumped into the frigid water.

"Stay put, Wade! I'm coming!"

An active life had given her firmly muscled arms, but her strength was no match for the effort it took Wade to remain stationary.

"Just a little longer!" she called. "I'm almost to you!"

They were close, but to Camile it looked as if an eternity separated them. She glanced behind her, noting the sorrel had reached the bank. He stood shivering beside the rushing river.

Two arm lengths separated her and Wade when her body jerked to a halt. The lariat squeezed painfully around her waist. Camile felt the burn against her tender flesh.

"I can't reach you! Swim!"

His green gaze traveled the short but seemingly impossible stretch between them. She read the message. It said his strength was failing him. Already, the current was beginning to carry him away from her.

"Get out!" he shouted.

Wade clearly needed incentive. Camile screamed, then let the current pull her under. She bobbed back up coughing as loud as she could.

"My feet are numb. I can't move them! The rope," she gasped. "It's cutting me in half."

Through liquid-drenched eyes, she saw his jaw tighten.

His lips moved. Camile couldn't hear what he said, but she felt certain he'd said she would be the death of him. Her heart began to race when he fought the current and swam toward her. To encourage him, she called, "I don't know if I tied the rope good enough to hold!"

"Stop complaining and reach out to me."

A tingle ran up her arm as she extended it forward. His fingers were inches from hers.

"Stretch," he panted.

Camile tried. The rope cut deeper into her waist. "I can't! The rope—"

That was all she managed before her body slammed into his. The air left their lungs in a loud whoosh. His arms went around her. Camile clung to his neck, close to weeping with relief. Then she realized they were moving.

"The horse!" Her head snapped in the direction of the bank. The sorrel was walking downstream. She glanced past Wade's shoulder. Ahead, the water spilled over a bluff. A narrow passage surrounded by jagged rocks. They were going to die.

"I'm sorry," she whispered. "I've gone and gotten us killed."

He followed her nod, then cussed softly. His hands fumbled for the rope attached to her waist. "Get behind me and hold on around my neck. I'll try to pull us out before we get there."

Impossible, she thought. "You pull your weight, I'll pull mine," she said. Fingers numbed by the cold water, Camile grasped the tightly stretched rope. Wade pulled himself in front of her.

"If your strength gives out, hold on to me," he instructed.

The process was grueling. Camile's arms were shaking. She wanted to give up and grab Wade, but knew her weight would be too much of a burden. She put one hand in front of the other, pulled, prayed, and repeated the process.

"We're almost there!" he called over his shoulder.

She knew he didn't realize how far behind she had fallen. Camile renewed her efforts, glancing toward the rocks. They were close. Too close. She wouldn't make it out. Relief spread through her when she saw Wade gain firm footing. At least she wouldn't be responsible for his death. He turned, extending a hand. His gaze shot toward her. The panic in his eyes was unmistakable.

"Hurry, Camile!" He grabbed up the rope and pulled fast and hard.

Rushing sounds of the falls filled her ears. She was still in the current. It sucked at her legs, the river unwilling to surrender another victim. The muscles in Wade's arms bulged as he tried to pull her from the fast-moving water. To her horror, she saw him stumble, one foot entering the river.

"Let go!" she screamed.

He shook his head, glanced toward the sorrel standing up ahead, and whistled loudly. The animal pricked its ears, then swung its head around. Wade whistled again. The horse turned and trotted toward him.

Camile gave a half-laugh, half-sob when he wrapped the rope in his hand around the saddle horn and mounted up. He kicked the horse out and raced away from the river. She found herself dragged through the water at an alarming rate. Water rushed up her nose, then her body scraped ground. Ground! She was out! She was safe!

After sliding to a halt, she lay there, face down in the

mud, coughing water. Strong hands propelled her up; then she was in Wade's arms. His hands were suddenly on her shoulders. Instead of holding her, he shook her.

"You little idiot! You almost got yourself killed!"

The anger reflected in his eyes warmed her frozen blood and sparked her own temper. "If it hadn't been for me, you'd be dead for sure!" she shouted.

"If it wasn't for you, I wouldn't have jumped in the damn river to begin with!"

"If you hadn't jumped in, I'd have made the bank on the sorrel! I wouldn't have had to risk my neck to help you!"

He made a sarcastic attempt at a laugh. "Who saved who?"

Temper building, she watched him approach the sorrel and pat his neck affectionately. He praised the dumb animal that had almost got them smashed against the rocks, but couldn't find a kind word for her.

"I should have left you," Camile muttered, pushing him aside to mount the horse.

"I should have let go of the rope," he grumbled back. "Saved myself the trouble of wondering when you'll try to kill me next."

She eyed the Colt he'd wrapped carefully in canvas inside his holster. "Keep a tight grip on that gun or you won't have long to wonder." Camile swung into the saddle, waiting for Wade to gather the rope still tied to the saddle horn. Once he replaced the lariat, she kneed the animal into motion, forcing Wade to run beside her.

"Stop and let me on behind," he barked.

"You know me. I never do as I'm told. The last time I saved your lousy hide, you took my horse and left me afoot. I'm not taking any chances *this* time. See you at the line shack."

Wade cussed her as she galloped away. She'd scared ten years off his life. Why had she pulled that fool stunt? he wondered. What was she in such an all-fire hurry to get home to, anyway? Hadn't she realized reaching the ranch would be the end of them? He would return to St. Louis and give up his dreams so that Camile might have hers. And what would she do? Talk her father into letting her run the ranch?

Marry a man who wouldn't understand her strengths? Her weaknesses? Her desires or her incredible spirit? Wade didn't know what drove her. He knew the demons that drove him. Demons he would continue to battle so that whatever haunted Camile would leave her be.

He might be tempted to stay, to see what became of her, if he could trust himself. If he could keep his hands off her. It was becoming increasingly more difficult to behave. But he would. Camile was an innocent, no matter how worldly she tried to appear. He would because he couldn't take what rightfully belonged to a more deserving man.

Regardless of how little he respected the man he once was, the man he'd become couldn't make love to a woman he'd deceived. At least that was what he told himself as he set off after her. He hoped Camile wouldn't call him on it.

The line shack was in sad need of repair, but the roof didn't leak and the walls were still sturdy against the wind. Camile had settled the sorrel in a crude lean-to around back, and now set about building a fire. Luckily, there were four rickety chairs that would do for kindling. The rotted wood broke easily beneath her hands. It helped to pretend she had hold of Wade.

"Sorry bastard," she muttered, throwing the wood in the grate, then striking flints against the rocks surrounding the hearth. After a fire burned, she spread the soggy blankets from her saddle pack on the floor to dry. Her gaze moved to the door. Rain fell outside. She shouldn't have left Wade. The shack wasn't far from the river, but he had to be bone-weary.

If he hadn't snapped at her, she wouldn't have become angry, and truth be known, Camile was angrier at herself than at Wade. She'd risked their lives over her selfish needs. When would she learn that impulsiveness always demanded a price? Desperation had driven her to brave the river for one night with him. Darkness was fast approaching, but she doubted the devil would be in the mood for dancing.

When the door burst open, compliments of Wade's boot, she felt certain she'd assumed correctly. He glared at her.

"Thanks for lighting a fire. Without the smell of wood smoke to guide me, I might have been wandering around all night in the rain." He slammed the door, then moved to the fire to warm his hands.

"You don't have a good sense of direction in the dark, do you? Riding over bluffs and such. I'm surprised I didn't have to come rescue you again."

His head turned toward her. Camile bit her lip. Arguing wasn't what she had planned for the remainder of the night. "I'm sorry for that stunt. I guess you're thinking I'm not the worth the trouble I cause again," she said softly.

"I'm thinking I'd like to strangle you." Wade removed his hat and tossed it on the blankets. His hand moved to his holster.

When he removed his gun, she took an involuntary step backward. "You aren't going to shoot me, are you?"

In answer, he rolled his gaze upward. "It's tempting, but I'm only removing the canvas I wrapped around the Colt to keep it dry." He peeled the protective covering off, then slid the gun back into his holster. "You scared the hell out me. Why did you jump in the river?"

She curbed her usual bluntness, trying to come up with a logical explanation. "I told you, I wanted to spend a dry night. I didn't think—"

"I know," he said, interrupting. "You never think, you just do. You don't realize the consequences of your actions until it's too late to turn back. Who the hell's going to take care of you after I'm gone?"

"You mean after you've run off to make your fortune so you can marry your fancy lady?" she snapped.

Slowly, he turned to look at her. "A lot can happen between St. Louis and Texas. I don't figure I'll be marrying Lilla Traften."

The tempo of her heartbeat increased. "Then why can't you stay? Regardless of what happens once I get home, my father will still need a good foreman."

"I can't stay."

"Why not?" she demanded.

"You know why," he answered softly. "Keeping my hands off of you would wear itself thin before long. I'm only hanging on by a thread as it is. You'll marry someone else someday and—"

"I told you, I don't want to get married," Camile declared. "I'm not a brood mare my father can trade to anyone of his choosing."

221

"You'll need a man," he argued. "One who will help you run the ranch. One your father approves of. One—"

"I'll have to consider that soon enough." Tomorrow there would be many things to consider. Tonight Camile would become a woman. She reached for the buttons on her shirt.

"What are you doing?" Wade asked, his gaze lowering to her fingers.

"I'm cold."

"You should get out of those wet clothes or you might catch a chill." He turned back toward the fire. "Tell me when you're decent."

Hurriedly, Camile stripped from her clothes. When she stood naked, she took a deep breath and said, "I'm decent."

Wade faced her. His mouth fell open. He wheeled back around. "Cover yourself."

"No. I want you, Wade. I can't say it any simpler."

His fist hit the rock wall that contained the fire. "Dammit, Camile. I want you, too. But you don't know me. I'm not who you think I am. We can't—"

Quick as lightning, Camile stepped up behind him and slid his Colt from the holster. He wanted her. She wanted him. It was that simple, and now she had to convince Wade. With shaky hands, she cocked the gun.

"Turn around."

His movements were slow. When his gaze fastened on hers and refused to lower, Camile steadied the gun on him.

"Take off your clothes."

"You won't shoot me," he scoffed.

"You know how I am. I don't think things through. I might shoot now and be sorry later."

His gaze narrowed on her for a moment. Camile imagined he was trying to decide if he should try to wrest the gun from her. Suddenly, he smiled. His hands moved to the buttons on his shirt. She knew what he was thinking. He remembered what had happened the last he stood naked before her. Langtry was in for a surprise. She wouldn't turn tail and run. Not this time.

Chapter Nineteen

"Slowly," Camile instructed. "Nice and slow with no sudden moves."

When inch by inch, bronze skin appeared between the gap of his shirt, she licked her dry lips. Camile swallowed loudly when he shrugged the shirt from his broad shoulders and let it fall to the dirty floor. Firelight played over the flat planes of his stomach and the bulging muscles of his arms. He was beautiful, although his work-hardened body held its flaws: a scar along his ribs, a small puckered place on his shoulder.

He bent, removed his boots and socks, straightened, stared her in the eye, and went for the fastenings of his pants. She supposed the shack could burn down around her and feel less heated than the sizzle between them while she waited. He removed the remainder of his clothing and

224

stood naked before her. Although she swore she wouldn't let her eyes widen, she knew they did.

"Come here," she whispered, cursing the tremor in her voice.

The smile Wade wore faded. "There are things left unsaid between us. You can see I want you. You're a beautiful woman, Camile. If all you need is for a man to tell you so, I have. Put down the gun and get dressed before there's no turning back."

There was no turning back. Camile had made up her mind to be with the man of her choice before her choices were taken from her. She bent, laid the gun on the floor, and stepped forward, her breasts brushing against his chest.

He flinched, started to step back, and obviously realized there was no place to run. Camile ran a finger down his chest.

"I'm looking for that last thread."

"Camile," he tried again. "Listen to me. You—"

She leaned forward and traced the copper circle of his nipple with her tongue, halting him in mid-sentence. Wade groaned. He placed his hands in her hair and tilted her face up. Their gazes locked.

"Damn you," he said, his lips brushing hers. "Damn you, Camile."

He kissed her, then. Not a gentle kiss, but the kind that made her head spin and her breath catch in her throat. Wade trailed kisses down her neck, cupped the fullness of her breasts, then lowered his head to graze her nipples. Her knees grew weak, as she supposed his did, for he bent, cupping the roundness of her bottom in his hands.

"You're beautiful," he whispered, then kissed her stomach before moving lower to the golden triangle between her legs. Camile's fingers twisted in his hair.

"Wade?" she questioned, unsure.

He knew words weren't going to soothe her virgin sensibilities. He had to show her. Wade kissed her deeply, savoring the scent and taste of her. He waited until her thighs trembled before taking the sensitive nub of her womanhood between his teeth, sucking softly. Her body tensed; then he heard her gasp of pleasure, felt her convulse against his mouth. When her knees buckled, he caught her, gently easing Camile to the blankets on the floor.

Wade ached with his need for her. A need he'd battled since the first night he'd run across her in Rosie's. Her eyes were filled with wonder when he looked into them, and were almost his undoing. He wanted to plunge into her—wanted to feel her wrapped around him, but held back. Camile was a virgin, and although he'd never been with an innocent, Wade had heard talk. Talk of screaming, blood, and pain. He didn't want to hurt her—he wanted to pleasure her. Slowly, his mouth lowered.

Past conscience and good intentions, Wade let passion rule, his lips making love to hers until he felt her stir again, until her arms were around his neck, the hard buds of her nipples pressed flush against his chest. She had beautiful breasts. They called to him, demanded he pay homage to their perfection. He nibbled his way down her neck, trailing his tongue over creamy slopes to circle her hard crests, to tease and torment before suckling each in turn. She moaned, arched her back, and dug her fingernails into his scalp.

Her responses drove him crazy. His hand moved over

the flat indention of her stomach, caressing the soft down between her legs. He stroked her until she rubbed against him, straining his control. Wade was painfully hard. He was hungrier for Camile than for any woman before, and he surrendered to desire, parting her legs with his knees.

She gasped when he entered her. He pressed his forehead against hers, battling his need to thrust deep, to bury his throbbing member all the way to the hilt. Clenching his teeth, Wade eased into her tight warmth, gasping along with Camile over the effort it took to hold back. His body was slick with sweat by the time he reached an obstacle. He stared down into Camile's wide eyes, kissed her tenderly, whispered, "I'm sorry," then plunged.

Camile sucked in her breath sharply. Her shocked gaze filled with tears. He groaned, the agony of hurting her and the ecstacy of complete immersion clashing with one another. Had she moved, even shifted, he could have easily spilled himself right then and there. Camile didn't move. She lay beneath him, stiff, unyielding. When her gaze narrowed, Wade suspected she might be about to wallop him one.

He took her limp arms from around his neck and placed them above her head, gently encircling her wrists, just in case. He'd die for Camile Cordell, but if she asked him to stop, he knew he didn't have the willpower.

But she didn't ask. Camile continued to stare up at him, her features pale, wary. Wade tried to allow her time to adjust, time for the shock to fade, but his body, well schooled to follow instinct, couldn't remain passive for long. He began to move, his eyes boring into hers, his thrusts slow and steady, until he felt her wariness ebb.

The pain was over. Now he could give pleasure. He

released her wrists, wedging his hand between their damp bodies to stroke the sensitive spot where they joined. She closed her eyes, moaning his name.

To Wade, she was the most beautiful woman in the world. She aroused him like no other, he supposed, because he'd never had his heart and soul tangled up with his lust, never been so desperate to give and take at the same time. When her legs wrapped around him, he battled her power. She caught his rhythm. His body screamed for release. He grasped her hips, driving his shaft downward to stimulate her as his fingers had done a moment earlier.

He drove into her again and again, fighting his own climax while waiting for Camile to find hers. Her nails dug into his back, her body bucked beneath him; then he felt her spasms and slipped over the edge of madness with her. He exploded with a fury that forced her name from his throat. He felt a burst of ecstasy so excruciating that he thought his heart had stopped, thought he'd surely died, and knew for certain he'd gone to Heaven this time. Camile was there.

She was trembling against him, pressed perfectly into the fit of his body, and her face flushed. A face that looked up at him, displaying the same awe he felt. This was wrong, Wade told himself. No matter how right she felt in his arms, he should have resisted. It was too late to turn back. He lowered his lips to hers, certain he'd lose the battle against loving her many times before the night ended.

Camile woke slowly, wondering for a moment where she was and why her body hurt in places she didn't know she had. She tried to move, but something held her pinned. A leg. Wade's leg. A contented smile crossed her lips; then she flinched. Even her mouth felt tender. Despite her discomfort, Camile snuggled closer to him.

"Wade," she said softly.

When he didn't respond, at least verbally, she turned to face him. His whiskered cheeks could use a shave and his hair, well, she supposed she must have lent a hand in its wayward inclination. She tried to smooth it down. He opened a green eye. It looked to have been soothed with sandpaper. Camile trailed her fingers over his lips, down his chest, past the flat planes of his stomach, and wrapped them around his sex.

"You're gonna be the death of me," he said tiredly, rolling on top of her. He removed her hand and pinned her wrists above her head. "We need to talk. There are things you need to know. Things you should have known before—"

The sound of the door being kicked open halted him in mid-sentence. Camile glanced toward the doorway. Standing there were Hank Riley, Jinx Callahan, Grady Finch, and two other Circle C hands. She stiffened over the threat of rifles aimed at them.

"Oh, shit," Wade and Hank said in unison.

"Get off of her," Hank said as he stepped inside. He kept his rifle pointed at Wade. "Put your pants on, Langtry. I ain't sending no man to the hereafter naked."

Shock claimed Camile. She would have been happy to see Hank under any other circumstances; however, at the moment, she was sorely at a disadvantage. Wade slid from her, careful not to uncover her nakedness, and obviously unconcerned over his own. He rose in all his godly splendor, walked to where his pants lay, and slid into them.

"Outside." Hank motioned him forward with the rifle, then cracked the door and called, "Get a rope."

Hank's instruction didn't register until Wade had proceeded the old foreman from the line shack. Get a rope? "Oh, God," she whispered. "They're going to hang him!"

She scrambled into her clothes, then frantically searched the blankets for Wade's gun. The sound of fists hitting flesh outside had her up and stumbling from the line shack in seconds. The scene she stumbled upon made her draw up short.

Wade was on the ground, Jinx sitting on his back while Hank and Grady tried to tie his hands. Anger coursed through her. There was blood on Wade's face, but then, she noted, he looked better than the other five men.

"Let him up!" she shouted, aiming the revolver at the men. When no one paid her any mind, Camile fired a shot into the air. The kick nearly sent her backward through the open doorway. She leveled the gun at the men again, having gained their undivided attention. "I said to let him up."

The ex-foreman snorted, then returned to tying Wade's hands. "Get inside. I know you ain't gonna shoot us."

"I will," she assured Hank. "Not to kill you, but to maim you. Wade taught me to use this weapon."

"Appears he's right talented at schooling," Hank grumbled. "I'm happy to see you alive, Cam, but I've got business to tend. Go back inside. I'll deal with you after I've dealt with Langtry."

"Y-you can't hang him," she stuttered. "I was willing."

Hank's face turned red. "I figured that much, girl. Figured he used those pretty-boy dimples of his to make you that way, too. Now I'm gonna stretch his pretty neck."

Her panic returned. Camile thought the Circle C men might have a notion she'd been raped. What was she supposed to do when whether she'd been willing or not, Hank intended to hang Wade? She'd once assumed an experienced man would be blamed for the seduction of an innocent, regardless of who did the seducing. The proof lay before her. Wade trussed up like a calf waiting for the branding iron. She had to save him.

"I forced him," she blurted out.

More than just Hank's face darkened. Grady coughed, or laughed, she wasn't certain. Jinx suddenly found the back of Wade's head more interesting than looking at her.

"You can't force a man," Hank said quietly. "Now, get inside. Wade went back on his word to me. He said you wasn't his type."

Hank had reminded Camile of the plans she'd once had in mind for Wade Langtry. Plans contrived in her ignorant past.

"That's why I stripped naked, pulled this gun on him, and ordered him to pleasure me," she said.

Grady choked in earnest. Hank's face drained of color. Jinx rubbed his forehead, still keeping his eyes trained on the back of Wade's head. The man he sat upon was suddenly staring at Camile, staring a hole through her. She averted her gaze.

"You ain't making sense," Hank said. "Whether a woman's to a man's taste or not, if she takes a notion to . . . well, she wouldn't need no dad-blasted gun. Besides, if he wasn't interested, I don't know why the hell you'd be so determined to . . . " He blushed again, refusing to finish.

"I planned it," she answered, amazed at the calmness of her voice. "I figured if Langtry ruined me, no man would marry me. Not even Ralph Lamar's knock-kneed son. I was desperate last night. I knew we'd reach the ranch today and my father would order me to marry. I imagined once I told him about me and Langtry, he'd reconsider bartering used goods. Figured he'd run Wade off, and I'd have another shot at running the ranch."

Her heart sped a measure at Hank's shocked expression. It almost stopped beating when her eyes met Wade's. They were deadly, cold as when he'd drawn down on the snake.

"Tell me you're lying," Hank demanded. He rose, stomping toward her. Although she wanted to crumble beneath his angry glare, Camile raised her chin.

"You know me, Hank. Is there anything more important to me than the ranch? Is there anything more important than winning?"

He held her stare long enough to make beads of moisture pop out on Camile's forehead; then he looked at her in a way he never had. A disgusted way. She fought the tears threatening to surface. Hank turned and walked away.

"Let him up," he said softly.

"Hold on a minute," Grady said. "William T. Ferguson was plenty mad when I told him Langtry and Cam weren't really married. He said he'd encouraged what was not legally blessed. Said he'd been pushing Langtry to plant his seed in her and if he succeeded, William figured her daddy would prefer a foreman for a son-in-law over a bastard grandchild."

Silence followed. All eyes turned toward Camile. She and Wade had discussed that possibility. Perhaps too late, but he'd told her he'd heard virgins couldn't get with child their first night with a man. Was that wrong?

"I don't think you have anything to worry about," she mumbled, feeling heat claw a path up her neck.

Wade groaned.

Grady sighed. "Forget the rope. Amos said if she said that very thing, it'd be best to fetch a preacher."

Her startled gaze flew to Wade. Jinx and Grady had him on his feet, but his hands were still tied behind his back. He had a black eye and a busted lip. His cold stare settled on her.

"Shoot me, Camile," he instructed her quietly.

Chapter Twenty

"Do you Camile Elizabeth Cordell take Wade . . . "

Preacher Graham's voice droned on inside her head. Camile stared blankly ahead at the sunset and thought it was a beautiful evening for disaster. Maria sniffled beside her. Her father sat in his chair at her back, a rifle draped across his lap.

Camile took her eyes off the sunset and studied her boots. She'd refused to wear a dress for this mockery of a wedding. It wasn't exactly that she minded being Mrs. Wade Langtry. If she had to have a husband, who better than Wade? The fact that he obviously didn't feel the same way bothered her.

Wade had settled down before they reached the ranch; he didn't request to be hanged or shot again, but he seemed different—suddenly a stranger to her. It was ironic that she'd used the very scheme she'd once considered to get rid of him, to save his life. But he didn't seem beholden.

"Humph!" Preacher Graham drew her attention. "I said, do you do all those things?"

"She does," Tom Cordell assured him. "Go on."

"I have to hear her say 'I do' before it's legal," the preacher huffed.

"Say it, Camile," Tom ordered.

The words stuck in her throat. She'd looked everywhere but at the man beside her. Camile stole a glance at Wade. He stared straight ahead. He didn't blink, no muscle twitched in his jaw, and the scar sat red across his cheek. Texas hadn't been kind to him. He was still handsome, but no one would call him pretty again.

"Go ahead," he startled her by saying. "I'm sure He knows as well as the next man, any woman who'd cheat at cards would lie, too."

"I do!" she snapped, Wade's attitude beginning to wear on her nerves.

Preacher Graham didn't seem anxious to continue his line of questioning with the stone-faced man standing next to her. He began all the same. When it came time for Wade to say, "I do," Camile steeled herself for a rebellion. But Wade never stumbled over those two words. He said them as if he married women on a daily basis and found it boring.

Heaving a sigh of relief, the preacher pronounced them man and wife. No slaps of congratulations followed the announcement. The ranch was silent as a graveyard. An awkwardness stretched until Maria finally grabbed Camile and proceeded to cry all over her. Tom wheeled forward, scowling at Wade but offering his hand.

"Come into the house and we'll have a shot of whiskey while the women fix something for dinner."

"No, thanks," Wade declined. "Camile and I'll be going into Tascosa for the night. I haven't had the opportunity to be alone with her for three days. I'm . . . anxious."

The veiled threat in his voice sliced through the sounds of Maria's sobbing. "Surely we can stay for a while," Camile suggested.

His gaze slid over her. "We need to talk." He finally smiled at her, although Camile couldn't confess she found any comfort in his lifeless expression.

"We can talk here," she offered weakly.

"It'll be dark by time we reach town as it is. You just promised before God you'd obey me. I'll get the horses."

As he headed toward the barn, Camile wished she'd paid attention to all the things she'd agreed to do. They rode from the ranch in silence—a silence that stretched until Camile tried to speak. The minute she opened her mouth, he glared at her. She promptly closed it, thinking once they reached town and the small hotel that did very little business, he'd be more inclined to listen.

It was almost dark when they made the outskirts of Tascosa. To her surprise, Wade reined his horse toward the hitching post of Rosie's rather than move down the street toward the hotel.

"Why are we stopping here?" she asked.

He didn't answer, just dismounted, tying his horse's reins before approaching her horse. "Climb down."

Camile didn't obey. She didn't feel like going into the boisterous cantina. "Why don't we go on to the hotel and settle in?"

236

He smiled. "A whore should spend her wedding night in surroundings that best suit her."

Her startled gaze went from his face to the cantina. She felt her face grow hot. "You bastard! I'm going home!"

"The way I see it, you are home." He took her leg with the obvious intention of pulling her from the horse. "You whored yourself for a piece of land, and you made me look the worst kind of fool by doing it!"

She kicked out at him. "I won't let you humiliate me this way!"

Undaunted, Wade dragged her down and slung her over his shoulder. She beat her fists against his back, but he never faltered as he stepped onto the planked boards to enter Rosie's. A boisterous laugh died, and conversation dwindled away as he approached the bar.

"Evening, Rosie," he said politely. "We need a room."

"This ain't no hotel, Langtry," Rosie said with a laugh. "By the way, good to see you again. It'd be better to see you without that cactus thrown over your shoulder. You know my rooms ain't for the likes of her. If you'll leave that baggage outside, I'd be more than happy to show you to a room."

"I'll pay for the room," Wade said quietly. "And whatever the damages come to."

When Camile tried to bite him, he slapped her bottom.

"The whole Circle C bunch would come down on my head if I let you take Cam Cordell to one of my rooms," Rosie argued. "Why don't you let me handle whatever she's obviously got you worked up over?"

"Her name's not Cordell anymore, it's Langtry, and the piece of paper in my pocket gives me permission to do whatever I damn well please with her."

"You married her?"

Rosie's obvious disappointment might have pleased Camile another time. All she felt at the moment, besides a stinging in her backside, was the need to kill Wade.

"Till death do us part, Langtry! It's gonna be a short marriage!" she ground between her teeth.

"For better or for worse," he countered. "You've never seen the bad side of me. Not yet."

"Last room at the back has clean sheets," Rosie said. "Keep her away from anything other than the bed. You might pay for what she breaks, but I'm the one who'll be cleaning up the mess."

The first thing that shattered was a porcelain washbasin of little cost, but of high sound quality. It missed Wade by inches. The water it contained soaked his hair and shirt. He smiled and continued toward Camile.

She backed away. "You don't deserve an explanation after humiliating me this way, but I want a chance to explain," she told him.

"You've already explained," Wade said, stalking her around the room. "You used me. I guess you only saved my life because if I died, your plans would go to waste. I don't like being made a fool of, and you're not going to like it, either."

"L-listen," she tried, her gaze darting toward the door. "You don't understand."

He blocked her exit. "I'm afraid I do, Camile. Now I know why you poured yourself into that gaudy red dress. You were trying to tempt me. You've been trying for some time. And here I thought it was because you cared for me."

"I do care for you," she assured him. "Or at least I do when you're being yourself."

"You haven't seen myself." His green gaze bored into her blue one. "Not the real me. The door swings both ways. You did what you had to do. Now I'll do what I have to do."

"Which is?" she demanded testily.

Wade studied her from head to toe, then turned toward the door. "Nothing for the time being. Good night."

"Good night?" she repeated, flustered. "You can't leave! Where are you going?"

His hand paused on the door handle. "When I pay for a woman, I like to know her terms before we get down to business. I'll find another whore to spend my wedding night with. Your price was too high for me."

Anger consumed her. If Wade spent the night with another woman and it became common knowledge, she'd never live down the shame. She would never forgive him. Despite the urge to hurl something at him, she fought her temper.

"Wade, I know you're hurt—"

"I'm not hurt," he said, turning to look at her. "I didn't give you enough of myself to be hurt. I'm mad. Damn mad. My price will be higher than yours."

Disbelieving, she watched him open the door and step outside. Camile hurried across the room. She placed her hand around the handle. It wouldn't turn. The sound of a key being placed in the lock ignited her barely suppressed anger. She allowed her temper full rein.

"Open this door, Wade!" she shouted, pounding on the wood.

When she received no response, she tried the handle again. The knob turned, but the door wouldn't open. Furious, Camile walked to a table littered with perfume bottles, picked one up, and hurled it against the door. Her husband thought her price was high the last time? Just wait.

* * *

Wade had ridden for over an hour when he reined his mount to a halt. He removed an object from his pocket. Moonlight danced upon the key. Someone would have to break down the door to get Camile out. He imagined the talk would spread fast in Tascosa. His conscience preyed on him. What he planned for her should be all the revenge he needed. He'd heard a bottle break against the door. By now, she would have worn herself out—was probably asleep in a bed he'd never intended to share with her.

He hadn't settled with Rosie, although he planned to wire her a sizable amount to cover the damages to the room. Why not slip back and unlock the door? Leave Rosie a few bills and pay Tom Cordell's attorney a visit? The truth was, he didn't know if he could go through with his plan. As angry as he felt at Camile, he'd lied to her from the beginning. Also, he'd lied to her when he'd said he hadn't given her enough of himself to be hurt. His heart said otherwise. She'd found a soft spot in him he didn't know he had. The proof—he turned his horse around and headed back toward Tascosa.

Broken glass crunched beneath his feet. The room reeked of cheap perfume. His wife lay on the bed, her long lashes casting shadows against her cheeks. The candles burned low. Wade placed the key on the bureau and turned to go. Camile moaned in her sleep. The soft sound tore at his insides. He doubted if he'd see her again after tonight. Negotiations would be handled by telegrams and parties less involved.

Unwillingly, his gaze strayed to her slender form. Her body curled into a ball. Against his better judgment, he went to Camile, pulling a quilt up over her. He pushed a curl away from her face. She was beautiful. Deceitful, he reminded himself. In love with the ranch, not with him.

"Damn you," he whispered hoarsely, his eyes stinging.

"Wade?" Her lashes fluttered open.

He froze. Another confrontation with his scheming wife wasn't part of the plan. Wade remained silent, hoping she would close her eyes and drift back to sleep.

"Let's not argue," Camile said. She lifted a hand and ran her fingers down the side of his cheek. "For better or for worse, remember?"

In sickness and in health, he mentally added, figuring what he felt for Camile was a sickness of sorts. He was still mad at her, hurt that she had so completely deceived him, and yet, he wanted her—responded without a will of his own to the plea in her voice. Her fingers moved to the back of his neck, applying pressure.

Wade fought her power over him, battled his desire. Accepting the invitation of her parted lips would be wrong under the circumstances. How could he want to strangle her and make love to her at the same time?

"Don't fight me," she whispered. "Not tonight. Tomorrow will come soon enough."

Tomorrow, he'd be gone. Tomorrow, she would fully understand the consequences of dancing with the devil. He told himself she deserved the same humiliation he'd felt that morning outside the line shack. The day he understood he'd been used as a pawn to further her goals. He would use her as she had used him—take what she'd so willingly offered. He had already paid the fiddler. Paid with his heart. Now, Camile would pay.

He allowed her to pull his mouth to her waiting lips. He

241

kissed her. Not tenderly as he'd done when he'd believed her innocent, but with raw hunger. He pumped all his anger and hurt into the merging of their mouths, challenging her to continue what she had thoughtlessly begun. She didn't push him away. Her hand slid from around his neck, moving to the buttons on his shirt.

No, he mentally warned himself. He would not love her with his heart this time. Lust ruled him. Let her see the real him, the savage her deceit had unleashed. He pushed her hands aside and rose from the bed. Gazes locked, Wade removed her boots, then her buckskins, not bothering with her shirt. He roughly parted her legs, pausing only long enough to release his rigid member before plunging into her.

She gasped, but didn't fight his impersonal assault. Instead, her legs went around his waist, her arms around his neck. He wanted to soften, surrender to the silken feel of her wrapped around him. Wade fought himself. Camile needed to see this other side of him. The side he didn't like. The side she would despise. He lifted her from the bed, their bodies joined, then landed with a jar against the wall.

Wade didn't apologize, Camile noted, just continued to plunge into her. He whispered things in her ear. Things no decent man would say to a woman. Things that made her cheeks turn red and her thighs quiver. His fiery passion unleashed hers. Camile clawed his back, sank her teeth into his neck, and still he kept plunging into her, driving her toward a place he'd taken her to before, though it had been a softer ride.

She shattered, there against the wall, wrapped around him, merged by skin and sweat. He lifted her, then eased her down on the bed, where he continued to thrust, slow, steady, with purpose. Within moments, he rekindled the embers of her fading climax.

The fire climbed higher, grew hotter, consumed her. It was torture. Wonderful torture, she thought, her head thrashing back and forth on the pillows. In one fluid motion, he rolled and pulled her on top of him, guiding her with his hands, teaching her to give pleasure—how to please herself, as well.

Camile's desire intensified, fueled by the heat in his eyes, the groans she stole from his lips. Faster, harder she pushed him, rode him, mastered him, and then she broke him. He thrust deep, shuddered, and exploded. Camile's release was divine. She flew up and away, moaning his name. Wade eased her down beside him. They lay joined, their breathing ragged, their hearts pounding.

Exhaustion claimed her. Tomorrow she would talk to him. Explain her reasons for lying to Hank and the others. She'd known earlier words couldn't penetrate his anger, but showing him how she felt might. The side of him she'd just seen was somewhat frightening, close to dangerous, totally untamed, and yet, she'd responded to him. She loved Wade Langtry.

All were aspects of him, and nothing he could do would change her feelings. She snuggled against his warmth, certain he hadn't made good on his earlier threat to spend time with another woman, hopeful of the future they would share together.

Camile thought he started to pull away; then she heard him sigh. His arms went around her. She was almost asleep when she felt his lips next to her ear.

"Damn you. You always win."

* * *

As Camile's gaze scanned her surroundings the next morning, complete with last night's destruction, she noted a disturbing absence. That of her husband. He'd gone to bring the horses around back, she decided, then rose, stretching sore muscles before scavenging the shambles in search of her clothes.

Today, she and Wade would talk. She swore it would be a day of new beginnings. It annoyed her to pause in her plans and search for a pair of thin cotton drawers as elusive as her husband.

When a light knock sounded at the door, she forsook modesty, pulling her buckskins up over her bare bottom. Assuming Wade waited outside, she flung the door wide. Rosie and Clive Atkins, her father's attorney, stood in his stead.

"Mr. Atkins has business with you," Rosie explained. "Wade told him to ask for you here."

Heat exploded in Camile's cheeks as Mr. Atkins glanced past her to the shambles of the room, his round eyes growing rounder. His nose began to twitch.

Rosie coughed. "You take a bath in that stuff?" She eased her way inside. "Good God, I told him surely whatever you'd done didn't cost that much. I'd have to say he shorted me."

"Where is he?" Camile wanted to know.

The woman shrugged. "Hell if I know. He paid me and left a good four hours ago. Maybe Mr. Atkins knows where he's gotten off to." She turned curious eyes upon the lawyer.

Clive Atkins shuffled uncomfortably. "Mr. Langtry, your h-husband," he stuttered, "got me out of bed before dawn demanding the deed to the Circle C."

"He what?" Camile whispered.

"Well, I told him I couldn't give it to him, the two of you not being married and all, but then he showed me the marriage license and said the place was legally his. What could I do?"

"The place is legally my father's!" Camile snapped.

"No." Atkins shook his head. "Tom deeded it to you after the accident. He was worried he might not recover. Anyway, the Circle C was legally yours, but of course, now it passes to your husband."

Camile could have accepted a shared partnership, but Wade's obvious haste to let her know he considered the ranch his for the taking left a bad taste in her mouth.

"From a simple foreman to a ranch owner. I don't think he suffered too much," she muttered.

"I'm afraid running the ranch isn't his intention, nor from what he told me, has it ever been." Mr. Atkins glanced at the floor. "He told me he planned to sell the ranch to the Wagner Cattle Company, of which he's a stockholder. He said a draft would be sent to your father." He paused, his face turning red. "And to tell you you'd already paid the fiddler. And paid him well."

She couldn't speak, couldn't breathe, couldn't believe what she'd heard. Wade? A stockholder in the same company that had sent a representative months ago? Wade? Her Wade, saying he had no intention of keeping the ranch? He'd never wanted a simple foreman's job, she suddenly realized. Her heart seemed to drop to her knees. The deed. The ranch. That was what he'd wanted from the beginning.

Tears stung the backs of her eyes. Wade had deceived her. Lied to her. Used her. It was the worst feeling in the world. To have given her heart to a man who'd never really wanted it—or her.

The temptation to fling herself across the bed she'd shared with Wade and cry her eyes out surfaced. Rosie's pitying expression and the lawyer's uneasy one made her stiffen her spine instead. Wade Langtry had made a fool of her. He'd broken her heart. Taken her father's ranch. He wouldn't get away with it!

Chapter Twenty-one

Camile stared out the study window. The morning sun glistened on the coats of horses grazing in the distance. Men rode in, men rode out. Nothing had changed. Nothing except that they were all waiting to be booted off the ranch. The men returned from the drive with little for their efforts. Dodge had been flooded with cattle, lowering the price. It was the second setback her father had suffered since her marriage to Wade Langtry.

Two months had passed and still no word from him. Not that Camile expected him to personally escort them from the Circle C—Langtry was too much of a coward. He would send someone else to do his dirty work, leaving her to bide her time until the showdown. Her stomach gurgled. Camile raced to the kitchen, then leaned over a bucket. It was the third day in a row she'd lost her breakfast.

"Are you ill again?" Maria rushed forward, placing the

dirty dishes she carried on a table. "You must go back to bed."

"No." Camile held up a hand to ward off the housekeeper. "It will pass. By noon I'll feel fine."

Maria frowned. "You are usually as healthy as a horse. I do not understand. . . . " The woman paled. "May God have mercy on us," she whispered.

"What?" Camile demanded. "What have I got?"

Shakily, the housekeeper pulled out a chair and sat down. "I have no children of my own, but my mother had six. Being the oldest, I came to know the signs well."

"What signs?"

"This explains much. The exhaustion, the lagging spirit, the crying, the sickness that comes only in the morning."

"It's Langtry's fault," Camile muttered. "No wonder I'm not feeling like myself. I'm sick with worry. He lied to us. Cheated us out of our ranch!"

"He did more than that," Maria said solemnly. "When was the last time you had your monthly flow?"

Camile tried to remember. "A while back," she said.

"Before or after you and Mr. Langtry . . . "

Heat rose in her cheeks. "Before."

"But not since?" Maria pressed.

"Now that you mention it, no." Camile turned to her. "That's strange."

"No. It is normal. You are going to have a baby."

Her knees nearly buckled. Maria jumped up and helped Camile to a chair. For the first time in her life, Camile thought she might faint. "I can't."

"In a few months, you will," Maria assured her.

"This can't be happening!"

"What's happened now?" Tom Cordell wheeled his chair forward.

The housekeeper and Camile exchanged a miserable glance. Maria hurried from the kitchen.

"Well?" her father demanded.

Camile lowered her gaze, the tears she couldn't seem to control of late brimming to the surface. "I'm going to have a baby."

Her father groaned. "Dammit, girl, when you make a mistake, you do it up right."

Straightening her spine, Camile lifted her face. "And when I make a mistake, I have to pay for it for the rest of my life. This time is no different than the last."

"You're a stubborn, willful girl, Camile. I've been too easy with you. Loved you too much for your own good."

A tear slid down her cheek. "You loved me too little. You haven't forgiven me for the accident. I've tried all these years to make it up to you. I've loved the things you love, lived the life you can't, tried to replace Clint. I've done it all for you, but it will never be enough. Never."

His expression turned to shock, then to pain. "You were only a child, Camile. I never blamed you. It was an accident. If anyone, I'm to blame. I spent more time with Clint. He was my son. The boy who would take my place when he became a man. I forgot you needed me, too. How could you carry the blame all these years? How could I not see what I've done to you?" Tears filled his eyes. "No matter what you do, Camile, I'll always love you. No matter what I've done in the past, it's been because of that love. I thought you needed a man. A softer life. A life your mother would have wanted you to have."

Pain squeezed Camile's heart. "All this time, I've tried

to make amends, tried to be who I thought you wanted me to be. I can't do that anymore. It's time I had my own life."

Tom nodded. "We'll leave here. Go somewhere else and start over. We'll tell everyone you're a widow, and the child—"

"The child will have his or her rightful inheritance," Camile interrupted. Her hand moved unconsciously to her still-flat stomach. "I can't let Wade take my child's future."

"I don't see how you can stop him from selling the ranch. The child belongs to him, too, Camile. Maybe if you told him—"

"No!" she shouted. Camile rose, then began to pace. "He mustn't find out. I paid the fiddler. I'm still paying. Wade Langtry is taking nothing else from me. I won't sit here any longer and wait for him to lower the ax. I'll take Hank with me."

"Take him where?" her father asked, clearly puzzled.

"To St. Louis. I'm getting my deed back, and I don't care if I have to kill Langtry to do it!"

"Hold on, Camile," her father sputtered. "You'd best not tangle with him again. He beat you. He beat us all."

"The contest isn't over." Camile felt more alive than she had since the day Wade had plunged a knife into her heart. "Not by a far stretch."

Tom opened his mouth, then lifted his hands in defeat. "I don't imagine I can stop you. Be careful, Camile. You're carrying my grandson."

"Grandson?" She lifted a brow.

"Don't think much of Langtry right now, but I figure if he's man enough to get my daughter in trouble this soon, he's man enough to throw boys."

A vision came to her as clearly as if he stood before her.

A little boy with dark hair, green eyes, and dimples. She would love her child. She wished she didn't still love his father. It would make the task at hand simpler. Camile set her jaw. She'd paid the fiddler. Now it was Wade's turn.

Anyone who was anyone had gathered at the immodest home of Miles Traften for an evening of social entertainment. Wade lifted a brandy snifter to his lips, watching Lilla Traften steal glances at him from across the room. He waited for her gaze to touch the scar, then dart away with disgust. She didn't do otherwise.

After the initial shock of seeing him again, the meeting two and a half months ago in which she'd fainted dead away, Lilla had put a brave face forward and tried to pretend his altered appearance didn't matter. Wade smiled when her eyes wandered in his direction once more. She returned his smile, although her bottom lip trembled slightly.

"What happened to you in that godforsaken country?" she'd gasped upon recovery. "I thought you said it was only business."

And so it had turned out to be, although he hadn't told Lilla the near of it, conveniently forgetting to mention he now had a wife—one Wade intended to rid himself of once the Circle C changed hands. He wondered how Camile had taken the news. His smile faded. What he would have given to see the look on her face . . .

He'd known to go while the going was good. If he'd hung around in Tascosa to personally deliver the blow, Hank or one of the others might have happened along and forced a confrontation. Whatever he thought of Camile, Wade wouldn't consider drawing against a Circle C hand. They were not to blame for Camile's scheming.

"I wish you'd been more careful around that cactus," Miles Traften said, interrupting Wade's thoughts. "Never heard of one doing that to a man's face."

Gregory Kline lifted a brow, indicating he doubted any cactus was responsible for Wade's maiming—not the kind that grew from the ground, leastwise. "What did you think of Texas women?" Kline asked.

Wade smiled slightly. "I found them about the same as you did. Gentle as a bullwhip."

Kline flushed. "Well, you obviously found a way around any hardships you encountered while in Tascosa. I heard rumors that the deed was in Camile Cordell's name. How did you manage to get the title transferred to your own?"

"She wanted to deal directly with me," Wade lied. "I bought her out."

"Ingenious strategy," Miles complimented him, then frowned. "Not a very good arrangement for the rest of us, but a smart move. I take it you bought cheap so you could sell high and double your profit?"

"The price was higher than I expected to pay," Wade answered quietly. "But when all was said and done, she got what she deserved."

"You might not," Miles said. "I glanced over the contract you gave me concerning the sale. I must say it took you long enough to present your terms. The contract is rather bold. Not only the price, but the added stipulation that Hank Riley and Jinx Callahan receive a pension from future profits of the ranch. The stockholders won't accept that condition."

"If they want the land, they will," Wade countered. "Hank and Jinx are too old to find work elsewhere."

"Still," Miles argued, "if you push the stipulation, they

might back out altogether. Then you'll be left with nothing but a ranch and no partners to help you survive. That isn't a life suitable for my daughter, is it?"

Glancing across the room at the woman under discussion, Wade shook his head. "No," he agreed dryly. "I can't see Lilla settling down in the Panhandle."

"Perhaps that isn't anything Mr. Langtry should be overly concerned with," Kline injected. "After all, he's never actually declared himself to Lilla. They aren't officially engaged."

"Lilla and I are none of your business," Wade warned him.

"Now, Wade, no need to get testy." Miles placed a hand on his arm. "Gregory has a point. There's been talk since you left. It seems the ladies of St. Louis have filled my daughter's head with doubts. Katherine Sims told her you were only stringing her along."

"Katherine wishes that. And so do you, don't you, Kline?"

Lilla Traften ended further discussion as she eased her way into the circle of men. "This is beginning to look suspiciously like a business meeting," she said, pouting prettily. "St. Louis's two most eligible bachelors are wasting all their charms on one another."

"Why don't you see to the ladies, Kline," Wade suggested. "I'd hate to send them all shrieking from the room with this face of mine."

An uncomfortable silence followed his reference to Lilla's feeble attempts at hiding her repulsion over his scar. Miles took Gregory by the arm and subtly steered him to the other side of the room.

"I apologized for my first reaction," Lilla reminded him in a quiet voice. "It takes a bit of getting used to. Things

253

feel different between us. Besides your face, you seem somehow changed since your return from Texas."

I'm in love with another woman. The thought startled Wade. He couldn't love Camile. Not after what she'd done. He'd given his heart for the first time and she'd ripped it from his chest and thrown it back in his face. She didn't love him. He was nothing more than an obstacle that stood between her and the Circle C.

"You also seem different," he said. He glanced down into Lilla's features. She appeared pale and scrawny to him. Her hair was the inky blackness of his own, her eyes dark. Beautiful, but without fire. "I've heard that you and Gregory have been seen together in my absence. Maybe it's not my new face that's responsible for your cool attitude."

She lowered her eyes demurely. "I have the right to see other men. You've never led me to believe you were seriously interested in a future together. I didn't realize what an object of gossip your failure to commit has made me."

"Why didn't you simply ask what my intentions were?"

When Lilla only blushed deeper and began fumbling with the skirt of her gown, Wade fought the urge to strangle her. Why couldn't she look him in the eye? Why couldn't she just come out and say what she wanted, and why the hell couldn't she speak above a whisper?

Instead, Lilla simply slid her arm through his in as daring a gesture as she would display while in public. "I've ignored my guests too long and now we're being gossiped about. Here comes Margaret to save us from scandal."

Wade inwardly groaned. Margaret Pendergraft taught lessons in charm and etiquette for the wealthy young ladies of St. Louis. The woman was the type to wear on his nerves easily. Tall and rather handsome for a matronly spinster, Margaret had the intolerable habit of thinking herself an expert on everything.

"Mr. Langtry. Lilla." She nodded. "Lilla dear, you know good and well it isn't proper for the hostess of a party to lavish more attention on one guest than she does the others. Let us resume a conversation. What is the topic under discussion?"

Wade glanced at the woman he'd once thought to marry, lifting a brow. Wade doubted she'd admit they were discussing their personal relationship.

"Texas," she said softly.

"Dreadful place." Margaret wrinkled her nose. "An untamed desert full of savages."

Lilla shuddered delicately. "The women, or so Gregory told me, are meaner than grizzly bears. He meant only to tease me, didn't he, Wade?"

"Dried up by the sun and beaten down," Margaret took it upon herself to answer. "Mark my words, a lady taken out of her element cannot survive. We are God's gentle creatures and need beauty and the comfort of other women surrounding us. You can't plant a rose under sand and expect it to grow."

At Lilla's polite nod of agreement, Wade fought the urge to laugh. He'd opened his mouth to suggest refilling the women's punch cups when the loud voice of the Traftens' manservant turned all heads toward the hall.

"Now see here, miss—sir, whatever the devil you are, you can't go in there!"

The hairs on the back of Wade's neck rose. His senses immediately went on the alert as a woman shoved her way into the ballroom. Margaret Pendergraft screamed.

"My heavens, what is it?" Lilla whispered.

"One of God's gentler creatures," Wade answered dryly. "It might be wise if you ladies took cover."

Blue eyes narrowed, Stetson pulled low, Camile scanned the group. When her steely stare found Wade, his hand instinctively moved toward his hip. The Colt wasn't there. Last time he'd seen it, Camile had been pointing the gun at Hank Riley.

"Looking for this, Langtry?" Camile drew the Colt strapped to her thigh. Several gasps followed. "I only want two things from you, and I don't care if I have to kill you to get them."

"Why don't we go outside and discuss this like men," Wade suggested flatly.

In answer, Camile fired a shot at him. The bullet bounced off the marble floor and ricocheted around the room. Screams of terror and a mass scramble to the floor resulted. Wade held his ground.

"You'll hurt someone, Camile," he said, "Why don't you give me the gun and we'll leave these folks to their party."

"I'll give it to you, all right. Right between the eyes! I want my deed back, and my underwear, too!"

Dire circumstances or not, a smile stole across Wade's lips. He knew it would rile her to take her cotton drawers. "I only took what's legally mine."

Her hand started to shake—whether from outrage or nerves, Wade didn't know. He knew he had to get her out of the Traftens' expensive ballroom.

"That's it. Keep coming," Camile taunted when he approached her. "If I shoot you, I become a widow and the deed's mine again."

He paused as a loud gasp split the charged air. Lilla, he

suspected. "If you kill me, you'll have to answer to the law," he said.

She frowned. Wade supposed she hadn't deliberated all the unpleasant consequences of murder.

"I don't want to kill you. You're not worth it, Langtry. I only want my ranch back. You as good as stole that deed from us."

Since Camile had already placed him in an awkward situation, Wade allowed his temper full rein. "I believe it was your failed plan that got me the deed. I had to be forced to say, 'I do,' remember?"

"I haven't forgotten anything," she ground out through her teeth. "Not the way you squirmed your way into my father's graces, not the way you lied to us—"

"Excuse me, Miss Cordell, ah, or I guess it's Langtry," Gregory said, lifting himself from the floor. "I don't know if you recall me, I'm Gregory Kline. We met in Texas."

She swung the gun toward the man. "I believe I do," she admitted. "Turn around and let me see your yellow-livered butt running for the hills and I'll know for sure."

A red stain settled over Gregory's face. "As I explained to you at the time, I'm a stockholder in the Wagner Cattle Company. These charges you're instigating against Mr. Langtry don't speak well of the company. Might I suggest we retire to a more suitable place to discuss them?"

"Kline, there isn't anything to talk about," Wade snapped. "It was her own fault that deed came into my legal possession."

"Mr. Langtry," Gregory warned. "I'm trying to assure your wife her claim will be taken into account so that she may *leave*."

"Me and this gun aren't going anywhere until I have

someone's word the stockholders will listen to my side," Camile said. "Someone whose word counts, which isn't you, Mr. Kline, and damn sure isn't Langtry."

"I'll give you *my* word if you'll go," Miles Traften said from the floor. "I'm the major stockholder in the Wagner Cattle Company. I'll send wires to the stockholders out of town and we'll grant you a hearing. Does that sound fair?"

"Miles, this isn't necessary," Wade said. "Camile is a scheming little witch, but she's not going to shoot anyone."

"Don't upset her!" Miles barked. "I want her out of my house! Now!"

Gregory stepped forward. "Do you have a place to stay, Mrs. Langtry?"

Camile eyed him mistrustfully. "I left Hank asleep in a chair at that fancy hotel where *he* lives." She glared at Wade. "We were waiting for that lying snake-in-the-grass, but I grew impatient and convinced the clerk to give me directions to where I could find him. I'm not staying under the same roof as Langtry."

"No, not under present circumstances," Gregory agreed. "It will take a couple of days for the out-of-town stockholders to arrive. I'm positive Miss Pendergraft won't mind putting you up until then."

Margaret Pendergraft's low groan collided with Wade's sigh of irritation.

"This is ridiculous," Wade ground out. "Camile's a good bluffer. She thinks she can get whatever she wants with threats and—"

"Langtry," Miles bellowed. "I gave my word and now I want her kindly removed from my home. Kline, see her out, and Miss Pendergraft, as well. Just so trouble doesn't erupt outside, Mr. Langtry will remain until after you've gone."

As Camile flashed him a smug smile and Gregory helped a flustered Margaret to her feet, it occurred to Wade that Miles had addressed him formally, and not in the warm manner he'd employed for over two years. Of course, the man was probably in shock.

A collective release of breaths followed Camile's departure. Wade stared after her, blood tingling. He'd forgotten how alive he felt in her company. How everything around him seemed to shift out of focus.

"Wade?" A whispered plea drew his gaze to the floor.

Lilla lay at his feet. Wade bent and assisted her up. As her round eyes searched his face, automatically darting away from the scar, he felt a twinge of guilt. He should have told her about Camile.

"Is it true?" Her voice trembled. "Is that woman your wife?"

"Yes, but—"

That was all Wade managed. Frail Lilla Traften drew back her fist and punched him soundly.

Chapter Twenty-two

Camile barely set foot inside Margaret Pendergraft's taste-fully decorated home when she felt the bile rising in her throat. Her eyes widened. She clamped a hand over her mouth.

"Oh, dear." Margaret took her arm and quickly led her through the house, calling over her shoulder, "We've made it inside just fine, Mr. Kline."

Not fine, Camile wanted to argue. Margaret led her to the kitchen, snatched up a crock, and held it under her face. Camile promptly lost what little dinner she'd eaten earlier. She wiped her mouth on her sleeve. "I feel like I'm going to faint," she whispered.

"Sit down." Margaret settled her into a dainty cane-backed chair. "Put your head between your legs."

"Do what?"

The woman shoved Camile's head down. "It will help. I'll get a cold cloth for your face."

"Thank you," Camile said from her awkward position. "I'm sorry. This usually only happens in the morning."

"Oh?" Margaret's voice sounded suddenly curious.

Camile cursed her loose tongue. "I meant, this never happens. I can't imagine what's wrong with me."

"Well, I can." Margaret lifted Camile's head and washed her face. "You're wearing an inch of dust, not to mention those disgusting clothes. Whatever point you were trying to make to Mr. Langtry, you should have used grace."

"Grace who?"

Margaret sighed loudly. "Never mind. My," she exclaimed. "There is a woman under all that dirt. And a very pretty one."

Not nearly as pretty as the dark-haired woman Wade had been standing beside when she'd stormed the social, Camile thought. Lilla Traften, she suspected. His fancy woman. "Me and Hank rode hard to get here. I didn't have time for a bath."

"I can tell." Margaret wrinkled her nose, then stared haughtily down at Camile. "Hank?"

"Hank Riley. A friend of mine," she explained. "Actually, more like a father to me."

The woman relaxed. "Well, I'll draw you a bath and help you into bed. You look exhausted."

"I am," Camile admitted softly. "But I can't stay. Soon as I rest a minute, I'd better find Hank. We'll get us a room somewhere for the night."

"Nonsense," Margaret scoffed. "Mr. Kline told everyone you would be staying with me until this matter can be resolved, and if I'm known for anything, it's my hospitality."

"But—"

"No arguments," Margaret interrupted. "Remove those filthy clothes. I'll throw them out."

"You will not," Camile assured her. "I like these clothes, if they are a bit tight." Unthinkingly, she undid the fastenings of her buckskins and breathed a sigh of relief. "There, that's better."

"Oh, dear." Margaret removed the crock and left.

After she'd gone, Camile could hardly keep her eyes open. She rested her head on the table.

"How far along are you?"

Her head snapped up. Margaret had returned, and now stood staring expectantly down at her.

"How far?"

"The baby. Not far, I'm guessing. You haven't lost your figure yet."

If her condition was that obvious, even to a stranger, Camile wondered how she would hide it from Wade. Easy, she assured herself. She wouldn't go near him until the stockholders meeting. Too tired to pretend otherwise, Camile said, "Not far. About three months."

"Does your husband know?"

"No. And I'd prefer to keep it that way," she warned her, narrowing her gaze on the woman.

"Can't say I blame you. Mr. Langtry has certainly become a surprise. Marrying a woman, getting her with child, then saying nothing of the matter to us, not to mention poor Lilla. He is practically engaged to her, you know."

Camile thought she might be sick again. A subtle cough turned her attention elsewhere. Gregory Kline stood at the doorway to the kitchen. She wondered how much he'd heard.

"Sorry to intrude," he said politely, his gaze roaming Camile. "You left the front door open, Margaret, and when you didn't return to bid me good night, I thought I should check on you. Is everything all right?"

"Everything is fine," she assured him. "I'm getting forgetful in my old age, but I'm glad you haven't left. Would you be so kind as to find Mrs. Langtry's friend and bring him here? A Hank Riley, waiting at the hotel where Mr. Langtry resides. You know it, don't you?"

"Yes. But for propriety's sake, wouldn't it be best if he stayed elsewhere?"

"Nonsense. I'll put him up in the cottage out back. The man is like a father to her."

"Then he would be an older gentleman," Kline pointed out. "What of your reputation, Margaret?"

She giggled. "I'm too old to have a reputation. You will collect him?"

"Of course." Gregory touched his hat in parting, then turned to Camile. "I would like a meeting with you tomorrow. These allegations you've brought against Mr. Langtry greatly disturb me."

"Why?" Camile asked bluntly. "Aren't you partners of sorts?"

"Of sorts," he agreed. "But I feel rather responsible for your plight, if indeed you speak the truth. I'm the one who convinced Wade to pursue the deed where I had failed. I certainly never suggested he do anything underhanded."

"In other words, you're trying to save your own skin," Camile said dryly.

"I'm trying to help you," he said less politely. "You do want your deed back, don't you?"

"She wouldn't be here if she didn't," Margaret injected.

263

Ronda Thompson

"The woman is exhausted from her journey, Mr. Kline. You can discuss this with her tomorrow."

"Until then." He tipped his hat in parting. "I will deliver Mr. Riley shortly. Good night, ladies."

He sneered slightly when his gaze met Camile's. She didn't like him. He reminded her of something scaly.

"Snake," she muttered when he left.

"I couldn't agree with you more," Margaret said. "Watch your back when dealing with the polite Gregory Kline. It's no secret he and Wade Langtry can't tolerate one another. I believe the reason is Lilla Traften. Maybe I should say her father's money. Gregory is a greedy man. He seldom does anything unless he benefits. Keep that in mind."

Camile's mind had turned to mush. She honestly believed she could sleep with her eyes open. "That bath," she reminded Margaret. "And a bed," she added wistfully.

"Come along." The woman helped her from her chair, steering her into another room and up a long stairway. "I'll have you settled in no time."

"Why are you being nice to me?" Camile asked.

Margaret appeared taken aback by her bluntness. "Because etiquette demands it," she blustered, then smiled. "The truth is, Mrs. Langtry—"

"Camile."

"The truth is, Camile, I haven't felt so alive in years as when you burst into that stuffy gathering and sent everyone screaming for their lives. I'm from Kansas," she whispered. "But no one here knows that. These people bore me to tears."

"Maybe you should move to Texas," Camile suggested. "We don't have many charm schools down my way."

"An interesting thought." Margaret smiled. "This Mr. Riley, he isn't by chance single, is he?"

She grinned back. "I ain't never met anyone more single than Hank."

Margaret appeared thoughtful, then frowned. "You haven't met anyone more single," she corrected. "I do so like a challenge," she mumbled, leading Camile up the stairs.

Later, bathed and tucked into bed, Camile stared at the ceiling. She assumed she'd fall asleep the moment her head hit the pillow, but worries plagued her. The racket downstairs and outside didn't help matters. She suspected Margaret was getting Hank settled. Camile closed her eyes. A face came to her unbidden.

Wade. Damn him, she hated the way her heart had lurched when she'd first spotted him in the crowd. It had taken her a minute to recognize him in his fine clothes. He'd looked like a regular gentleman. Handsome, more than handsome. But she preferred him in his hat and boots. She shouldn't prefer him in anything. She shouldn't be thinking of him with or without his clothes. Getting her deed back should be her only concern.

Still, she kept seeing him in her mind—kept recalling the feel of him, the taste and scent of him. His fingers on her skin. His lips on her neck. Camile's eyes opened abruptly. A hand clamped over her mouth.

"Hello, Camile."

She immediately tried to struggle up. Wade held her down.

"I just want to talk to you."

Her teeth found flesh.

"Dammit," he swore, jerking his hand from her mouth.

"Get off of me!" she growled. "You have nerve, Langtry. Sneaking in here. What did you do, gnaw a hole in the wall and crawl inside like the rat you are?"

"It wasn't that difficult. Margaret is showing Hank to the cottage out back. She left the door wide open. As for having nerve, you've got more than I do. You should have stayed in Texas."

"And done what? Bided my time until you sent someone to throw us off the ranch? You know me better."

"I should have figured you'd show up," he admitted huskily. "I forgot how stubborn you are. How well your body fits against mine. How good it feels to be inside of you."

Camile squirmed beneath him. She hated him, but her body obviously didn't agree. Her blood burned hot in her veins. Her senses were acutely aware of everything about the man on top of her. Aware also that he'd used her, deceived her, humiliated her.

"You'll have to count on your memory from now on," she said. "Get off of me, Langtry, and get out."

"I like your fire, Camile. I like all of you, except your sharp tongue and your scheming nature."

"You're a fine one to talk. You lied to me from the beginning. You never cared about being foreman. All you wanted was to convince my father to sell." Her fingers curled into claws. She was furious all over again.

As if he sensed a threat, Wade encircled her wrists and raised them above her head. "I guess we're cut from the same cloth. You did what you had to do. I did what I had to. Now it's over. I'll see that your father gets a fair price."

"I'll see you in Hell," she shot back. "I'm going to get my deed back, and like the last time, I'll do whatever it takes to win."

His fingers tightened around her wrists. "Would you?" he asked softly. "How bad do you want it, Camile?"

He had referred to the deed, hadn't he? She felt her heart beating against his. Felt the warmth of his mouth hovering above. Her breasts were aching. She suddenly couldn't think clearly.

"Bad enough to give yourself to me? Right here? Right now?"

"No," she managed to whisper. "Because I can't trust you to deliver your part of the bargain."

Softly, his lips brushed her ear. "Haven't I always delivered? If we don't belong with one another, we fit perfectly together. Ignorance was bliss, wasn't it?"

The jolt traveled to her toes when his mouth finally fastened upon hers. Camile wanted to surrender to the seductive timbre of his voice. She remembered the things he'd whispered to her when they shared a room at Rosie's—would never forget their first night in the line shack. Wade could be tender, or he could be rough, but either way, he was good. His deceit had also buried a knife in her heart.

Wade wasn't the man she thought him to be. Ignorance *had* been bliss, but she wasn't stupidly in love with him anymore. Camile twisted away, silently cursing the ragged sound of her breathing.

"No, Langtry. I learned my lesson the last time. You don't play fair."

"If you pursue this, I'll have no choice but to play dirty."

"I have no choice, either. You've backed me into a corner. I can cheat with the best of them."

"Maybe in Texas," he agreed. "You're a long way from home. You made a good impression on these people tonight. Storming a social gathering. Shooting a gun. They know me. They don't know you."

"I imagine by now, they're smart enough to figure they

don't know you as well as they thought. You didn't tell your fancy lady you already had a wife, did you?"

When he didn't answer immediately, Camile suspected it was her turn to cut him.

"I don't plan on having one for long," he said, twisting the knife he'd buried.

"That suits me. The quicker I leave you behind, the happier I'll be."

Amidst the tangle of their bodies, the heat rising between them, Camile knew war had been declared.

"Here's a little something to remember me by," he said.

He kissed her. She allowed him to delve into her mouth with his tongue. Even allowed his hands to slide down her arms and cup her swollen breasts. She couldn't allow him to bunch the nightgown Margaret had given her to wear over her legs. She knew what would follow. Her hands settled over his.

"Consider yourself forgotten," she told him.

He released her, rose from the bed, and walked away. The lamps burning in the hallway silhouetted his dark shape against her door.

"I let you win once," he said. "I won't make the same mistake again. Consider yourself warned."

Wade slipped into the shadows and disappeared as mysteriously as he'd appeared. Camile wondered for a moment if she'd dreamt him. No. She still felt the pressure of his mouth against hers—smelled his masculine scent. Still loved him—had to beat him at his own game. How, was still a matter very much undecided.

Chapter Twenty-three

Gregory Kline called late the next afternoon. Camile met with him in the parlor. She was scrubbed, combed, and wore clean clothes—her own—much to Margaret's disapproval.

The man eyed her buckskins and fringed jacket distastefully. "Mrs. Langtry—"

"Don't call me that," she told him quietly.

"Camile, is it?"

"Don't call me that, either."

"What should I call you?" he blustered.

"In a hurry. Say what you have to say and leave."

He promptly dropped his polite facade. "I admire a woman who doesn't mince words. I especially admire a woman who managed to get the best of Wade Langtry. You have no idea who you were dealing with."

"I had no idea at one time. Now, I know him for the snake-in-the-grass he is."

Gregory smiled. "Believe me. You still have no idea."

"What do you want?" Camile asked, the man already wearing on her nerves.

"Your ranch. I plan to help you get the deed back so you can sell to me."

She straightened in her chair. "Why would I do that?"

"Because I want you to."

The man was crazy. Camile laughed. "I have no intention of selling."

"But you will. Otherwise, I'll have to tell the man you just referred to as a snake-in-the-grass that he is going to be a father. If I recall, you didn't want Margaret passing the news along."

Her sarcastic humor fled. Gregory Kline had heard too much last night. "Are you blackmailing me?"

He smiled. "I'm rather good at it."

"And if you'll *recall,* I'm rather good with a bullwhip. A knife, too. I have a gun upstairs. I imagine at this range, it'd make a big hole in your chest."

"But killing me wouldn't make the stockholders sympathetic to your plight," he pointed out. "And you do have one. Langtry deceived you, used you, filled your belly with his child, stole your deed, then abandoned you. If you play your cards right, you can beat him."

"I don't need your help," she said. "I've played poker before."

"But I need yours. I want Langtry ruined. I want him run out of this town. I want—"

"Lilla Traften," she finished.

"Thanks to you, I consider her already mine. And more importantly, her father's fortune. My grudge against Langtry is personal. I don't like scum passing themselves

270

off as gentry. Now you, Camile, are at least genuine. Too genuine. We'll have to change that."

Having heard all she intended, Camile rose. "This meeting is over." She started from the room, but Kline grabbed her arm.

"Do you want me to tell him?" he asked.

She tried to act as if she didn't care. "Go ahead."

"You do realize once it's common knowledge you're carrying his child, no court in the country will sever the marriage. If there's no possibility of the marriage being dissolved, your property still becomes your husband's. See what a dilemma you're in?"

Camile swallowed. "I'd as soon Wade have the deed as you," she informed him.

"I tell you what. I'll let you keep the ranch if you'll ruin Langtry for me. I stand to forfeit a great investment if the Wagner Cattle Company can't obtain your property, but then, I'll have Lilla soon. I can stand to lose my money. Her father has an abundance."

"I get to keep the ranch?" Camile didn't trust Kline anymore than she trusted her husband. "If I ruin Wade?"

"Yes."

"How?"

Kline rubbed his hands together. "We'll talk about that later. The stockholders have already arrived. The hearing has been set for tomorrow, which doesn't leave us much time. Miles will be entertaining tonight. I will escort you to the affair. You—"

"Hold on a minute," Camile said. "I'm not going to no shindig."

A long sigh of irritation sounded from Gregory. "You must. I want everyone to see a different Camile Langtry

271

than the one who stormed Miles' social last evening. A less capable Camile. I will speak to Margaret. It seems the two of you have become fast friends. If she cares about your plight, she'll see that you arrive at Miles' home a changed woman."

Being bullied didn't set well with Camile. Nor did dragging Margaret Pendergraft into her troubles. "I am what I am, Mr. Kline. A fancy dress won't change that."

"It can't hurt," he insisted. "I'll pick you up at seven. If you want your secret to remain one, and if you want your ranch back, come dressed for the part. Good day."

Seething with helpless rage, Camile watched him leave the room. She heard him speaking with Margaret. Moments later, the woman appeared in the parlor.

"Mr. Kline has just informed me I am to make you presentable for a gala tonight. Have you thrown in your lot with him?"

"I guess he failed to mention he's blackmailing me. He said he'd tell Wade about the baby if I don't help him ruin him."

"And you don't think your husband deserves some grief for what he's done to you?" Margaret asked.

"I didn't say that, but we've been fighting our own battles from the beginning. I can't figure why Kline wants to stick his nose in my business. He's got a bone to pick with Wade, and he wants me to do the picking."

Margaret groaned. "Please do not mention nose and picking in sentences strung so closely together. Mr. Kline hasn't given me nearly enough time to turn you into a lady."

"I've never cared to be one. No offense to you, Margaret, but if that pale-shouldered, finger-crooking, silk-swishing Lilla Traften wasn't such a lady, Wade would have been sneaking into her bed last night instead of mine."

Her hostess gasped. "Do you mean to tell me Wade Langtry was here last night? Upstairs? In one of my bedrooms?" She fanned her face with her hands.

"He came to warn me. More or less said these people won't accept me."

"Did he? I mean, did the two of you . . . "

"We declared war on one another," Camile said, failing to mention that she and Wade had an odd way of doing battle.

"Hmm." Margaret eyed her up and down. "We're almost the same height, both slim, although my womanly curves have shifted. I think I can alter a few of my things for you. If it's a war your husband wants, we'll give him one."

Camile had done some damage. Wade felt curious gazes trained on him. Miles had invited him to his home. However, Wade suspected the only reason was because of his affiliation with the cattle company. The man didn't have much choice. Any discussion over the matter of the deed had been forbidden. This was strictly entertainment, and Wade admitted he was slightly amused.

Lilla hadn't spoken to him, but she'd been sneaking glances at him since his arrival. She wasn't at all like Camile. That hellcat would have marched right up and asked him point-blank why he'd married another woman. Of course, there was speculation going on. For the deed, he'd heard one group whisper. Because she probably pulled that gun on him and forced him, was another suggestion moving around the room.

That one would work to his advantage tomorrow. He

wasn't looking forward to a confrontation with Camile. At least not a public one. Their private arguments were another matter. He'd crept into Margaret's home to warn his wife, but once he saw her, felt her beneath him, inhaled her intoxicating scent, his thoughts had been ruled by the front of his pants.

She heated his blood like no other woman. Maybe the attraction stemmed from them being two of a kind. Ruthless. Lying. Stubborn. Determined. Beautiful . . . A woman had entered the ballroom. A vision. He craned his neck to see over the crowd, as did every man in the room. Conversation dwindled away.

Wade wedged his way through the crowd. The vision wore delicate lilac lace. The fabric hugged her womanly figure, displaying a fair amount of creamy bosom—seductive yet innocent. Short, glossy curls framed her angelic face. Her eyes were the color of a Texas sky, her lips petal pink. He knew the feel and taste of that mouth well. Damn Camile. What was she doing here? And why had she outfitted herself in full female armor?

"That can't be your wife," Miles commented beside him, his tone shocked. "Why, she's lovely."

"If you'd have looked closer last night, you'd already know that," Wade responded tightly.

Society people were strange. They couldn't seem to see past a person's clothing. Wade had seen past Camile's the first night he met her—seen beyond and beneath them since. Still, he responded to her much the same as he had the night she'd worn a gaudy red dress that left nothing to the imagination. Come to think of it, the dress she currently wore didn't, either. He supposed because the material was expensive, the cut wasn't considered indecent.

His hands balled into fists at his sides. He knew what every man in the room was thinking. They were thinking they'd like to get her out of that dress and into bed.

"I can't believe Gregory brought her here."

Wade tore his gaze from Camile, looking down into Lilla's pale features. She had subtly placed herself beside him. He hadn't noticed who Camile had arrived with, only that she'd walked into the room and managed to captivate everyone. And without a gun this time.

"I'm sure Kline is only doing his duty," he drawled. "You shouldn't be jealous, Lilla. Camile *is* a married woman."

Lilla blushed. "First your treachery, and now his. I'll be the laughingstock of St. Louis."

His gaze softened. "I never meant to hurt you, Lilla. To be truthful, I never loved you."

"Love isn't the point," she said under her breath. "Love has nothing to do with marriage. I wanted you because every single young woman in St. Louis wanted you. You were considered a good catch, and my father approved. That was enough."

Her declaration didn't make him angry. He'd wanted to marry Lilla because of what she represented. Respectability. Maybe because at one time, a woman of her station wouldn't have looked at him twice. If Camile had broken his heart, had filled him with a need for revenge, she'd taught him a lesson in love. What he'd wanted from Lilla wasn't enough—would never be enough.

"I hope someday you find out differently," he said.

She turned red again. "My God, Wade. You're in love with her. It wasn't nearly so bad when everyone assumed you were only after her deed, or that she'd somehow forced you into marriage, but if they realize you're actually enamored with that blond ruffian, I am totally humiliated. What could she possibly have that I don't?"

"At one time, I would have said fire," he answered, then smiled. "But it seems you have some spark to you after all. As for being in love with her, don't worry, Lilla, that will remain our little secret."

"It won't if you don't stop staring at her that way," she growled. "Your tongue is practically hanging out of your mouth."

He clamped his lips together as she stormed off. Camile was now surrounded by men. Conversation had thankfully resumed; otherwise, others besides Lilla might have heard him declare his feelings for his wife. Feelings that confused Wade. How could he still be attracted to her? After she'd used him, planned his downfall from the beginning, why did she still own a piece of his heart? A chunk of his soul? She put every woman in the room to shame. What made her all the more attractive was that Camile didn't know how beautiful she was—how irresistible.

Surrounded by admirers, men, he imagined, who weren't asking her how far she could throw . . . or spit, Camile appeared very uncomfortable. Wary of the attention she received. What was she doing here? And why was she with Gregory Kline? Wade intended to find out.

"You're doing fine," Gregory muttered, smiling and nodding to people as he guided Camile toward the refreshments.

She wanted to snatch her arm from his fingers. When he'd arrived at Margaret's home, he'd looked at her differently. Looked at her as if he'd never seen her before. It made her skin crawl. "I've had all of this I can stand," she mumbled. "Get me out of here."

"In due time," he said. "You've made quite an impression on most of the men gathered this evening." His gaze lowered to her partially exposed breasts. "Or I should say, that dress has. When you have a face and figure like yours, speaking more than two words isn't necessary in the company of men. The women, however—"

"I don't care about the women," Camile snapped. "Their opinion of me doesn't matter."

"A handful of the stockholders are from St. Louis. They'll go home with their wives tonight and discuss Camile Langtry. You must make a good impression on the women, as well. Appear frail, helpless, wronged. Prey on their female sensibilities."

Frail? Helpless? Camile couldn't—she wasn't that accomplished an actress. Still, she'd obviously done a good job of it when she'd convinced Hank and the others she'd planned Wade's seduction—though not for the reasons they all believed. The reasons Wade believed. She tried not to search for him among the crowd. When last she'd seen him, he'd been looking down into Lilla's pale features, his expression soft.

Unconsciously, Camile's fingers dug into Gregory's arm. Jealousy ripped through her. The thought of Wade touching another woman, whispering the things he'd whispered to her, drove her beyond reason. And she wasn't thinking rationally. The man had lied to her, used her, abandoned her. Why should she care what he did or with whom?

"Ladies, may I present Camile Langtry," Gregory said, pulling her into a small group of women.

The ladies immediately scattered. To her embarrassment, she and Gregory were left standing alone. Not totally. One woman remained. Camile sized her up. Lilla Traften sized Camile up.

"I assume introductions are unnecessary," Gregory said with a laugh.

Neither woman smiled.

"As hostess, Lilla, you are obligated to see that Camile is introduced among your guests," Gregory said.

"I don't recall my father inviting her," she responded stiffly.

"But he invited me," Gregory pointed out. "Camile is my guest."

Two bright spots of pink exploded in Lilla's cheeks. For a moment, Camile thought she looked as if she'd throw a temper tantrum; then a polite mask settled over her face.

"You are correct, Gregory. I won't cause more gossip by failing in my duties as hostess. Come along, Mrs. Langtry."

Camile's feet, stuffed inside a pair of Margaret's dainty shoes, refused to budge. Gregory gave her a forceful shove.

"Try to say as little as possible," he warned softly. "Just smile and nod."

She forced a fake smile on her lips, nodded, and followed Lilla into the crowd. The introductions did not go well. Wade had been right. She didn't fit in among these snobbish people. The women eyed her warily, said little to her, then promptly ignored her. Camile tried to be polite, even telling one woman her hat reminded her of a prairie chicken's nest. Her compliment sent the woman huffing away. Lilla had begun to look as if she was enjoying herself. Kline had deserted Camile, and she couldn't count on Wade to rescue her from this fiasco.

"I'd like to leave," she said to Lilla.

"But of course you would," she countered smugly. "I'll show you to the coat room to retrieve your wrap."

This time, Camile didn't hesitate to follow Lilla. She worked her way through the crowd, remembering to smile and nod, smile and nod. Once they entered the small coat room, Lilla said she'd locate Gregory and have him meet her there. Camile found her matching lace shawl. She couldn't wait to return to Margaret's comfortable home. To be honest, she couldn't wait to get back to Texas.

"Running scared?"

She wheeled around. Wade stood propped against the door of the coat room. She noted he'd closed it, blocking any escape. Her gaze drank in his handsome features. She smothered the emotions his nearness stirred.

"Margaret's shoes are killing me," she answered calmly. "I can't breathe in this dress."

"I can't breathe either. I've been waiting for you to fall out of the front of it all night."

She glanced down. "Margaret assured me it was decent."

"Maybe on Margaret."

He shrugged from the door and approached her. Camile fought the instinct to back away. She'd been ridden roughshod over since her arrival in St. Louis. Lilla Traften's snobby guests might send her running, but Wade wouldn't get the best of her. Even when he stood before her, thoughtfully eyeing her décolletage, she didn't cower.

"She doesn't have as much to pack into it." He frowned. "Come to think of it, I don't remember you being quite that endowed, either."

Draping her shawl around her shoulders, Camile hoped Wade wouldn't ponder her ripening figure too seriously—

he might arrive at the reason for her swollen breasts. "I've grown up in the last few months," she explained.

"But you haven't outgrown your scheming nature. What are you and Kline up to?"

"I don't know what you're suggesting," she answered, and it wasn't an out-and-out lie. Camile wasn't sure how Kline expected her to ruin Wade. "He thought I should meet the stockholders before tomorrow."

He smiled. "Was the disguise his idea, or yours?"

The small room seemed to be shrinking. Wade had moved closer. She was too aware of him as a man and too unaware of him as a lying, back-stabbing opportunist.

"I'll do what I have to do to win, Wade. You know that about me. But at least I'm fighting this battle for honest reasons. I'm fighting for my home. What's your reason? Greed?"

"You couldn't understand my reasons. You would have had to have lived my life. See what I've seen. Fought my demons. Your need for the ranch might stem from a love of the land, but mine stems from desperation. Remember that tomorrow."

He turned toward the door. Camile could breathe again, although her heart felt trapped in her throat. Tomorrow, whatever the outcome, the battle between her and Wade would end. One of them would become the victor, but both of them would go on with their lives. Separate lives. The realization lowered her spirits.

"Slipping off to the coat room with the very man you've brought allegations against wasn't a wise move."

Gregory had arrived. Camile clutched her wrap around her tightly. She wished Margaret would have come with them. The woman had begged off so Hank wouldn't be left alone. Something odd was going on between those two. If Camile didn't know better, she might suspect they were sweet on each other.

"I didn't slip off with him," Camile finally responded. "He cornered me. He wants to know what we're up to."

Kline smiled. "I'm sure he does." He retrieved his coat and hat. "And you must be curious as to how we're going to ruin him. Although I'm greatly disappointed in your efforts this evening, we do need to discuss my plans for tomorrow. Has Margaret found you something suitable to wear to the meeting?"

"Black," she whispered. "I'm wearing black."

"Fitting," Kline agreed. "After we behead Langtry in front of the stockholders, you can consider yourself a widow." He took her cold hand and placed it on his arm. "It's time to sharpen the ax."

Chapter Twenty-four

Her toes were no longer crammed inside Margaret's shoes, but Camile felt far from comfortable. She and Gregory were alone in the parlor. Although she'd tucked her bare feet beneath the hem of her dress, she couldn't hide the amount of flesh her gown exposed. A fair amount that Gregory Kline seemed to have trouble ignoring.

"You were saying?" she reminded when he kept staring.

"Ah, yes, back to business, although I must say, you look fetching in that gown. I never really looked at you before tonight. I'm not certain exposing all your womanly charms was to our advantage. It might make one wonder who took advantage of whom."

"You don't really care, do you?"

He smiled. "How well you've come to know me, and in such a short time."

She shrugged. "I know a snake when I see one."

His face turned an angry shade of red. "And here I thought we were partners. Might possibly become more than business associates before the night's end."

Camile stiffened when his gaze raked her meaningfully. "You thought wrong. I'm tired. Let's get this over with."

He laughed sarcastically. "You balk at my advances when the man whose child you carry is nothing more than a killer?"

If he expected her to answer, Camile didn't know what to say. Wade had killed two men. Both out of self-defense. How could Kline know about that? Gregory nodded sadly, as if he mistook her confusion for shock. He opened the valise he'd carried into the house, removed a sheet of paper, and handed it to her. Wade's face stared back at her from a wanted poster. He wore a beard and his hair was longer, but it was Wade.

"Wade is a wanted man?" she whispered, stunned.

"Unfortunately, no. The poster was a ruse to gain him entrance into a gang of outlaws. Wade Langtry was a bounty hunter who went by the name 'The Wolf.'"

Camile had heard of him. His quickness with a gun was legendary. She couldn't see Wade in the role. Hired guns didn't teach women to make biscuits. They didn't save lives, they took them. Even as her mind tried to reject the glaring truth staring up from the wanted poster, Camile recalled his grace with a gun. The way he surveyed a room when he entered, always alert. He was a man with a past; maybe she'd known that about him instinctively. She just hadn't known how much of a past.

"He's killed a lot of men," she said quietly, mostly to herself. "Men who deserved killing."

"And one who didn't," Gregory added. "When he first

283

arrived in St. Louis, I thought I knew him from some-where. As time passed, I assumed I was mistaken. After all, he can be quite deceiving, can't he?"

"What do you mean, one who didn't?" Camile demanded, ignoring the statement.

Gregory sighed, then joined her on the settee. "I'm get-ting to that." He patted her arm. "Be patient."

She moved as far from him as possible. "Patience isn't one of my strong suits. I'm at my rope's end with you. I see where this is leading. No one in St. Louis but you, and now me, knows about Wade's past. You want me to make cer-tain they find out."

"You're a smart girl."

"Not very. I can't figure out why you need me. Why don't *you* tell everyone?"

"There's a small matter of blackmail involved," Gregory whispered conspiratorially. "I didn't get the goods on Langtry until after I returned from Texas. Part of me wanted desperately to expose him, and part of me under-stood a man of his talents could prove useful. If he got that deed, and by any means necessary, I agreed to keep his secret."

"And I suppose you're a man of your word?" Camile's tone held sarcasm.

"No," he answered. "I'm a man who doesn't want to be on the receiving end of Wade's gun. If I told, he might pos-sibly shoot me, but you—"

"What makes you think he won't shoot me?" she demanded.

Gregory scooted closer to her. "Because after watching him tonight, I believe Langtry has a soft spot for you."

Camile knew exactly where the spot was, and it wasn't

soft. Once, she'd thought desire and love were the same thing. Now, she knew differently.

"You can say you came by the knowledge accidentally," Gregory continued. He lifted his valise, dumped a stack of papers on the floor, then placed the wanted poster on top. "Dear me," he exclaimed. "I've dropped my private papers."

She was not amused by his antics. Camile felt ill. Wade worming his way into her life for deceitful purposes wasn't the worst of his sins. Men like him were usually considered animals. No better than the prey they hunted. This disturbing development should make her blood run cold, her heart harden against him. Instead, she felt tears gathering. She saw him as a starving boy, one with no family, no one to turn to—nothing but a gun. No wonder he didn't want to discuss his past.

"He could have just as easily walked the wrong side of the law," she said.

Gregory's mouth fell open. "You're defending him? After all he's done to you? All he plans to do to you tomorrow? Are you daft?"

The tears threatening to mist her eyes were blinked back. Camile straightened. "In Texas, if we don't welcome his kind with open arms, we respect them, and respect them plenty when we need help. We fight for every inch of ground we have. For our cattle, we battle wolves, coyotes, snowstorms, and the worst predator, rustlers. A friend of my father's had a problem three years ago. He tried to locate The Wolf to solve it for him. Word was, the gunman had dropped out of sight. Retired. He tried to leave it behind. Build a respectable life—"

"Respectable?" Kline blustered. "His kind don't deserve

a respectable life. He used his blood money to buy himself a place in this town. He used Miles Traften to gain valuable information about investing, and he used his daughter to settle himself in deeper. To maintain his facade of respectability!"

"And you used him." Camile stood, her anger mounting. "You blackmailed him, and now you want to stab him in the back!"

"No, that's your job," he sneered, also rising. "Unless you want to lose your ranch. Possibly lose more. He could take the child away from you, although I doubt he would give a damn about it. Langtry has no love for children. I know. I saw him shoot one."

Her hand flew to her mouth. "You're lying. Wade wouldn't—"

"He did," Gregory interrupted. "One night in Atlanta. That's where I once knew him. I was there on business, drinking at a local saloon. He was there, too. We both left the establishment at the same time. I remember standing on the sidewalk outside, breathing in the night air. Langtry headed past an alley next to the saloon. I heard a gun cock, then saw him wheel around and shoot. The supposed gunman he killed was a twelve-year-old boy."

Bile rose in her throat. Camile clamped her hands over her ears. Gregory pried them away and continued.

"Langtry was cleared because there were other witnesses. People who heard the gun cock. That boy had come to kill The Wolf—kill him for killing his father a month before. He was the son of a man who had tried to rob the local bank. Unfortunately for the man, Langtry was inside when he shot a clerk."

"Then the man was an outlaw," Camile said shakily.

"No. Only a poor man trying to feed his starving family. He did, however, murder the clerk, which I suppose warranted his death. I doubt Langtry lost any sleep over killing the father, but the son, the sight of that boy, brought him to his knees. I was rather fascinated by the scene. A hardened killer weeping over the worthless son of a worthless man. Maybe he looked down at the boy and saw what he himself had become. I don't know, but he'll never redeem himself. Not in my eyes, and not in this town's. Not after everyone learns the truth."

When Camile's head began to spin, she had no choice but to sit. She stared blankly ahead, her thoughts a jumbled mess. The truth sickened her, saddened her, confused her. She should feel repulsion for Wade and what he'd done, but instead, she felt compassion and pity. What a burden he carried, and how well she understood the price of impulsiveness. She'd paid it at the age of eight—was still paying.

Her fingers moved protectively to her stomach. Would Wade try to take the child to punish her for the crimes he believed she'd committed against him? She thought she knew him once, and now she realized in subtle ways he'd tried to tell her about himself—tried to warn her. She hadn't listened. Her heart had trusted him—loved him—believed in him.

"Why is my ranch so important?" she asked.

"The only steady source of water runs through your property. Although you've been generous to the other ranchers in the area, you might not be as generous to us. If you wanted, you could dam the river and force everyone else out."

"We wouldn't do that," she assured him.

"We can't gamble on your good will. The company has

Ronda Thompson

already purchased a great deal of land in the area. Without yours, it could prove useless. Langtry knows that. Unfortunately, so do the others. You must be very convincing tomorrow. Understand?"

Could she sacrifice Wade for the ranch? No. The ranch itself wasn't the reason. She must sacrifice him for her father's sake, for Hank and Jinx, who were too old to gain employment elsewhere. For her child. She came to get the deed. She came because she felt used, humiliated—had wanted revenge. But still, she'd never meant to totally ruin Wade. Greed never drove him. Security, a chance to leave his past behind—that was what drove him.

"Kline, you let me handle it the way I see fit at the meeting. Maybe there won't be any call to bring up Wade's past."

He reached for his hat, picked up the documents, and turned a cold stare on her. "A secret for a secret. I don't want him to show his face in this town again. Let him win, and I'll tell him your secret. Then where will you be? He'll not only have control of the ranch, but of you, as well. I know your type. You don't want him under those circumstances."

She hung her head in defeat. "Kline, Hank Riley's always saying what goes around comes around. I hope in your case, it's true."

"I'll be there to guide you tomorrow," he said, shuffling toward the door. "Don't disappoint me."

"I won't," she whispered, slumping back against Margaret's dainty settee. Wade The Wolf? She still couldn't believe it of him. *"I draw like a man who's had to do it to survive."* He'd said that once. What a nasty business survival could be. And how obsessive a dream.

His dream didn't stem from a love of money, but from a need for security. A need to distance himself from his past. As a boy, he'd dragged himself up from poverty by whatever means available. Could she judge him? Could anyone who hadn't lived the life he'd lived, seen the things he'd seen, fought the demons he'd fought?

A tear slid down her cheek; then she began to weep in earnest. Camile cried because she lacked the courage to tell him she carried his child. She wept for all that might have been, and all that would never be. But mostly, she cried over what she must do to him tomorrow.

The stockholders of the Wagner Cattle Company gathered in the home of Miles Traften. The study seemed the most appropriate place, easily accommodating thirteen men and the woman they were expecting. Only after a good number of St. Louis's respected ladies encroached upon the proceedings—claiming poor Camile deserved support—did the meeting move to the ballroom.

Wade suspected the ladies insisted for no such reason. They came because they wanted to be entertained. And he supposed he and Camile were at least that—entertaining. They were both out to fool the good people of St. Louis. Both out to win. Wade wasn't certain what strategy to use in order to ensure his victory. He counted on Camile drawing first blood. He also counted on her to get herself into trouble. At that, she never failed.

A hush fell over the noisy group when she entered. Wade had to give her credit. Camile was dressed in black taffeta. Her hair curled attractively around her face, a face made paler by the darkness of her gown. She looked soft, delicate, helpless—everything he knew she wasn't. He'd abandoned his facade of respectable gentleman for the meeting, wearing his comfortable cowboy garb.

He couldn't fight in restrictive clothing. And he figured this might turn into an all-out range war. Hank Riley and Margaret Pendergraft stood behind Camile. Both sent a glare in Wade's direction before finding seats among the spectators.

When Gregory Kline escorted Camile to a chair among the stockholders, the gentlemen rose, a gesture of respect. Wade figured it was a good thing he was already standing. Her cool blue eyes met his from across the room. He rolled his gaze upward, letting her know he didn't buy her act for a moment. Her lack of response bothered him. There was no fire in her. None of the anticipation he'd expected for the upcoming battle. He noticed the dark circles beneath her eyes. Maybe the dress alone wasn't responsible for her waxen complexion.

Wade became alarmed. Was she ill? His gaze darted toward Kline. Had that snake touched her? He relaxed, immediately dismissing the possibility. Gregory Kline was a man of small stature, reed-thin, with very little spine. Camile would make fast work of him.

Another possibility surfaced. Camile didn't think she could win. She'd given up before the battle began. Again, he dismissed his notion. Camile Cordell . . . Langtry, the Prickly Pear of the Panhandle, never gave up. It wasn't in her nature.

"Gentlemen . . . and ladies," Gregory Kline called over the noise that erupted once Camile was seated. "Shall we get the proceedings under way?" When murmurs of approval followed, he turned to Wade. "Mr. Langtry, would you like to begin?"

He didn't respond. Not until the women quieted. "Normally, 'ladies first' is the rule," Wade answered, pleased when Camile's gaze snapped up. "But I'll let her start all the same." The spark he'd expected to ignite in Camile's eyes failed to appear. She nodded.

"Gentlemen," she said softly. "As I'm sure you've been made aware, Wade Langtry professes claim to a deed—"

"Speak up!" Wade interrupted. "For Christ's sake, the woman's normal tone of voice is a shout. I can't hear a word she's saying."

"Mr. Langtry," Gregory warned. "Please refrain from any attempts to frighten your wife. Mrs. Langtry, could you please speak a little louder—we're having trouble hearing you."

"I'm sorry," Camile said.

Wade felt a measure of relief when a degree of emotion registered in her face. Although why she'd been looking at him when she apologized, and why she looked so truly honest, puzzled him.

"Gentlemen," she began again. "Wade Langtry came to the Circle C Ranch under the guise of a foreman. He never made my father an offer for our ranch, or tried to negotiate a sale, and that in itself indicates he meant to use deceitful practices to obtain my deed."

Feminine as well as masculine heads turned toward Wade. After a moment, he realized a response was expected from him.

"While her claim is true enough, I had good reason to keep my identity and my purpose for being at the Circle C a secret. Gregory Kline can attest to the fact that Camile, then Cordell, ran him off the Circle C with a bullwhip when he tried to approach her father about selling."

Wade paused for effect. A gasp issued, quickly stifled by the offender's hand.

"I believe the woman under discussion made a rather crude remark the night she stormed this very room waving a gun," Wade continued, "verifying she'd met Mr. Kline before."

"Maybe the remark should be repeated for the benefit of those not present at the affair," a stockholder suggested.

Wade watched all heads swing back to Camile.

"I don't recall the remark," she mumbled, seemingly more intrigued with fondling the seed pearls on her black dress than with the proceedings.

"Mr. Kline?" Wade asked.

"I don't recall the remark, either," he said uncomfortably.

Pushing away from the wall, Wade approached the stockholders. "I believe Mr. Kline rose from the floor and asked if she remembered him. She then told him to turn around and let her see his yellow-livered butt running for the hills and she'd know for sure."

"Oh, my," a female whispered.

"Were those your words?" the stockholder asked, flustered.

"I believe they were," Camile admitted without emotion.

Gregory Kline joined Wade, addressing the stockholders. "Mrs. Langtry's been known to have bouts of protectiveness concerning the Circle C that are not always . . . rational. I most certainly never feared her. If I thought the Cordells were dangerous, I wouldn't have asked Mr. Langtry to speak with them on our behalf again."

Miles frowned, but appeared accepting of Gregory's assurances. "Mrs. Langtry, would you explain how Mr. Langtry came to be in possession of the deed and why you think you were wronged? Mrs. Langtry, did you hear the question?"

Camile glanced up from plucking at the seed pearls of her gown. What had Miles Traften asked? Her mind wandered, recalling the day when she'd ridden the buckskin. How Wade had made the comment about "ladies first." How had he come by the deed? That was the question asked.

"I believe that's obvious," she answered. "He married me, securing legal title to my property."

"I thought the Circle C belonged to your father," Miles said.

"My father transferred the deed after an accident left him crippled. I wasn't aware he'd done so until my father's lawyer informed me of the transfer the morning after the wedding. The same morning Wade Langtry presented him with our marriage certificate and demanded the deed."

"And you, Mr. Langtry?" Gregory turned toward Wade. "Were you aware the deed had been transferred to Camile Cordell?"

"Yes," he answered stiffly. "Tom Cordell told me as much the first day I arrived at the Circle C."

A grumble from the spectators erupted, quickly silenced by a glare from Kline. When he turned back to Wade, he smiled. "Did you deliberately set out to marry Camile Cordell, thus ensuring ownership of the Circle C?"

In the silence that followed, Camile abandoned her pearls to look up at Wade. His gaze scanned the stockholder's faces before moving over the spectators, then settling on her.

"When the wedding was decided, and not by me, I asked her to shoot me. Does that sound willing?"

293

Ronda Thompson

Lilla Traften giggled. Margaret Pendergraft sat within elbowing distance of the woman, and elbowed her with force. When Lilla's giggle turned into an unfeminine grunt of surprise, Camile almost smiled.

"If you didn't wish to marry Camile Cordell, please explain how it came about that you did," Gregory pressed Wade.

"That's one you should ask Camile. The ladies present may wish to retire before she answers."

His suggestion, Camile noted, put glue to the spectators' chairs. Not one woman left the room. Her stomach began to knot up. This was the part she dreaded. The part where lying was a necessary evil. Camile took a deep breath.

"Wade Langtry seduced me," she said quietly.

Chapter Twenty-five

"What?" Wade shouted.

"Mr. Langtry, please!" Miles Traften warned. "I'm sorry, Mrs. Langtry, we failed to hear you again. Repeat it, please."

"Yes, please do," Wade demanded, storming across the room to stand before her. "I surely didn't hear you correctly."

She couldn't look at him, didn't want to see the shock she knew would be etched on his features. Damn him. How many times had he said any woman who'd cheat at cards would lie, too? "I said, 'Wade Langtry seduced me,' " she repeated loud enough to cause mayhem.

"Ladies!" Gregory Kline warned the raised voices. When order returned, he regarded Wade with a smug smile. "Mr. Langtry, have you something to add?"

"I'm afraid I do." His deep tone raised gooseflesh on Camile's arms. "It appears my wife and I clearly have a

295

difference of opinion as to which of us was the seduced and which the seducer."

"Would you care to elaborate?" Gregory asked impatiently.

"I'm afraid I would." He walked away from Camile and approached the stockholders. "In my opinion, when a woman strips naked and forces a man to look at her while pointing a gun at him, and then goes a step further and orders him to shuck his clothes, as well, it's pretty clear the woman was the one who started it!"

"Oh, dear!"

Margaret Pendergraft's exclamation started a buzz of female voices. Gregory Kline turned pale before he shouted for order.

"Mr. Langtry, what are you suggesting?" he demanded.

The rumble of noise came to a sudden halt. Camile swore half the ladies leaned forward in their chairs.

Wade's jaw muscle began to twitch. "I'm saying Camile Cordell got what she asked for. What she'd been asking for from the day I set foot on the Circle C. She had plans. I'm the one who was seduced, not her."

"Plans?" Gregory blustered. "While your motive for seducing Mrs. Langtry is evident to all, I don't see why she would—"

"I didn't see it, either," Wade interrupted. "Not until her plan backfired on her and got us married. She's the one who should be on trial. Not me."

Gregory's smug expression had faded. He looked desperate. "That is your opinion, Mr. Langtry. Your word against hers. I—"

"I have a witness," Wade interrupted. He smiled at Kline. "I'd like Hank Riley to stand."

A gasp exploded from Margaret Pendergraft. Hank Riley slowly lumbered to his feet, staring at Camile as if she might just blurt out what he should say or do. She inwardly groaned. Hank was as honest as the day was long. It wasn't in his nature to lie—not even for her. Anger brought Camile to life.

"Leave Hank out of this," she said to Wade. "We've always fought our own battles."

"And I've told you I don't always fight fair," he responded quietly, then turned toward Hank. "Hank, tell everyone what Camile said that morning outside of the line shack."

The witness glanced nervously at Camile, at Margaret, then finally decided on his feet. Hank played with the hat clutched between his hands and cleared his throat several times. Camile expected someone to suggest getting a rope if he didn't say something soon.

"Mr. Riley, will you please explain how you came to be what Wade Langtry calls a witness, and what it was you heard?" Miles insisted.

"Well," Hank started, and a gush of relieved breaths followed that simple word. "How I came to be there is a long story. Camile and me got banned from the drive on account of a run-in Camile had with this feller named Jim Cummings. We was at Rosie's, that's a combination cantina and whorehouse." Hank stopped abruptly, his face turning red. He glanced around him. "Excuse me for being so blunt, ladies."

"Just go on!" Lilla Traften bellowed.

The cowhand nodded. "Anyway, Langtry stopped Cummings before he got too far with Camile, and beat the bastard senseless. Then Wade told her daddy about what had

happened and got me and Camile banned from the drive."
Hank's face was turning blue. "I've got to catch my breath,
so nobody yell at me!"

No one dared. Camile began her plucking again. She
thought she heard the toe of Wade's boot tapping impatiently against the marble floor.

"Cam didn't take being hobbled too well," Hank went
on. "She and Langtry had this competition going, both
having to top each other so Wade could keep the foreman
job, or Camile would get control of the ranch. So Cam runs
off and joins up with the drive."

"Do you think we could get to the part about the line
shack?" Gregory interrupted, receiving a glare from all for
doing so.

"I'm getting to that," Hank assured him. "Cam handed
just fine from what Grady told me, but then one night
women visited the campsite and men got distracted. Cam
and Wade was in a wagon doing what nobody knows for
sure, except Cam dressed up like a wh—woman to rile
Langtry, and I guessed it worked. Then these three no-
goods, Jim Cummings being one and Lenny, this scum
Cam cut up one time—"

"Mr. Riley," Gregory warned. "Please get on to the part
about the line shack."

"Mr. Kline, please stop interrupting!" a woman shouted.
She nodded at Hank to continue.

"Lenny's partner, Sam, was in on it too and they took
Cam. Clubbed Wade over the head, cut him up like he is, and
took off with her while every man was otherwise distracted."

"Oh, dear." Margaret gasped as if caught up in a tale she
was afraid would end badly even if the victim sat not three
feet away, plucking the seed pearls from her dress.

"Yeah," Hank agreed. "I, being at the ranch, didn't know all this trouble was going on. Tom decided me and Jinx should meet up with the drive in Dodge and bring Cam home. When we ran into Grady and he told us, it turned me plumb sick. He said Wade was out tracking her and it didn't take long to find the bodies. I wasn't sure how many was in on it, so when I busted into that line shack, I didn't know what I'd find. I found—"

Lilla Traften chose that moment to engage in a fit of sneezing. She was promptly clubbed over the head with a purse by the lady sitting beside her.

"You found?" Miles prompted.

"I found them," Hank said. "You know . . . together?"

Margaret Pendergraft began fanning herself, and Miles Traften mopped his forehead with a starched handkerchief. Camile found she'd plucked more than half the pearls from her dress and they were scattered all over the floor.

"Now, will you please tell them what she said when you threatened to hang me?" Wade insisted.

Hank sought solace in his boots again. "She said we couldn't hang him 'cause she forced him."

A storm broke open within Miles Traften's ballroom.

"But I don't believe her!" Hank shouted over the noise. "At first, I thought she might pull a stunt like that on account I said once if the two of them ever got caught doing what they weren't supposed to be doing, Wade would get run off the ranch, and no decent man would want to marry her, which was fine by Cam. But then later, I didn't think that no more."

"Why?" Gregory pounced upon a crumb of saving evidence.

"I been thinking on it a while. I don't reckon Cam would

299

go to those lengths for the ranch. She might for matters of the heart, but not for the ranch."

"Christ!" Wade ground between his teeth. "The man's like a father to her. You don't think he'd want to believe she's capable of whoring her body for a piece of dirt, do you?"

Camile stiffened. Wade obviously believed she could, and once, that had suited her. It didn't anymore. She knew his reasons now. Why he'd done what he had. But he didn't know hers. She couldn't tell him she loved him, not when he didn't feel the same. She couldn't throw herself on his mercy and beg him to let her keep the ranch for the sake of their child. That left her one option. To finish what she'd started.

"We've heard his side," Gregory said. "Mr. Riley only witnessed the morning after and nothing firsthand of Langtry's ridiculous claims. I think Mrs. Langtry should tell us her side of what truly happened that night in the line shack."

Wade's movement caught her eye as he returned to lean against the wall again. He settled himself, crossing his arms over his chest while fixing her with his intense green eyes.

"Mrs. Langtry, have you nothing to say in your defense!" Gregory demanded rather than asked.

Deliberately, Camile stared back at Kline blankly, enjoying his discomfort. She nodded. "You must first understand the kidnapping left me in shock. Then the ordeal with the river further weakened my spirit. You see, the rain caused it to rise. Wade almost drowned and I had to save him."

"I believe it was the other way around," Wade countered.

"All right," she amended. "First he tried to save me, then

I had to save him, then I guess it was his turn again. The point is, the effort it took to pull ourselves from the current drained my will and left me shaken."

"You had to save Mr. Langtry's life?" Miles asked.

"More than once," she answered, searching for more pearls to pluck.

Gape-mouthed spectators turned their attention toward Wade.

"I saved her just as many times as she saved me," he offered flatly. "Camile enjoys a good contest."

She abandoned her pearls. "If it was truly being judged as a contest, you'd have lost because your rescues were, for the most part, only an interruption to possible danger and not out-and-out life-and-death circumstances."

Wade pushed away from the wall, the muscle in his jaw twitching again as he approached her. "I've gotten you out of more fixes than I can remember. If memory serves me, none of them were minor!"

"Maybe." Camile shrugged. "If I hadn't roped you before you went over the bluff, you'd definitely be dead. If I hadn't placed myself at your back while Sam held a gun trained on you, you might or might not have been fast enough to outdraw him. But if I hadn't jumped in the river and pretended I couldn't get out without your help, you would have drowned!"

"Mrs. Langtry." Gregory broke the stare-down between the two. "This is all quite fascinating, but you've led us away from the original purpose of deciding what in truth took place in the line shack. That is the issue, and not which of you is the more adequate at rescue."

"I'd say we're evenly matched," Camile said softly.

"No," Wade argued. "Rosie warned me the first night I

301

laid eyes on you, you didn't fight fair. I should have remembered that and refused to listen to the part of me that wanted to believe your scheming lies. There are some things a man can't fight. You used that against me."

Camile flinched. He didn't look angry. He looked hurt. His expression confused her. If he only cared about the deed, if he'd only been angry because she'd made a fool of him, why did she see the same pain reflected in his eyes she'd seen in her own? The pain of losing more than land or money? The pain of losing someone you loved? The stockholders as well as the spectators were suddenly forgotten.

For Camile, there were only the two of them and the ranch be damned. She wouldn't have him thinking she'd used herself for any purpose other than the sharing of love.

"You were right not to trust me at first," she admitted. "The ranch and proving myself to my father meant everything to me. But later, after we got to know each other, you could have told me, Wade. You could have told me the night in the line shack and I would have listened. I know who you were, what drove you to do this."

The softness that crept into Wade's eyes hardened. His gaze flew to Gregory Kline. "You son of a bitch! You told her!"

"I never told her," Gregory said, turning pale. "I don't know what you're suggesting. Mrs. Langtry, maybe you'd better explain what you mean concerning your husband's reasons."

Camile tried to hold Wade's stare, but he walked away, returning to lean against the wall. His face said it all. His past was about to catch up with him.

"Mrs. Langtry?" Gregory prompted.

The ranch, Camile reminded herself. The baby. But it

was no good. Nothing seemed as important as keeping Wade's secret. Proving to him she could be trusted. It had dwindled down to choices. She knew the one that must be made.

"I've said all I intend to say, Mr. Kline," she said with steady resolve. "The stockholders will have to make a decision based on what they've been told."

"Mrs. Langtry, you surely have something of importance to add!" Gregory insisted, a panicked edge to his voice. He leaned in close to her. "Or would you prefer I did the talking?"

"This discussion is over." Wade's voice made all heads turn toward his direction. "I retract my claim to the deed. No one belongs on that ten-thousand-acre stretch of Hell more than Camile Cordell. It's hers."

Stunned, Camile watched him approach her. "Now we're even, again," he said, placing the Stetson over his dark head and, for all appearances, looking as if he intended to leave.

"Wade," Camile whispered weakly.

"Langtry, I think you and I should have a few words," Gregory Kline said, glaring at Camile.

"If you have the guts, Kline, come speak to me at the Lucky Lady, where I intend to get good and drunk while I can still afford it. It's over as far as I'm concerned."

"Langtry!" Gregory called.

"Stop!" Lilla Traften rose. It wasn't Wade Langtry the brunette leveled her gaze upon. A fortunate choice, since he never paused before leaving the room.

"It's over as far as I'm concerned, too, Gregory. With him." Lilla nodded toward the empty doorway. "And with us. Today made me realize how wrong Wade and I were for each other. How wrong you and I are for each other. I never knew him, not really. I liked the way he looked and the way the other women envied me, but I never loved him." Her dark gaze settled on Camile. "Not like she obviously does. And he didn't love me. Not the way—"

"Lilla," Gregory warned. "We'll discuss this later."

"No," she insisted. "I owe her an apology for my behavior last night. We all do. I didn't know what love was until I heard their story. I want a man who truly loves me. One who would risk everything for me. That man isn't you, Gregory. And he isn't Wade Langtry. Camile has won more than her ranch. He told me last night that he—"

"That he what?" Kline pressed. "That he not only deceived her, but he fooled the rest of us?" His face became an evil mask. "Did he tell you who he was—"

"Kline," Camile warned. "Do you want to admit you blackmailed him into getting the deed? Or that you tried to blackmail me, too?"

"What's this talk about blackmail?" Miles Traften asked, moving into the circle. He glanced between Gregory and Camile expectantly.

"Nothing," Kline said, lowering his gaze.

"I certainly hope not," Miles countered. "The stockholders and I have a proposition for Mrs. Langtry. I want her to know that we're trustworthy and if there is one among us she doesn't trust to deal with her fairly, the obstacle will be removed. Do you consider Mr. Kline an obstacle, Mrs. Langtry?"

She smiled. "I'm not sure. Are you going to be a problem, Mr. Kline?"

Gregory's face paled. "No."

"Then let us have our meeting," Miles suggested.

"Excuse me, Mrs. Langtry. Gregory, help me escort the other ladies from the room."

Frustration clearly stamped upon his features, Gregory followed Miles toward the women. Hank and Margaret rushed forward.

"You won," Margaret said, hugging her. "You have your ranch back."

Camile stared blankly over Margaret's shoulder. "I didn't beat him," she whispered. "He let me win. That bastard gave up!"

"Cam," Hank said with a sigh. "You two have been butting heads since you first laid eyes on each other. Langtry did the right thing. He let it go. Maybe it's time you did, too. Why don't you call things even and quit?"

She opened her mouth to argue, but Miles rejoined them, indicating the waiting stockholders with a sweep of his hand.

"Shall we? Oh, and I'd like you to stay, also, Mr. Riley."

Business be damned, Camile wanted to speak to Wade. And as soon as she concluded her meeting with the stockholders, she would. It wasn't over yet between them, not by a far stretch.

Chapter Twenty-six

Camile's knees were shaking when she entered the Lucky Lady. She had dressed in her comfortable buckskins and fringed jacket again. It took her eyes a moment to adjust from light to dark. The usual smoke hung in the air, the usual smell of liquor, but not the usual sound of loud voices. This was a tamer atmosphere than Rosie's.

A sudden halt of muted voices assured her she'd been noticed. Camile scanned the faces staring at her curiously. The man she came to see stood at the bar, his back to her. When Camile approached Wade, he didn't turn, but continued to sip the contents of the shot glass he held.

"This isn't Texas, hellcat," he said before she reached him. "Decent women aren't allowed inside the saloons."

"I don't know why," Camile countered. "I've seen Sunday socials livelier than this poor excuse for a watering hole."

Her observation brought a scowl of disapproval from the man behind the bar. "Mr. Langtry, would you like to have this woman shown out?" he inquired indignantly.

Wade lifted a brow. "If you want to take on the Prickly Pear of the Panhandle, be my guest, Jacob."

The man's dark eyes rounded. "Sorry, ma'am. You can stay as long as you don't shoot anyone."

"I've decided I'm too hotheaded to wear a gun." Camile placed Wade's Colt on the counter. "I'm returning this."

He frowned. "Figure I'll need it?"

She shrugged. "Your secret is still safe. Kline's been hobbled. I told Miles he blackmailed you, but he wasn't interested in the details. He was more interested in cutting a deal with me."

"You sold out?" he asked, turning to look at her.

"Sort of."

"How do you sort of sell out?"

"I made an agreement with the stockholders. I sold my water rights for a large portion of stock in the company. The ranch is mine. I just own a portion of the water rights."

Wade studied her, almost as if he were memorizing every line, every groove, every inch of her. "I have to hand it to you, that was a smart move."

"Why did you hand it to me?" Her eyes locked with his. "It wasn't like you to quit while you were ahead."

He turned back to his drink, not bothering to bring the glass to his lips, but merely swirling the gold liquid around the glass. "It's what you expected, wasn't it? You offered me a deal. Your silence and my reputation for the ranch?"

"I don't remember making any deals. I wanted you to know I could play fair."

"You lied. You sat there and said I seduced you. I can't

307

count that as playing fair. I suspected you only hesitated to give me time to make my choice before you dropped the ax on my neck."

"What if I would have?" Camile asked, then lowered her voice. "So what if you earned your living the hard way when life was hard? You learn from your past mistakes. You don't let them eat your insides away, and you can't run from them."

The glass in his hand hit the counter with enough force to splash whiskey over Jacob's spotless bar. Wade pulled her toward a secluded corner. Heads turned, but the distance allowed Wade and Camile privacy for at least words.

"I killed a kid, Camile," he said hoarsely. "A twelve-year-old boy. Now tell me how proud I should be of my past."

She'd never seen such a look of suffering in a man's eyes. Camile drew back.

"Does it disgust you to know you gave yourself to a child killer?" he went on. "I bet even that damned all-important ranch wasn't worth knowing you invited the lowest form of scum inside of you. You want me to face that? I see it every time I look in a mirror."

"Wade, don't," Camile whispered. She hated what life had done to him. What he'd done to himself. His was the worst kind of punishment, a self-execution that would last a lifetime. The same sentence she'd once placed upon herself.

"Don't what? Make you listen to the truth? You see why I would never want you to know? Why I'd lie, cheat, steal, do anything to keep from facing the man I became? To keep from becoming him again?"

He paused, wiping his hand over his forehead as if the

gesture would remove the memories. "I killed his father a month before. Got caught in a holdup while I was in the bank. The man shot a clerk. I figured he deserved to meet his Maker. Maybe the man stole to feed his starving family, and maybe he stole for greed. The thing is, after I killed that boy, I realized it wasn't for me to decide. I realized I was no better than him. I would steal to feed my family. I would kill for someone I love. I deserved to take the bullet that night in Atlanta. Not the boy."

There were no words to give him comfort. Camile silently cursed a demon only he could fight, and the silence that stretched between them. Survival had extracted a price from Wade Langtry. The sacrifice of one boy to find the human hidden within himself.

"You don't know how alike we are," she finally said. "I killed a kid, too. My brother. The same day I put my father in a wheelchair. I thought I could ride the stallion, but he threw me and my brother tried to save me. He was killed— my father trampled. I see now, through you, what I did to myself all those years. I wasn't waiting for my father to forgive me. I was waiting to forgive myself. You have to let go of it, or the guilt will run your life. The guilt will decide who or what you become."

The pain in his eyes intensified. Gently, he touched her cheek. "You should have told me. You thought becoming your brother would replace him in your father's eyes, make the guilt go away. I guess I thought if society could accept me, in time I might learn to accept myself. Whatever you did, at least you did for love."

Her heart slammed against her chest. He knew. How could he not? A woman didn't risk her life to save a man

309

she didn't love. She wouldn't give up all for his sake or accept the pleasure and the pain of him unless she loved him. "Yes, I did it for love."

His fingers brushed the fullness of her lips. A shiver of anticipation raced up her spine. Did the softness in his eyes mean he felt the same?

"The land will never want you the way you want it, Camile, but I envy you the honesty of loving it. Go home. You've proven you can fit into any setting. You were always a diamond. Texas needs you, although it will never tell you it does."

After Wade walked to the bar, she approached him, anger burning her cheeks and tears threatening her eyes. "I also came to tell you Miles Traften said he knows a good man who can see that you and I are free of one another. But before I go, I'll give you some advice. God knows you've given me enough since the first night we met."

She took a steadying breath as he turned to face her. "When you operate a ranch, you get all kinds," she said. "Men who come and go. Some running from something, some running to it, but my father believes in fairness. He thinks what a man becomes is more important than what he was. You'd do well to think more like him. Good-bye, Wade."

She walked to the swinging doors, then hesitated. "I knew about Atlanta before you told me. I can forgive you for what you did, for all you've done. I hope you can forgive yourself."

Camile pushed the doors wide. Her long strides carried her quickly to her horse. She swung up into the saddle, not daring a look at Hank. Tears streamed down her cheeks as she reined the animal toward Texas.

"It took you a while," Hank said. "I was hoping the two of you got yourselves straight. Figured he might follow you out and come on home."

"You figured wrong!" Camile snapped, then sniffed. Most unladylike, she drew her sleeve across her nose. "If he wants to stay in this boring place, it's fine by me. If he wants to marry some woman who'll have him falling asleep at dinner in less than a year, that's fine, too. Wade can run from his past, but sooner or later, the road ends."

"Hell. Didn't know he was in for such a bad time of it," Hank countered, his tone dry. "It's a damn shame. He made a good hand, didn't he, Cam?"

She nodded, angrily dashing the tears from her cheeks. "Ranching comes natural to him, anyone can see that. We could use his help with that five-hundred-thousand acres we have to oversee for the stockholders."

Hank rubbed his chin. "Too bad you can't do what's best for the ranch and ask him to come along. He'd know about the baby before long. Guess that'd be the end of your road, too."

The fire went out of her. Hank was right. Asking Wade to help her with the ranch wouldn't do as a ploy to buy her time—to make him love her someday.

A small crowd caught her eye from the planked sidewalk. Several of the ladies who'd attended the meeting watched her in silence. Their solemn faces said it all. Camile Langtry planned to leave the deed undone.

"Damn him!" she swore, yanking her horse around. "I have to save him, again."

"What have you got to save him from this time?" Hank shouted in confusion.

"From himself!"

The horse made the godawful-est racket as she rode up the plank steps, charging through the swinging doors. Shouts of concern followed. Glasses crashed to the floor as men dove for cover. Jacob, the barkeep, crossed himself before disappearing behind the bar. Camile felt right at home. Wade stood where she'd left him, calmly sipping his drink as if unaware a woman had just ridden a horse into the Lucky Lady.

"Forget something?" he asked, dismissing the improbability.

"Yeah." She swung a lariat overhead. "You."

The rope sailed smoothly over his head. Pulling the slack tight caused his drink to fall to the floor. He turned, lifting a dark brow. When he remained silent, waiting, Camile wondered what the hell she thought she would say to him.

"You have to come with me," she blurted out.

He smiled slightly. "Give me one reason worth spit why I should."

She could give him two, but Camile wasn't ready to tell him the truth. "Five hundred thousand acres, Wade. They think I can run five hundred thousand acres! I need your help."

His smile faded. He shook his head. "Not good enough, Camile. If anyone can do it, you can. You don't need my help."

"This life will bore you to death," she tried.

"You're not exactly good for a man's health," he countered. "It would take something more convincing to make me come with you."

She was beginning to panic. "Texas needs men like you as much as it needs women like me. I can't force you, Wade, but I want you to come. I need you."

Fire sparked to life in his green gaze. Beads of moisture popped out on her upper lip. Humbling didn't come easy to the Prickly Pear of the Panhandle. He walked toward her, loosening the rope while shrugging from its confines.

"You need me, or the ranch does?"

The road had come to an end. It branched in two separate directions. The truth, or more lies. She had no right to withhold his child. In time, they would both heal him.

"I need you," she admitted softly. Her hand moved to her stomach. "We need you."

His gaze followed her fingers, then widened. He swallowed. "You weren't going to tell me?" he accused.

Camile couldn't stand the hurt in his eyes. "I was afraid. I thought you might stay with me because of the baby. I needed to know you'd stay with me because you wanted to."

"Dammit," he swore. "We can't keep lying to each other. Keeping secrets. Hurting each other!"

She nodded, tears slipping down her face. "No more secrets. No more lies. No more competition."

Wade removed his hat and ran a shaky hand through his hair. He replaced it and stared up at her. "Prove it, Camile. You know what I need to hear. Say it."

He didn't have to act so angry about the fact she loved him. "How do I know you won't laugh at me?" she asked warily. "How do I know you don't want to hear me say it so you can humiliate me? Get the final revenge?"

His gaze rolled upward. "You're gonna be the death of me," he said, then reached up and hefted her from the saddle. "I knew the first night you stuck your boot in my throat, my life would never be the same. You've turned me every which way. Stomped on my feelings and broken my heart. I

313

would have given you the ranch. I would have asked you to marry me that night in the line shack if I believed you could forgive my past. I did wrong, Camile. We both did by not being honest with each other. It's time to make amends."

His heart rested in his eyes. He loved her. Camile knew it surely as the sun would rise tomorrow. "Maybe you should make amends first," she suggested.

Wade pulled her into his arms. "Life with you will be one hell of a ride, Camile. Show me that once in a while you'll let me win."

If her bearing remained stiff, her gaze steady, warmth spread through her and softened the woman within. Camile smiled. Her arms slid around his neck.

"I love you, Wade. More than land and cattle. More than life itself."

He gazed tenderly down at her. "I love you, too, hellcat. Looks like this time, we both win. Let's go home."

A cheer sounded when he swept her up, placed her in the saddle, and climbed on behind her. More shouts greeted them from the streets. Hank sat his horse, grinning broadly, Margaret Pendergraft beside him in a buggy loaded with valises.

"Where are you going, Margaret?" Camile asked when they pulled up beside the couple.

"Texas." She cut her gaze toward Hank. "You can't very well ride a horse all the way home in your condition."

"She's right," Wade said against her ear. "You have to take care with that hellcat you're carrying. No more stunts until after the baby comes."

"Is that an order, Langtry?" Camile questioned stiffly.

His arms tightened around her. "Just a suggestion. I don't want to be your boss, Camile. I want to be your partner."

Those were sweet words. She relaxed against his broad chest, reveling in his warmth, in the future that lay ahead for them. "I guess about now you're wondering what you've gotten yourself into."

"That's what I should be wondering," he countered; then she felt his breath against her ear. "I'm wondering if you could feel and taste as good as I remember."

Heat wound a path through her body. She'd been fighting her attraction to Wade since first seeing him again. Fighting her heart. The battle between them had ended, and as Wade had said, they'd both won. It felt wonderful to surrender to true love.

"Do you reckon we should go to your room at that fancy hotel and pack up your gear?" she asked, turning to smile seductively at him.

His smile was just as wicked. "I reckon so, Prickly Pear."

Cougar's Woman
Ronda Thompson

On the journey to meet her fiancé in Santa Fe, Melissa Sheffield is captured by Apaches and given to a man known as Cougar. At first, she is relieved to learn that she's been given to a white man, but with one kiss he proves himself more dangerous than the whole tribe. Terrified of her savage captor, she pledges to escape at any price. But while there might be an escape from the Apaches, is there any escape from her heart? Clay Brodie—known as Cougar to the Apaches—is given the fiery Melissa by his chief. He is then ordered to turn the beauty into an obedient slave—or destroy her. But how can he slay a woman who evokes an emotion deeper than he's ever known? And when the time comes to fight, will it be for his tribe or for his woman?

___4524-9 $4.99 US/$5.99 CAN

Dorchester Publishing Co., Inc.
P.O. Box 6640
Wayne, PA 19087-8640

Please add $1.75 for shipping and handling for the first book and $.50 for each book thereafter. NY, NYC, and PA residents, please add appropriate sales tax. No cash, stamps, or C.O.D.s. All orders shipped within 6 weeks via postal service book rate. Canadian orders require $2.00 extra postage and must be paid in U.S. dollars through a U.S. banking facility.

Name_____
Address_____
City_____State_____Zip_____
I have enclosed $_____ in payment for the checked book(s).
Payment <u>must</u> accompany all orders. ❑ Please send a free catalog.
    CHECK OUT OUR WEBSITE! www.dorchesterpub.com

WESTON'S *Lady* BOBBI SMITH

There are Cowboys and Indians, trick riding, thrills and excitement for everyone. And if Liberty Jones has anything to say about it, she will be a part of the Wild West show, too. She has demonstrated her expertise with a gun by shooting a card out of Reed Weston's hand at thirty paces, but the arrogant owner of the Stampede won't even give her a chance. Disguising herself as a boy, Libby wangles herself a job with the show, and before she knows it Reed is firing at her—in front of an audience. It seems an emotional showdown is inevitable whenever they come together, but Libby has set her sights on Reed's heart and she vows she will prove her love is every bit as true as her aim.

___4512-5 $5.99 US/$6.99 CAN

THE LADY'S HAND
BOBBI SMITH
Author of *Lady Deception*

Cool-headed and ravishingly beautiful, Brandy O'Neal knows how to hold her own with the riverboat gamblers on *The Pride of New Orleans*. But she meets her match in Rafe Morgan when she bets everything she has on three queens and discovers that the wealthy plantation owner has a far from gentlemanly notion of how she shall make good on her wager.

Disillusioned with romance, Rafe wants a child of his own to care for, without the complications of a woman to break his heart. Now a full house has given him just the opportunity he is looking for—he will force the lovely cardsharp to marry him and give him a child before he sets her free. But a firecracker-hot wedding night and a glimpse into Brandy's tender heart soon make Rafe realize he's luckier than he ever imagined when he wins the lady's hand.

_4116-2 $5.99 US/$6.99 CAN

The Snow Queen
ANNE AVERY

When Boston-bred Hetty Malone arrives at the Colorado Springs train station, she is full of hope that she will soon marry her childhood sweetheart and live happily ever after. Yet life amid the ice-capped Rockies has changed Michael Ryan. No longer the hot-blooded suitor Hetty remembers, the young doctor has grown as cold and distant as the snowy mountain peaks. Determined to revive Michael's passionate longing, Hetty quickly realizes that no modern medicine can cure what ails him. But in the enchanted splendor of her new home, she dares to administer the only remedy that might melt his frozen heart: a dose of good old-fashioned loving.

_52151-2 $5.99 US/$6.99 CAN